# Skin

ALLY WAGNER

Embrace the Skin you're in

*To my heart and anchor, thank you for loving and*
*supporting me at my worst.*

*To Kimberly, thank you for believing in me when I didn't.*

*To Michelle, thank you for pushing me*
*to be the best version of myself.*

# *One*

"Cain, I don't know about this." Kee mumbled as she anxiously scanned the busy streets and sidewalks of downtown Los Angeles. Tonight was the 25th anniversary of the Monster Movement and most of the preternatural were out celebrating. She could easily spot the vampires trying to blend in with the humans in the crowds, their movements too fluid to ever be anything living. She could point out the various types of wereanimals by the subtle way they scratched and picked at their limbs, their skin itching to be shed with the full moon less than a week away.

*I hate crowds,* she thought almost angrily. *We've been dating for over a year, he should know this already.*

"It'll be fine, Kee," he assured her as he led them to Shifters.

Shifters was a bar that employed wereanimals, but catered to all species. Before the preternatural creatures were granted their own rights, the bar posed as a cover for monsters to meet up and socialize without the worry of discovery. After the Monster Movement passed, it became one of the most successful bars in LA. Monsters and humans flocked to it every night for the fun, energetic atmosphere. The success of Shifters encouraged other preternatural clubs like Byte, Tips, and Brews to come into existence.

It was also the place Kee met Cain.

She technically hadn't needed the second job at Shifters since her surveillance job paid the majority of her bills, but she wanted something to keep her busy on her days off. So, with a little white lie about her heritage in management, she had been hired on the spot. On her second day of training, she served Cain when he and his coworkers had come in for beers after work.

Their physical attraction to one another had been undeniable, but their personalities had clashed. Cain was twenty-seven, confident, strong, and a little hard-headed while she was three years younger, timid, cautious, and reasonable. Cain had hit on her suavely and relentlessly, and she hadn't known how to react. She had been new to the job, still trying to find her footing, so she had shied away from his advances. He had left the bar nursing a bruised ego.

A couple weeks later, he came in again with some friends and had been sitting in her section. When she saw the handsome werewolf, she grinned, determined to make up for their disastrous first meeting. She sauntered over to their table and smiled flirtatiously at him, asking how he had been. In response, he made a snide comment about moving to a different part of the bar.

Instead of brooding at the cold brush off, she mustered the scraps of her courage, smiled kindly at him, and then told him to go fuck himself. He hadn't been expecting it, seeing as how she had been so evasive before, but it instantly piqued his interest again. She agreed to let him take her out on a date to apologize. They officially started dating soon afterward.

Kee smiled fondly at the memory. They had a rough start to their relationship, but she wouldn't change it for anything. She loved Cain, and he was good to her.

Someone's shoulder connected with hers, the impact tearing her from her thoughts as she stumbled behind Cain. "Sorry!"

She immediately apologized as she regained her footing.

"Watch where you're going!" The warlock sneered at her, the distinct scent of clove and cinnamon giving away his lineage.

Whatever pathetic retort she had died on her tongue when a deep growl came from beside her. She looked up at Cain and frowned when his dark blue eyes gleamed with his wolf's presence. She squeezed his hand until his attention was drawn back to her. "It's okay. It was my fault, Cain. I was lost in my thoughts."

"Damn right." The warlock sniffed, chin raised high as he continued on his way.

Cain shook his head after the man left and shuffled Kee to the edge of the sidewalk to avoid the passing crowds. He turned and cupped her face in his large, worn hands. "He could have easily dodged you, Kee. You can't let people push you around all the time."

She looked down, eyeing the cracks in the cement beneath their feet. "It's a busy night, Cain. People are bound to bump into each other." She mumbled.

He sighed and bent so he could press his forehead against hers. "Alright, what's wrong?"

Kee closed her eyes and leaned into him, trying to siphon some of his strength. "I'm nervous about meeting your pack." She admitted, her brow furrowing. She was scared. She didn't like packs and hated alphas even more. Unfortunately, tonight was the night she finally ran out of excuses to not meet the LA wolf pack.

"They will love you, just like I do," he told her confidently, his hands sliding down her neck to rest on her shoulders. "Just be yourself."

She pulled back and shot him a dubious look. "You want me to tell them I'm a shapeshifter?"

He pursed his lips together, glancing around them to make sure no one overheard. "That's not what I meant and you know it," he chided as he straightened, removing his hands from her to run them along his short, dark brown hair. "Your personality will be enough, Kee. I know you can be anxious when meeting new people, but these are members of *my* pack. They're closer to me than my real family."

Pack or not, werewolves did not like shapeshifters. No preternatural creature did. Wereanimals of every kind had one specific animal they correlated with, one beast that called to them on the full moon. Shapeshifters did not. That's what made them dangerous and, unfortunately, targets.

"I understand that, but you know that werewolves are the ones who helped wipe out my kind. I'd rather *not* repeat history." She saw a muscle tick in his cheek, but she knew he understood.

"You won't. Just give them the same modified version you gave me when we first started dating." His voice didn't hold any contempt, but she knew he was still bitter about the lie she told him.

"And what happens when the truth comes out, Cain? Remember when I told you the truth? You didn't speak to me for two weeks!" She reminded him.

"That was two months into our relationship and it was a shock." He ran a hand down his face in frustration. "I thought we agreed not to bring this up again?"

She crossed her arms over her chest. "We did. Look, all I'm saying is that they'll think I'm not good enough for you."

He wrapped his arms around her. "You're perfect for me no matter what they think. We will tell them the truth later. I want them to meet you and get to know you first."

She hugged him back, but didn't reply. They would reject her right off the bat if they knew she was a shapeshifter. In all reality, they may very well try to kill her. She wasn't one of them. Never would be. She was an anomaly. A danger.

Kee tightened her hold on him as she searched for some thread of bravery within her. This was important to Cain. He didn't ask much of her in their relationship, so when he swallowed his pride and begged her to do this, she knew she couldn't say no. No matter how much her instincts were telling her otherwise.

She took a deep breath and stepped back from him. "Well, do I at least look presentable enough to meet your pack?" She asked as she put her hands on her hips.

Cain looked her over, taking in her dark blue skinny jeans that disappeared into short, black boots. His eyes roamed to her fuchsia, long sleeve shirt and lingered on the laces that crisscrossed above her small cleavage. Her dark blonde hair was down, parted to the side, and fell to the small of her back. Her eyes were lined with black, making the grey stand out.

He leaned down and pressed a kiss to her lips. "Delicious, but I prefer you naked and wet. Just like how I had you before we left." He whispered huskily before pulling back with a suggestive grin.

Heat rushed to her cheeks at the reminder of the quickie they had in the shower earlier. She playfully swatted at his arm and stepped away to drink in his appearance. He was wearing dark jeans and a forest green flannel with the sleeves rolled up to his elbows, the tattooed Celtic knots and ropes visible on his left forearm. He finished off his look with dark brown boots and a cheek dimple that made her heart flutter. "You look pretty yummy yourself."

"You can eat me later," he grinned. "Come on, I don't want to keep them waiting."

Kee fished her phone from her back pocket to put it on vibrate and frowned when she found there weren't any messages waiting for her. Lucas still hadn't replied.

*Where the hell is he?* She knew the head vampire for LA County was more than capable of taking care of himself, but she had never gone so long without hearing from him. Especially after giving him the surveillance report he asked for. *I hope he's okay.*

With a sigh, she muted her phone and tucked it back in her pocket. "Alright, I'm ready." She gave Cain a smile when he took her hand in his and together they walked into the bar.

Shifters was split into two sections. One side had a horseshoe shaped bar with high tables scattered around it while the other side consisted of low tables and a dance floor. It was Friday night and the bar was packed with wereanimals celebrating the anniversary of their legal freedom. She stuck close to Cain's back, relying on him to maneuver them through the crowd. The scent of alcohol and sweat hung in the air, bodies pressed against each other as they danced to the eccentric beat of the loud music.

She tried to not stumble behind Cain as she followed him towards the back of the building where the VIP room awaited them. Inside, there were high tables with bar stools, a small stage for dancing, and one set of sofas with a glass coffee table. The lights were at a dimmed brightness, music set to a tolerable level for the werewolves who weren't partying the night away. She had been in this room many times, but it was her first time being a guest in it.

"We have to greet Warren and Natalie first." He told her as he began leading her to the white leather sofas.

She stepped closer to him when she suddenly felt the attention in the room shift to her. She glanced around them, trying to count how many potential threats there were. At one of the tables, she couldn't help but notice one of the four werewolves were in their wolf form. A man at the table had his boot on the wolf, using the animal as a footrest. She inhaled sharply as the wolf met her gaze, a whine in his throat. She saw the boot flex with the sound, making the wolf quickly look away and shut its eyes.

When she looked up at the table, the three were staring at her, making her quickly look away so they wouldn't take it as a challenge.

Still, she could feel their gaze sliding over her body, their judgement and scrutiny pricking her skin like needles. She squeezed Cain's hand, her heart beating hard in her throat.

*This was a bad idea.* She thought miserably.

"Cain, my dear, you made it." A velvety smooth voice spoke once they approached the couches. Kee looked up to see a beautiful blonde lounging on one of the sofas, her gold dress accentuating her curves in all the right places. When the woman made eye contact with Kee, she fluidly sat up and smiled with perfect white teeth. "Oh, you finally brought your girl!"

"Yeah, it was time she met the pack." He replied with a wide smile. He let go of Kee's hand and walked over to the man sitting on the other couch. His black hair fell over his shoulders as the two clasped forearms and grinned before speaking in low tones to each other.

Kee clasped her hands in front of her, not sure what else to do with them. Her pulse was loud in her ears, making it hard to hear what they were saying. She could only watch as her boyfriend talked to his alpha for a few minutes before going over to the woman. Cain bent down and pressed a kiss to the blonde's cheek, closing his eyes when she rubbed his head affectionately like one would a dog.

Kee blinked when the three suddenly looked at her expectantly.

"Come here, let me introduce you," Cain gestured towards the alpha as he straightened, an excited smile on his face.

*Fuck, it's happening.* She swallowed a dry lump in her throat and took a few steps forward to stand in front of the alpha and Cain.

"Kee, this is Warren Erickson, our alpha, and his mate Natalie Erickson," he said with a proud smile. "Warren, Nat, this is Keira Quinn."

"I-it's nice to meet you." She bowed her head nervously, not making eye contact. She jumped slightly when a warm hand wrapped around her trembling one.

"Look at me," Warren's voice was deep and full of power, making the hair on the back of her neck rise. When her eyes met his, he gave her a small smile and nuzzled the inside of her palm in greeting. "It is nice to finally meet my beta's chosen woman, Keira."

She flushed and resisted the urge to pull her hand back. *Don't. Just keep calm. Don't embarrass Cain.* "Please, call me Kee," she said with a small, forced smile. "And it's very nice to meet Cain's pack. I've heard so much about you guys."

His hand tightened around hers as he held her gaze. "Good things, I hope."

"A-always." She stuttered, his gaze making her uncomfortable.

"You seem nervous, Kee," Warren commented in a light tone, but then his stare hardened, his expression turning cold. "Could it be because you neglected to meet with the alpha of this territory when you moved here?"

Cain frowned and stepped forward. "Warren—" He cut himself off when Natalie grabbed his elbow and pulled him down to sit next to her on the couch.

"You knew this was coming, Cain," she whispered gently. "Warren said he would go easy on her in respect to you, but he has to ask her some questions. It is pack protocol for a new wolf to meet with the city's alpha when they move here. She's beyond overdue to meet us. A year is very lenient, Cain." She soothingly rubbed his arm when he sighed, "Trust him."

Kee blinked at the alpha, not expecting such a direct question. She had moved to Los Angeles from Riverside a year and a half ago at the persuasion of Lucas. She hadn't even known Warren existed until Cain.

"Honestly, I wasn't aware I had to." She could taste her heartbeat as she saw the other members of the pack move towards them. Some had pulled up chairs from the tables, others sat cross legged on the floor, but none dared to sit on the sofas next to the beta, alpha and his mate.

"Oh?" Natalie asked curiously, still keeping her arm threaded through Cain's. "Does that mean you were recently bit?"

There were two ways for a wereanimal to become one. One way was to be born between two wereanimals, though a pup making it to full term was rare, and the other was to be bit by one in their beast form on the night of a full moon. Wikipedia had at least gotten that part right.

Kee could feel her palm sweating in Warren's and her embarrassment just heightened her anxiety. Why didn't he let go? She was the only one in the room standing and it didn't help her fraying nerves. She broke eye contact with Warren and glanced at his mate, but tilted her head down to make sure she didn't offend her. "Umm, no, I was born as a shifter."

*Just not as a werewolf,* she refrained from adding.

"Then why don't you know pack protocol?" A man behind her asked.

She felt her stomach twist when she saw Warren's light blue eyes hardened as he glanced at the one who dared to speak out of turn. She could feel the man's fear as he shrunk back, cowering under the stare of his alpha. She felt Warren's fingers squeeze around hers and was forced to meet his gaze once again. His eyes were like ice and she felt her chest grow cold in response, despite the heat coming from his hand.

"I don't come from a pack." She was sure she had said it quietly, but the silence of the room made it seem like a shriek.

"No? You're a lone wolf then?" Natalie questioned lightly as she reached with her free hand to lift the fruity cocktail from the glass table. She looked at Kee over the rim of her glass, watching her carefully as she studied the possible new addition to their pack.

She nodded, eyes still locked with Warren's as they continued to stare into hers. She shouldn't want to pull away from him, but every fiber in her body was telling her to. She felt as though he were staring into her soul, peeling her layers away and making her feel exposed. Vulnerable.

*Is this the power of an alpha?* She almost scoffed. Of course it was. It was just like all those years ago. Perhaps it was the wolf blood that ran in her veins that made her fall victim to it.

"Lone wolf status or not, you should know pack dynamics. Not coming to me the moment you decided to enter my territory was a great insult to me." Warren finally spoke again. "Or, did your parents not belong to a pack? I assume they were both wolves as well?"

"Yes, they were. And, my father did," Kee admitted solemnly. Her hand flexed within Warren's as the bad memories resurfaced from his prodding. They were bad because of her, because of the damn shape-shifter gene. "But they refused to acknowledge my mother after I was born."

Warren didn't immediately comment as he continued to hold her gaze. He felt her small hand twitch in his and the look in her eyes made him understand that these were painful memories. Perhaps he would give her a pardon after all. "Why?" He asked, but this time his tone was gentle instead of pressing.

She finally tore her gaze away from his, looking down at their joined hands instead. "Because of me," her brow furrowed as she tried to word it carefully without lying. "They couldn't accept her because I wasn't a wolf." *More half-truths.* "They thought she cheated on my dad since my wolf gene hadn't shown up."

Warren rubbed circles on the top of her hand with his thumb, his alpha nature automatically trying to comfort a hurting wolf. "But it manifested late."

"Mhm," she watched his thumb trace circles on her skin, her

fingers shaking with the need to snatch her hand away. "The damage was already done though."

"What do you mean?"

The painful memory was strong enough to break whatever spell Warren had put her under. She vehemently shook her head and finally pulled her hand from his as she tried desperately to rebuild her mental walls. "I don't want to talk about it."

Knowing Kee had hit her limit, Cain quickly stood up, forcing Natalie's hand off his elbow. He went to her and folded her into the security of his arms. She pressed her face to his chest and he gently stroked her hair. He glanced at the pack members staring at them and let out a low warning growl, his lip curled up into a sneer. Not wanting to piss off their second-in-command they looked away, got up, and dispersed.

Satisfied, he rested his chin on her head, still petting her hair. "It's okay, Kee."

She gripped a fistful of his flannel in her hand and clenched her jaw tightly. She was angry. Mad at Warren for resurfacing the memories she tried so hard to suppress, and disappointed at herself for still reacting that way. It was in the past. She refused to shed any tears about it, but that didn't make her heart hurt any less.

# *Two*

Two vampire lords stood across from each other in an abandoned field on the outskirts of downtown Los Angeles, a mix of their followers creating a wide ring around them. The clearing ran along the side of the city's water runoff, the Metrolink tracks about a mile or so away. Their arena for the night was littered with shattered concrete, dumped trash and broken furniture. It was the only empty area that was close to LA, yet faraway enough to not cause damage, or involve any humans.

When the Monster Movement passed, it praised and flaunted equal rights for all. The reality, unfortunately, was a different story. Most law enforcement officers were prejudiced, the vast majority still unaccepting of the new members of society. Because of this, preternatural creatures handled their *business* without police involvement. What consequence was it to the humans if the monsters killed each other? As long as the fights were far enough from the population to avoid human involvement, and all left over bodies were disposed of, the police turned a blind eye.

That was why the vampires chose the dumping ground out by the railroad.

It was eerily silent in the field and yet the thirst for blood was almost blaring. Each vampire gathered in the clearing was still, more so than any mortal could ever be. Their wide eyes were shining in the moonlight, never blinking in fear of missing the fight that was soon to occur. Their excitement was like an electric current in the air, a blanket of charged energy that wrapped them all in a coil of tension. Which side would win? Whose leader would prevail? Who would get to tear out the others' throat and bathe in their blood?

"There is still time to yield to me, Lucas." The slightly shorter male offered with a wide, condescending smile, his fangs gleaming. He had his arms crossed over his chest, his tight blue tank top stretched and strained against the firm muscle. His blonde hair curled behind his ears, pale gold eyes shining with arrogance.

"I will not submit to someone who will doom our kind, Alexander." Lucas replied calmly, emerald green orbs never leaving his opponent. His hands were tucked in the front pockets of his black slacks, his face blank and impassive as he waited for Alexander to finish his ridiculous speech.

"Doom? No, no, I plan on revolutionizing our fellow vampires! Can't you see? By uniting as one, we are that much closer to enslaving the humans forever!" He spread his arms open and gestured at the vampires surrounding them. "Just think, being able to take a drink whenever it pleases you! Owning your own personal blood bank!" A triumphant grin spread across his face when cheers from half of the surrounding vampires echoed in the night around them.

Alexander met Lucas' gaze. "See, Lucas? Together we can convince the Lord of California, then eventually the Council!"

When the United States government decreed preternatural creatures as members of society, the Council was formed to represent them so that they could talk to the President and his cabinet as equals. It was made up of a single member from each type of monster: one vampire represented all the undead, one werewolf to speak for all the wereanimals, one warlock to answer for all the magic users, and one elf to give voice to all the rare woodland creatures.

For months the Council and President deliberated on potential rights until they finally achieved a common ground. Each species was responsible for their kind. There was an established ladder of command within each of the preternatural races that progressed from city, county, and state. For example, if the LA alpha couldn't control their city's pack, then the alpha for all of Los Angeles County would have to interfere. If it went past that, then the alpha for California would have to step in. If it went beyond that, then the Council would be forced to take action.

That was what happened between Lucas and Alexander. Lucas, ranking higher than Alexander as his lord, had to eliminate the threat to the rest of the vampires. There would be no revolution under his ruling.

"It sounds to me as if you have trouble getting volunteers to feed from," he commented lightly, which earned him snickers from the crowd at his back. A small smirk tilted up the corner of his lips as he slid a hand through his short, black locks. "If you could control your power, perhaps you would not have this issue."

A snarl marred Alexander's face at the insult, nails elongating in anger. "I can control it just fine."

"We will see."

Without replying, Alexander rushed at Lucas, throwing a fist at his face. Lucas caught his wrist and jerked him closer, bringing a knee up to the blonde's stomach. Alexander twisted away from the knee and brought his other elbow down towards Lucas' head. Lucas swiveled to the side, letting the elbow crash down on his left shoulder, the impact fracturing his collar bone.

Cheers went out through the spectating vampires, but Lucas

ignored them as he took advantage of Alexander's closeness. He circled his left hand around Alexander's neck and, using the hold he still had on his wrist, gave a hard pull on Alexander's right arm to dislocate it from the socket. Lucas crushed the blonde's throat when he let out a wail but quickly released his hold when Alexander's claws slashed at his chest.

When he was free, Alexander stumbled back a few steps before regaining his footing. Alexander grinned when he noticed the blood staining Lucas' shirt. Feeling smug, he flared out his aura, the invisible power sweeping out and ruffling the spectator's clothes and hair. The weaker vampires flinched back from the oppressive power, but Lucas' coven remained unmoved.

Alexander's grin faltered slightly when he saw Lucas briefly touch the open wound on his chest and inspect the blood on his fingertips with mild curiosity. When Lucas began to walk towards him, Alexander bared his fangs and cracked his knuckles before charging in once again.

Lucas dodged the attacks as he approached the smaller vampire, his movements as fluid and graceful as a dancer's. When he was close enough to Alexander, he didn't try to escape the claws that slashed across his stomach and shoulder. He pressed his hand against the blood steadily seeping down his torso and coated his palm thoroughly in it. Lucas met Alexander's confused gaze and held up the bloody palm. A golden fire ignited within it, causing the vampires around them to instantly retreat a few yards.

Vampires were sensitive to fire, their skin easily combustible once caught in a flame. It was why the sun caused such a problem for them. Newly turned vampires instantly burned, but the older ones, though weakened, could withstand it as long as they weren't directly in the light.

"That isn't possible." Alexander sneered. Anger remained in his tone, but uncertainty and fear shone in his eyes.

"Oh, but it is." Lucas replied with a cruel smirk. He uncurled his fingers, fire twisting into a ball before bouncing towards his panicked enemy.

Alexander frantically threw himself to the right, easily avoiding the flame. He clenched his jaw, lips curling into a snarl once again. The attack had been too easy to avoid, too predictable. More fire came at him, causing him to roll to the left this time. When he leapt to his feet, he looked at his lord with uncertainty. "The Curse of Apollo," he stated quietly. "I didn't think it meant *this*."

Lucas scowled at the name that was branded on him centuries ago, but otherwise ignored it. "Give up, Alexander. Unless, of course, you wish to burn?"

"I'll take my chances!" Alexander was going to slice Lucas into little pieces before the flame could ever touch him. He would win this fight, take over all the wereanimals, and then conquer humanity. He would make the Council see it his way. If not, then the warlocks and elves were just another obstacle in his way.

Alexander rushed at Lucas once again, swiping and kicking as fast as he could, desperate to land a blow and win. But, he wasn't fast enough. Lucas sent him sprawling with a kick to his stomach. The only wounds Lucas had were the ones he had inflicted on him earlier in the fight.

His eyes narrowed when he realized that he had been played. "You let me hit you earlier."

"Indeed," Lucas coated his other hand in his blood and held it out as a flame sprang to life in his palm. "I needed the accelerant." He put out the new fire by making a fist and then looked at his opponent seriously. "Also, I wanted to see how strong you really were. I have to admit that I am disappointed, Alexander."

Alexander blinked and Lucas was on him, tackling him to the

ground. Lucas sat on his chest, pinning his head down with a tight grip on his throat. Alexander's eyes widened as Lucas lowered his fire to hover over his face. The scent of burnt hair filled his nostrils as strands of his blonde bangs shriveled away to ash. A screech ripped out of his throat as the skin on his forehead and cheeks sizzled and melted away from the muscle and bone. His hands grabbed Lucas's forearm, trying desperately to push him off so he could escape the nearing flame. When his opponent wouldn't budge, Alexander let go and exposed his wrists to Lucas, a sign of submission among vampires.

Lucas pulled his fire away and just barely loosened his hold on the blonde's neck. "Something you wish to say?" He asked casually, his tone borderline mocking.

"I yield." Alexander hissed through clenched teeth, his face wracked with pain as it tried to heal itself from the damage. It would take days for his muscles to knit back together, and even longer for the skin to regrow over it. When the flame came back towards his face he shouted again, "I yield!"

Lucas pulled his hand back and extinguished the flame, but bent down so his face was inches from Alexander's. "Do not ever oppose your reigning lord again, Alexander. You are relieved of your title and a new vampire will take over the Pasadena coven. Go against me in the future and the consequences will be dire."

He then dipped down and bit into Alexander's wrist with his fangs, tearing through the tendons and veins as he acknowledged the submission. He spat the chunk of flesh out when he pulled away and stood up, leaving Alexander to cradle his gushing wrist to his chest while his other hand cradled his scorched face. Lucas stepped away and turned towards his vampires. They were staring at him eagerly, their bloodlust almost palpable.

A fellow vampire approached Lucas, his eyes a light hazel that complimented his shoulder length brown hair. "What are your orders,

Lord Lucas? Will we immerse in blood tonight?" He asked, his voice still holding a slight Italian accent even after a century.

"No, Giovanni, we will not," he looked at his brethren and saw their scowls of disappointment. "We are not going to kill them. Wiping out a large number of our own people will accomplish nothing. Go feed, fuck, or whatever else you may have to do to calm your thirst, but you are not to kill them." When they hesitated, he expanded his aura until it crashed over them. At the power, the vampires quickly did as told, disappearing in flashes from the field.

Gio stayed near his lord and maker, a frown on his lips as he watched Lucas' face pale by each passing second. "Lucas," he began more casually once the other coven members dispersed. Lucas was his vampire father, he was allowed to be familiar with him. "You need to feed. Let me bring you someone. Your wounds will heal faster."

"No, it is fine. I will find someone on my own." He glanced back at Gio's concerned frown and put a reassuring hand on his shoulder. "I will meet you back at Byte."

"The bar is downtown. Please, allow me to accompany you there." He offered.

Lucas would have to get to the city to feed, but he was wounded and covered in blood. He didn't want to show up at his establishment in such a weakened state. He knew there would be willing people to feed from there, but he didn't want to deal with the crowd, or the questions. Maybe he could just find a place to rest in the city before dawn came.

*I happen to know someone who lives closer.* He thought with a small smirk. He had to visit her regarding her latest report anyways.

"I will be fine, Giovanni. Watch over our people. Make sure they do not disobey me." His eyes turned icy. "If they do, remind them what I did to Alexander's face. I will accept no other outbursts."

"Yes, but what if they ask about the new lord for the Pasadena coven?" He tilted his head slightly. "Without a lord in the city, they will just do what they wish, laws be damned."

"It will merge with ours until I find someone suitable. I am the Lord of Los Angeles County, so I will assume the Council will have no qualms about it." He squeezed Gio's shoulder. "I will see you tomorrow night, Giovanni."

"Yes, sir." He replied dutifully as he watched Lucas disappear in the blink of an eye.

# *Three*

Warren stood, straightening to his six foot two height. He saw Kee flinch at his closeness and chose to put his hand on his beta's shoulder instead of hers. "Why don't you go get some fresh air?"

Cain nodded once and laced his fingers with Kee's. "Let's go outside, babe."

She didn't respond, just let him guide her from the room. She kept her head down and ignored the werewolves as they continued to gawk, murmurs echoing around her. When they got to the bar area, she ignored her coworker's questions and kept her gaze on the beer splattered floor as she followed Cain. After they exited the bar, he led her around the corner and to a small alleyway beside the bar. When he brought them to a stop, she pulled away from him and braced herself against the chipped, brick wall to take a deep breath.

Cain gave her a few minutes to breathe, leaving her alone while she put herself back together. In the past year of dating Kee, he knew when to give her space. He respected that she didn't like to cry, that she didn't give in to weakness. She was wary and timid with most things, but she never let herself go into a crying fit. However, there were times when he thought she should, that it was okay to do so. He feared that all her bottled up emotions would overflow one day and swallow her whole.

After a few more minutes, she turned around and leaned back against the cold wall. "Well, that wasn't what I expected." She commented dryly.

"I'm sorry," he apologized with a heavy sigh. He leaned against the bricks next to her, hands shoved into his front pockets. "I didn't think he would do that."

"Does he do that to everyone?" She asked quietly, kicking a chunk of broken asphalt to the side. It skipped across the alleyway, making a stray cat jump at the sudden intrusion.

"Yeah," he responded softly with a sigh. "Alpha's can sense lies and his dominance compels you to answer him."

"Kind of like what Lucas can do?" She looked up at him and didn't miss the scowl that passed across his face. She sighed and looked away. "Sorry to bring him up."

"I know he's your boss," he mumbled as he ran his hand through his hair. "I just don't like vampires, Kee."

She gave a one shoulder shrug, not willing to fight with him about the subject again. "I don't know what to tell you. I've worked for him before I even moved here. He's part of my life."

Almost two years ago, she had unexpectedly run into the vampire when she was running from two drunk werefoxes. He didn't spare her a glance until he stumbled across the talent she tried so hard to hide. He had chased off her pursuers and then finally looked at her. *Really* looked at her. She had been ready to fight him, ready to protect herself, but it proved unnecessary. Unbelievably, he offered her a job working for him.

She wanted to refuse. She knew vampires were dangerous and Nana had always warned her to stay away from them. But, being hired as *her*, without having to hide who she was, was too thrilling to pass up. With the exception of Nana, it had been the first time someone didn't hurt her, or show disgust, after learning what she was. It was refreshing and she had wanted to hold onto that feeling.

"I know, I know," he sighed heavily. "To answer your question, I guess it's similar to a vampire's compulsion, but they can't physically take control over someone like vampires can. Alphas give orders and, with their aura, the wolves feel compelled to obey. They can persuade you to tell the truth and detect when you're not. However, alphas can only do it to members of the pack, potential pack candidates, or wolves that are way less dominant."

She pointedly ignored that last bit. "I wanted to pull away from him, but I didn't want to insult him and make you look bad," she admitted as she looked at the hand Warren had held captive. "But after a while it was hard to break away."

Cain kept his eyes on her, a small frown on his face. "I'm sorry it turned out like that, Kee. I really didn't think he would question you. I knew they wanted to find out more about you, but I didn't expect it to go the way it did."

"Well, I hope he's happy." She couldn't keep the bitterness from her tone. "Not only do they know part of my past, but now I seem like a little bitch. Great first impression." Sarcasm practically dripped from her words.

*Gods, I'm so embarrassed. How can I face any of them again?*

His brow furrowed. "No one thinks that of you. You have a sad past. You're allowed to get emotional about it."

She threw her hands up in frustration. "I didn't want to get emotional at all, Cain! I just wanted to meet your pack and maybe have a good time! I knew this was a bad idea! Just look at what happened!"

"Then why did you agree to it?" He asked, anger seeping into his tone.

She pushed off from the wall so she could turn and face him. "Because you asked me to! You made such a big deal about it being so important to you!"

"It is important to me!" He snapped back. "They're my pack!"

"Which is why I did this, damn it! Don't you see?" She shouted in frustration and turned from him, her hands balled into fists. She took another deep breath and released it slowly. "I think this was a mistake." She mumbled it, but she knew his sensitive wolf ears would pick it up.

The blue of his eyes darkened as a growl rumbled in his chest. He took that as rejection. Rejection of his pack, which was practically his life. He stepped away from the brick wall and glared at her back. "Maybe it was then."

She scoffed without turning to look at him. *Good to know he agrees.* "You stay with your precious pack; I'm going home."

"You're just going to leave?" Cain asked incredulously.

"What else am I supposed to do, Cain? I can't go back in there without being embarrassed or judged. I can't take all the looks they were giving me when we left. I just—I can't do this." She told him as she ran her hand through her hair. "I want to go home."

He let out a frustrated sigh. "I drove, Kee."

"I'll walk." She strode out of the alley, heading up Figueroa Street and away from Shifters. She heard his angry growl echo behind her, but didn't hear his footsteps following her. *Good.* She really didn't want to be around him at the moment. She pulled out her phone from her back pocket and checked the time, 1:04am. She was definitely going to stop for a drink on the way home. She had about a five and a half mile walk ahead of her, so the extra fuel couldn't hurt.

A little over two hours later she was walking up her apartment stairs on Olympic and Arlington. She smiled and bent to pet a small, black and white kitten as it passed her on the narrow stairway, its mother following close behind. She had always been partial towards cats. Maybe that explained her first change.

*No, not the time to think of that.* She shook her head, the alcohol she had consumed earlier making her a little dizzy with the action.

Walking to her door, she stuck her key in the lock and grabbed the handle. Almost instantly, every fiber in her body told her something was wrong. Adrenaline immediately chased away her buzz. The hair on the back of her neck stood on end in warning, her skin breaking out in goosebumps. She had taken a few martial arts classes at her great-grandmother's request when she was younger, but she didn't have the normal lycanthrope strength like others did. The agility and speed, yes, but not the same degree of inhuman strength.

Wary, she slowly turned the knob to her apartment door and opened it. The lights were off, as she had left them, but that didn't mean anything. With a racing heart, she reached blindly along the wall until she found her living room switch and flipped on the lights. She quickly scanned the entryway, looking for any person or thing that didn't belong. When she didn't see anything, she silently closed the door behind her.

As quietly as she could, she slipped off her boots and socks, wanting the traction of her bare feet on the wood floor if she needed to fight. She set them down without a sound and walked through her living room on the balls of her feet. After doing a quick once over of her small white kitchen, she headed towards the left side of her apartment. She started to walk towards the hall that led to her bedroom but suddenly stopped when she stepped in something wet. Balancing on one leg, she brought up her knee and glanced down at the bottom of her foot. Her brow furrowed when she saw a smear of blood on her skin. She lowered her foot back down, eyes now focusing on the trail of blood on her dark wood floors. She traced the trail with her eyes, finding that it led from her balcony door and down the hall towards her bedroom.

Something was in her apartment and it was either very hurt or very hungry.

Kee padded back to the kitchen and grabbed the biggest knife she had out of the drawer closest to the fridge. She then went back to the hallway and followed the blood, keeping her footsteps silent. As she neared her bedroom, she saw the door was cracked open, blood smeared on the handle. She put her hand on the door, took a few deep breaths to try and steel her nerves, and pushed the door open. When no one jumped out at her, she turned on the light. The breath she was holding rushed out in relief when she saw nothing had been waiting for her in the dark. But, she did notice that her queen-sized bed with sage green bedding was missing a pillow.

With a furrowed brow, she looked down at the drops of blood again and saw they led towards her bathroom. The door was closed, another blood stain on the handle. Her instincts flared in warning again as she saw a stream of light from under the door. Whatever had broken in was in her bathroom. She stood frozen in fear for a few minutes, her stomach bunched tightly with nerves.

If the thing inside didn't know she was there, did she have the upper hand? Should she just call the authorities? She scoffed, *Yeah, right. The LAPD doesn't deal with monster distress calls.*

No one was *supposed* to receive special treatment based on their race, but it wasn't uncommon for human police to be extra strict on monsters. Preternatural creatures were treated more harshly, suffering larger fines and longer sentences. There was no life in prison for them, they were condemned to death and executed within ten days of sentencing. No excuses.

*Yeah, fuck that. But that means I have to go in or leave. And, quite frankly, I have nowhere else to go at 3:30 in the morning.*

She wrapped her fingers around the knob and clenched the knife tightly in her other hand. She could do this. With a shaky breath, she twisted the knob and flung the door open with a loud bang. She darted into the small room, knife ready to slash at her intruder. When she didn't see anyone she felt some of the tension leave her shoulders. Maybe they just stole her pillow and left? However, her grey eyes darted to the closed shower curtain. With an audible swallow, she reached for it.

"Miss Quinn."

She screamed at the sudden, slightly accented voice and stumbled backwards onto her ass as the shower curtain slid open. She dropped the knife and fumbled with it until she finally caught it in her hand, the blade biting into her palm. She ignored the sting and wrapped her hand around the handle again, holding it protectively in front of her. She gasped when she realized it was Lucas who was reclining in her white bathtub, the pillow from her bed tucked under his head.

"Oh, my fucking gods, Lucas, you scared the shit out of me!" She shouted at him before resting her free hand over her racing heart.

"Did I?" He hummed with a small, pleased smile on his face.

She glared at him from her kneeling position. "You mind explaining why the hell you broke into my apartment?"

"Is it really breaking in when you choose to leave your sliding glass door partially open?" The vampire countered lightly as he looked over at her from his makeshift bed.

She set her butcher knife down and ran her uninjured hand over her face in exasperation, still trying to calm her racing heart. "Yes, it is. Especially when you weren't invited in."

He tensed at her words. "Are you rescinding the invitation into your home?" If she did, he would literally be forced to leave and that would leave him in a very bad situation.

She groaned softly and ran her hand through her hair. "No, of course not," she sighed. "But, an explanation please? And no theatrics, Lucas. I've had a bad night." She cupped her face in her palm and looked at his face peeking up from her bathtub.

She had to admit that she had always thought he was handsome. His jet black hair was usually kept cut in a gentleman's fashion, the top longer than the bottom and sides. Normally, he kept it neatly parted and swept to the side, but tonight it was messy, strands of it brushing against his forehead. His eyes were like emeralds and lined with thick black lashes. He was just shy of six feet tall, forcing his knees to bend in order for him to fit in her small bathtub.

"Hm, you could say I also had a bad night, which is why I am here." He replied as he gingerly touched his chest.

Kee perked up at his gesture and crawled closer to the bathtub. As soon as she was close enough she sucked in a breath. "Lucas, you're hurt! Is this why there's blood all over the place?"

If he had a shirt on earlier, he didn't anymore. His pale flesh was slashed open from his right collar bone to the bottom of his left rib cage. A long, deep gash ran along his left shoulder, which was also sporting a nasty bruise around his collar bone, and a large cut ran across his lower stomach.

"Very observant of you," he commented blandly. He scanned the formerly white walls of her shower and bathtub, noticing the decent amount of blood smeared everywhere. "I suppose I should clean this."

She scowled at him when he looked up at her with an amused smirk. "This isn't funny. What happened to you? Hold on, I may have bandages somewhere." She moved to stand up, but he put a hand on her shoulder, keeping her in place. "We need to treat them." She protested.

"They will heal on their own, Miss Quinn," he told her. "They would have healed faster if I had fed after the fight, but I did not have the strength to do so."

Granted, he knew some humans who would have thrown them-selves at his fangs, desperate to get bit by someone of his power level, but he always tried to stay clear of them. Honestly, he just didn't want to show up at Byte looking as he did. Plus, Aubrey had been getting on his nerves as of late.

She frowned at him. He was too weak to feed? Lucas was strong, so whatever happened tonight must have drained him. "What happened?" She asked softly, meeting his eyes.

He held her gaze for a second, not removing his hand from her shoulder. "Do not look so sad, no one got the better of me," he smirked at her. "I beat Alexander in our fight. That is all. You were closer than Byte." He knew other beings who lived in Los Angeles as well, but none he trusted as much as her. "I am planning on sleeping here until nightfall."

*That explains the pillow.* "That's fine," she adjusted her weight on her knees. "But, I didn't know you were fighting tonight. I haven't heard from you in three days. Why didn't you tell me?"

He lifted a brow at her, the humor draining from his face. "Why would I? It did not concern you. You are my employee, not a vampire who has sworn loyalty to me." He tried to avoid mixing the two.

Her eyes hardened into a scowl, despite the slight burn his words caused her. "And if you had died? Then what?"

He gave a single, elegant shrug with his good shoulder. "I suppose you would have eventually found out when I did not come to you with a new surveillance job." The only reason he had found out about Alexander's little plan was due to Keira's spying.

She broke eye contact with him and looked down at her knees. "That's cold of you, Lucas."

The vampire tilted his head slightly as he looked at her. "Is it?"

"Yeah. I guess I thought we were, I don't know," she rubbed her hands on her knees and flinched when she felt the fabric stretch her cut. She looked at the wound she had accidentally inflicted on herself as she replied quietly to him, "*Friends?*"

"Friends," he echoed, but his eyes were fixated on her hand. He zeroed in on the blood that was smeared on her flesh and flared his nostrils as the scent swarmed them. It had a unique smell that called to him, inviting him to indulge in its intoxicating taste. He felt his fangs throb in need. "You need to leave." He snapped abruptly as he tore his gaze away from her hand, his hands clenched into fists.

Kee reeled back like he had slapped her. *Is the idea of being friends with a shapeshifter such a disgusting thing?* And here she thought he was different.

She put her hands on the edge of the tub and used it as leverage to stand. "Fine, but let me at least clean your wounds. They look bad, especially this one." She bent over the tub as she reached down to touch the slash across his chest. Before she made contact, his hand wrapped tightly around her wrist, making her flinch. She peered up at him and felt her heart jump to her throat when crimson stared back at her. It was never a good thing when a vampire's eyes changed color, especially a lord.

"I get it, I'll go." She said hastily, trying to pull her hand back from his.

Lucas held firm as he pulled her hand towards his mouth, his tongue running along the cut on her hand without hesitation. His eyes widened slightly at the flavor. He would admit that he had always been curious as to how she would taste, but he had never dreamed it would taste like this. Her blood was sweet, but had a prominent tang that lingered. He had fed on wereanimals before, but none of them made his spine tingle or his skin flush. It was because of what she was, he was sure.

He heard her gasp as he leisurely stroked the cut again with his tongue, but he didn't stop. He normally had ironclad control, but he was wounded and weakened from the fight. He should have taken Giovanni's offer, but he underestimated the damage done to his body. Using his curse hadn't helped either.

He tugged on her wrist, bringing her hand flat against his mouth so his tongue could trace the lacerated flesh again and again. He needed more. He pushed his tongue into her cut, trying to get all the blood he could from it. She called his name, but it was drowned out by his blood lust, the haze rolling over him and muting his senses.

His tongue was cool and the smooth, firm strokes of it on her palm made her stomach do a funny flip. She closed her eyes, biting her bottom lip as he continued to lap at her cut. Her eyes flew open when she was suddenly jerked forward. Her free hand shot out to brace herself against the cool tile of her shower. Again she called his name, but when he didn't respond to her, she forced her hand into a fist, closing him off from the wound. His eyes stared at her fist, his lip lifted in a snarl.

"Lucas!" She called frantically, her voice raising several octaves as his eyes traveled up to her wrist, the gaze turning ravenous. "Don't!" She shouted when he bared his fangs.

She let out a short, pained scream as he sunk his sharp fangs into her wrist without warning, easily tearing through the sensitive skin. He drank as blood poured into his mouth, the liquid all but scorching his throat as he swallowed. He gripped her wrist tighter, forcing out more blood as he greedily drank, ignoring the pleas of his name.

"Lucas, stop!" Kee cried as she felt her strength begin to leave her with each hard suck. She struggled against his hold, but it was like a band of solid steel. She glanced over her shoulder at the knife a few feet away and cursed at the distance, she would never be able to reach it. "Lucas, *please*, stop!"

After a few minutes of her uselessly pleading for him to stop, her arm gave way from the wall, no longer having the strength to support herself. She slumped down ungracefully as her knees buckled, falling on top of him in the bathtub. She was sure she landed on his wounds, jarring them and possibly splitting them further, but still he didn't stop. Black spots formed in front of her eyes and her anxiety heightened, filling her chest with an ice cold fear. He was going to kill her if he didn't stop. She had to think of something, anything, to get him to stop.

*Shift.*

Her mind whirled through the heavy fog, trying to concentrate long enough on a certain image in her mind. But what image? What animal? What skin did she create? Images of the black and white kitten suddenly flashed before her eyes. She locked on to it, her mind replaying the scene over and over again until she felt her body ignite in that familiar heat. Her eyes flashed gold, mirroring those she saw in her mind, before closing tightly as her body shifted.

Lucas was forced to stop when his mouth was suddenly filled with soft fur. His eyes faded back to green as he came back to his senses. He blinked and tried to get his bearings. A tiny, pained mewl instantly drew his attention to his hand. He was holding up a tiny, furry arm, the body awkwardly hanging from it. He quickly released the arm and adjusted his hold so that he held the small kitten in both of his hands. Glassy, golden eyes glanced at him before sliding shut, her head falling forward.

"Keira," he called softly, frowning when she didn't respond. He tightened his hold on her just enough so he could check for a heartbeat. He found one, but it was slow. "Damn." He cursed at his slip of control and set her down on his rapidly healing chest, lying her body on top of his heart as it beat with her unwilling sacrifice.

Keira's blood had turned on his blood lust, something he hadn't lost control of in nearly a century. How? How had he lost control to this extent? If she hadn't shifted into this new form, would he have drained her? It was very possible.

As regretful as he was that he had lost control in his time of need, he would not lie and say he hadn't enjoyed it. Her blood was something he had never tasted before. It filled him with raw power, so much so that even though dawn was swiftly approaching, he did not find himself tired in the least bit. His muscles and bones didn't ache with the need to sleep, to go underground and hide until dusk. He had skipped going to sleep plenty of times, a small benefit of his curse, but he felt as if he could walk around all day in the sun and not feel a single repercussion.

His wounds were healing faster than what was normal after a feeding, his strength fully recovered as well. He frowned as he realized he felt almost a little stronger, as if his muscles and power were on a high from the feast. This was bad. After a taste of her he knew he would crave more in the future. He clenched his jaw and looked down at the small kitten on his chest. No, he couldn't do that to her again, she was too valuable to him. He lightly pet her soft fur, his brow furrowed as he realized he would have to smooth this out with her.

That is, if she didn't take off running first.

# *Four*

"Mommy! Look at the kitty!" *A seven year old Kee exclaimed, pointing to the black cat that sat on their front porch, licking its paw.*

*Her mother laughed at her excitement, smoothing out her daughter's short blonde hair.* "Yes, it's a pretty kitty." *Trinity commented as she handed her daughter a small cup of apple juice.*

*Almost every afternoon after school they would have tea parties on the porch while daddy was at work or with the pack. They would get a worn picnic blanket, spread it out on the wooden deck, and eat peanut butter and jelly sandwiches cut into tiny triangles.*

*Trinity hummed softly as she watched Kee drink her juice.* "Honey, how do you feel?"

*She blinked at her mom.* "Fine," *she replied, distracted by the cat as it curiously crept closer, mewing softly. She held her hand out, reaching to pet the silky black fur.*

"Don't pet strays, Kiki" *she said before her eyes hardened with concern.* "You don't feel itchy at all? Or, like you need a really good stretch?"

*She looked at her mom again. Her long reddish-brown hair was braided in a thick rope that hung over one shoulder, the bright bow Kee had picked out clipped at the end of it.* "No, why would I be itchy? I feel fine, Mommy!"

*Her mother sighed and looked away, her brow furrowed in worry. "It's the full moon tonight," she murmured and then glanced back to the house when the phone rang. "That must be your dad. Stay here, I'll be right back." She could only hope her mate brought good news about the pack.*

*"Okay, Mommy!" She smiled when her mother stood and stroked the top of her hair before disappearing through the front door. She turned back to her sandwich, finishing off the triangle and licking the lingering grape jelly off her fingertips.*

*Hearing a meow, she quickly looked at the cat who now sat directly in front of her, staring at her as it swished its tail. She glanced over her shoulder at the house and then back to the cat. She hesitantly reached out and pet it, smiling as she touched the soft fur. The cat leaned its head in towards her hand, purring contently as it closed its eyes.*

*Kee had always liked cats, but Daddy hated them. She pouted as she pet the cat, knowing she would never be allowed to have one. It wasn't fair! Why didn't Daddy like them? She didn't want a dog like he suggested! She wanted a cat! Cats were pretty, soft, and just so cute! She wanted one!*

*She felt her body suddenly tense, heat spreading like wildfire across her flesh. She looked down at her hands as her skin tingled with sharp, painful pricks. Her bottom lip trembled when her hands convulsed and twitched. A startled scream escaped her lips when they started to shrink and sprout black fur. Moments later she was sitting at equal height as the cat, crying her eyes out, but the sounds that came out were meows. At the noise, the cat ran away, but she was too scared to care.*

*"Keira?!" Her mom shouted as she came running outside. She looked at the clothes on the patio and she smiled, tension leaving her shoulders.*

*'Mommy, help!' Kee tried to say as she strained to grab the hem of her mom's jeans, but her paws didn't have thumbs. Her mom stepped away from her, still shouting her name. 'Mommy!' She cried again.*

*"Kiki, honey, where are you?" Her mother called, running down the three steps of the porch to run around the yard of their small, two story*

house. *"Baby, it's okay! I know your shift is scary the first time, but it's normal! Just come out and I can help you!"*

*She ran after her mom on all fours, trying to get her attention. 'I'm here! Mommy, I'm right here!' She was wailing, but the voice came out as high pitched mews. Why wasn't she helping her? Didn't she see her? Her limbs shook as she ran, the new body and movement rapidly draining whatever energy she had left.*

*"Shoo!" Her mom snarled at the cat who persistently followed her and batted at her ankles. "Keira!"*

*'Mommy!' She sobbed, her little lungs heaving with fear and anxiety. She finally collapsed from the strain, her furry legs giving out under her. She cried out as her body felt as if it was being stretched, like her arms and legs were being pulled in all directions. She felt and heard her bones crack and pop while her muscles burned beneath her skin. She screamed in pain, her meow turning into a very human screech.*

*At the shriek, her mother instantly turned around to see her daughter lying naked on the grass, sobbing hysterically. "Kee!" She quickly ran to her trembling form and hugged her, trying to calm her down as her daughter all but hyperventilated. "Honey, it's okay. Where did you come from? I was looking for your wolf form, but all I saw was that…cat," she trailed off as her body went rigid with fear. "Oh, oh no."*

*At another hiccupping wail, Trinity snapped out of her fear to focus on her daughter. Kee needed her and she would always come first. She scooped her up and held her close, rubbing her bare back as she continued to sob. "Shh, it's okay," she cooed, carrying her into the house and upstairs to Kee's room. She set her down on the twin bed and wrapped the fluffy pink blanket around her. She sat down next to her and rubbed Keira's arms through the blanket, trying to calm both of them down. "Baby, what happened?"*

*"I don't know!" Kee cried, pulling the blanket tighter around her and burrowing herself into her mother's side. "I was scared, Mommy! It hurt! It hurt really bad! A-and I cried for you, but you couldn't see me!"*

*Her mother took a sharp inhale. "Were you chasing after me?" She asked quietly. When she nodded, Trinity's eyes filled up with tears. She tightened her hold on her daughter as she hugged her. "Oh, Kiki..."*

*Kee hadn't been able to sleep that night. She had stayed up and stared wide eyed at the ceiling, scared to go to sleep. She heard the creak of the front door and sat up. 'Daddy must be home!' She thought excitedly. He would make everything better. He always comforted her when she was scared. He was the best daddy ever!*

*She climbed off her bed, clutching her wolf stuffed animal to her. She slipped out of her room and hurried down the stairs, wanting to launch herself into her dad's arms and have him swing her around like he always did when he came home. She reached the kitchen but froze on the other side of the wall when she heard her mother crying.*

*"You have to be mistaken Trinity." Her father told her in a tight voice. "There's no way. Shapeshifters were wiped out nearly two centuries ago. Almost every other race of monster agreed on it. They were too dangerous to be allowed to live. You know this."*

*"I know what I saw, Liam! Think about it! It explains her late shifting and her not being affected by the full moon." Kee's mother pressed with tearful eyes. "She's not a werewolf like us."*

*"That's impossible!" Liam barked defensively. "Unless you cheated on me with some werecat?"*

*She glared at him through her tears. "Don't you dare accuse me of that! I have been nothing but loyal to you! You're my mate and I would never do something so vile!"*

*He sighed heavily, running his hand through his dark blonde hair. He took a few deep breaths before pulling his mate into his arms as she choked on a sob. "I know, I know, Trin. I'm sorry. This is just—fuck I don't even know. It's not good."*

*She wrapped her arms around his waist, holding him just as tight. "What's Christian going to do?" She mumbled into his shoulder.*

*He tensed at the mention of their alpha. "I don't know. You know how old fashioned he is." He replied honestly as he stroked her long, curly brown hair.*

*Trinity pulled back to look up into light blue eyes. "Liam, you can't let him hurt her. She's our daughter."*

*"I know, but this is our pack, Trin. I've been part of them since I was born. This is our family. I'm his beta and I have to do what he tells me."*

*She stepped back from him, her brow furrowed. "But this is our daughter." She stated firmly. "She's your blood."*

*He clenched his jaw. "Is she? Then why isn't she a wolf?"*

*"I don't know!" She cried in frustration. "But this is your daughter and she should come before our pack! She's confused and scared, Liam! She needs us. She needs you, her dad! Fuck the pack and help your daughter!"*

*Liam surged forward with a snarl and cupped her jaw with a firm grip. He pushed her back against the kitchen wall, his hips caging hers. "You can't say that, Trinity." He bit out through clenched teeth, his wolf shining in his eyes. "That's mutiny. If anyone heard you say that you know what the consequences will be."*

*She scowled up at him defiantly, never one to quite submit to her mate when she was supposed to. "You going to tell your precious alpha on me?"*

*His eyes softened as his beast pulled back. "Of course not." He dipped down and pressed a soft kiss to her lips. The hand that was on her throat slid up to caress her cheek. "I wouldn't do that to you."*

*"Mommy? Daddy?" Kee cried as she finally turned the corner to the kitchen to face them.*

*Liam stepped away from his mate so they could turn towards their daughter. Trinity held out her hand to Kee, and she scrambled over. She hugged her mother around the legs and stared up at her dad with pleading, glistening eyes. She would never forget how he reached out to pet her head, hesitated, and then dropped his hand back to his side.*

*"Kee!"*

Kee was startled awake when she heard someone other than her parents call her name. Her eyes snapped open and she stared blankly up at the ceiling, her mind reeling. Finally, she blinked out of her shock, trying to push back the bitter memory. It was then she noticed Cain hovering over her, his dark blue eyes wide with worry. "Cain?" She mumbled, trying to rub the sting out of her eyes.

"Oh, thank gods." The werewolf sighed in relief as he sat on the edge of her bed, running a hand through his hair and down his face. "Fuck, you had me worried."

"Worried?" She echoed softly as she sat up. She felt her comforter fall around her waist, leaving her bare to the cold. Her brow furrowed as she pulled the blanket back up to her chest. When had she gotten naked? Wait, when did she even get home? A wave of dizziness suddenly hit her and she flopped back against the bed. She pressed her hand to her forehead to try and stop the world from spinning. Had she drank that much? She only had three drinks. Right?

"I knew you were mad at me, but damn it, Kee, you could have at least wrote me back letting me know you were safe," he turned to her, looking like a wounded puppy. "I figured you were just angry. I went to visit you at Shifters, but your coworkers said you were a no-show for your bartending shift. I almost lost my shit; I thought something happened to you."

"A no-show? What time is it?" She asked, sitting up once again and reaching for the iPhone on her nightstand. She didn't remember setting it there last night either. She unlocked her phone and saw seven missed calls, five from Cain and two from her manager. She cleared them and looked at the time. "It's 6:43pm?!"

His brow furrowed. "Are you saying you've been asleep since last night?"

"Yeah, but I don't remember going to sleep." She admitted as she clicked on her text messages. She had six from Cain, one from her coworker, and one from Lucas. She tensed, the memories from last night rushing back to her like a broken flood gate.

She hesitantly glanced at her wrist and sucked in a breath to see two bruised, swollen puncture wounds on her wrist, the cut on her palm barely visible anymore. Her gut twisted as she remembered the feeling of Lucas drinking her blood. The firm, sure strokes of his tongue had made butterflies burst in her stomach. However, her chest grew cold when she realized he could have, and very well may have, killed her if she hadn't shifted.

She shuddered at the thought.

"What the hell is this?" Cain asked as he grabbed her forearm, bringing it closer so he could inspect the puncture holes in her small wrist. His eyes darkened, his lip lifting into a sneer as he glanced back up at her naked form. "Is this why your apartment reeks of blood? What did you do, Kee?"

Her eyes widened slightly at the rough edge to his voice. Fuck, the last thing she needed to deal with was Cain's wolf. She slowly put her phone down back onto the nightstand without checking the message. Grey orbs met fierce blue. "Cain, it's not what you think." Even to her that sounded cliché, despite it being the truth.

"We get into one fight and you turn into a blood whore?" He growled, his dominant aura expanding and pressing down on her. A blood whore was someone who gave both blood and sex to vampires for a price. Was that what she did for the lord of the city? Had she lied about her surveillance job this entire time?

She could feel his jealousy and possessiveness feeding his inner alpha, making it surface as he tightened his hold on her forearm. His fingers pressed into her skin, but not hard enough to leave a bruise. She hardened her eyes, trying to hide the unease she was beginning to feel. Cain had never hurt her before, never given her a reason to fear him, but she knew when to be cautious when dealing with a werewolf.

"I said it's not what you think," she repeated sternly, trying to pull her arm from his vice-like grip. "You know me better than that."

Cain grabbed her other wrist when she tried to push him away. "It was your boss, wasn't it?" He asked, his voice cold as it rumbled with the presence of his wolf.

She scowled at him, but her heart was racing, causing her head to swim in dizziness. The loss of blood was taking its toll on her. "I refuse to talk to you when you're like this," she met the dark blue eyes of his inner wolf. "Get off me." She warned.

"Did you tell him that too?" He questioned sarcastically, his energy expanding out to press down on her again, trying to get her to submit to him.

She tried again to pull her wrists free from him, but his hold was tight. Why couldn't she have the strength of a werewolf? She heard another rumble in his chest, his aura pushing down on her harder. "You can't make me submit to you, Cain. I'm not a werewolf! Nothing like that happened! Now, get off me!"

He ignored her demands and bent towards her, his nose running along the soft skin by her neck and then down towards her breasts. He released a vicious growl and bared his teeth. "His scent is all over you! How can you say nothing happened?!"

Kee felt a rush of adrenaline hit her as her fear spiked. Taking action, she quickly flung her head forward, slamming her forehead into his. When his grip loosened from the shock and the disorientation, she ripped away from his hold and leapt off the bed. Her knees instantly buckled, and she tried to brace herself against the nightstand, but ended up sending everything on it to the ground with her. Her body was already weak from Lucas' feast last night and the impact with Cain's head hadn't helped.

She quickly looked up and shrank back when she felt Cain move off the bed. She had never dealt with his wolf acting like this before and she was painfully reminded of her father's rage. It scared her. "I think you should go until you've calmed down, Cain. I'll explain things once you're yourself again. I'm not dealing with your wolf."

Seeing the fear in her eyes made his feet freeze, his stomach dropping. Why was she looking at him like that? Did she really think he would hurt her? *Had* he hurt her? His heart twisted at the thought. Still, his eyes went to the blood on the floor and then back to her naked form. His hands clenched into fists, his back rod-straight with confusion and anger as his wolf paced inside him. "Just tell me if you slept with him."

"Of course I didn't, Cain," she mumbled, pressing her hand to her forehead when she felt something wet trickle down between her eyes. She pulled her hand away and looked at the smear of blood. "How could you even think that of me?"

He felt the relief run straight down to his beast, calming him down. His jealousy cooled but didn't extinguish completely. Why was she naked? "Kee, tell me what happened."

"No. Just go home, Cain." She said with an exasperated sigh. She moved to stand up, once again trying to use her nightstand as leverage to stand.

He moved to help her, but she quickly shook her head and shied away from him. His hands balled into fists again. "Fine," he murmured dejectedly. "I'll talk to you later."

"Later," she echoed, not watching as he left. Hearing the front door shut, she collapsed onto her bed and rubbed her hands down her face. She was going to give Lucas a piece of her mind for getting her into this fucking mess. At the reminder of the unread message, she reached for her phone on the nightstand, but instead found it shattered on the floor. She groaned and mourned the loss for a second before flopping back against her pillows again. For the moment, she was just too exhausted to care.

# Five

"Kee."

The shapeshifter looked up from the bar at Cain's voice. She saw him freeze before he grabbed a chair at the bar, his body tense as they stared at each other hesitantly.

She drank in his appearance. His short, dark brown hair was a little messy, his clothes dirty from working outside all day. She saw his eyes gleam with uncertainty as if he didn't know if it was okay for him to sit or not. They hadn't spoken in a couple days since her phone had shattered, so she could understand why he felt that way. She would have tried to go to his house, but as an iron worker he usually worked long hours during the day. And, since she had been promoted to bartender, she was expected to close the bar the nights she didn't work for Lucas.

She shook her head and then quickly made her way out from around the horseshoe-shaped bar. Ignoring the man with him, as well as the other patrons at her bar top, she stood on her tiptoes and threw her arms around his neck. Almost instantly, she felt his arms encircle her waist, holding her firmly against him. "I love you." She whispered.

He and his wolf relaxed at those three words. "I love you, too." He told her and bent down so he could place a kiss on her lips.

Kee kissed him back and then pulled away when someone cleared his throat loudly. She gave an embarrassed laugh and looked at the other werewolf. He was taller than her but shorter than Cain. He was heavily built with bulky muscles that could be seen through his black work shirt. Much to his irritation, she often teased him about working out too much. He had blonde hair that was cut close to his head in a military fashion and dark brown eyes. He was Cain's best friend and the only member of the pack that she knew on a personal level.

"Good to see you, too, Noah."

He held up a hand in a mock salute. "Hey, Kee. Please tell Cainy-boy here that you're not mad at him. I'm real tired of his ass moping around all fucking day."

She laughed again as she turned back to Cain. "I'm not mad at you," she said. "My phone broke when I knocked it off the nightstand, and I don't have your number memorized." She admitted.

The beta blinked at her before laughing. "I'll admit that I don't know yours either. It's sad what technology has done to us." He smiled at her and then cupped the side of her face lovingly, his thumb brushing along her cheek bone. "I'm just glad you're not mad at me. Especially with how we left things. And for how...*we* acted." We, being him and his wolf.

She rubbed her cheek against his palm. "I'm not mad at you. I just haven't had a chance to go get a new phone yet." As she went to give him another hug, she noticed the sulking wolf behind him. His fur was light brown with streaks of darker brown on his paws, ears, and tail. She realized it was the same one that had been under the table at Shifters when she met his pack. Despite him being practically the size of a small pony, she hadn't noticed him all. She frowned when she realized his aura was almost nonexistent.

She looked at Cain. "Is he okay?" She asked, nodding towards the large wolf sitting behind him.

He sighed and stepped aside so the wolf was in view. "His name is Conrad. He recently joined the pack."

"Hi, Conrad," she greeted with a warm smile. However, it slipped when his amber eyes glanced at her before looking away, his ears slanted down in a submission. "Did something happen?"

Cain exhaled softly. "I don't know for sure, but he won't go into his human form." He looked back at the light brown wolf with a frown. "A werewolf that spends too much time in their wolf form sometimes isn't able to shift back. They bond too closely to their beast and forget their human form. It happens mostly with submissive wolves."

"And, you think that's what's happening?" She asked and then jumped when a werecat at her bar slammed his cup down on the countertop, shouting at her for another round. "I'm coming, hold on!" She snapped as she moved back behind the bar.

Cain and Noah each took a seat at the bar top, Conrad sitting back towards the wall where he wasn't in anyone's way. "I don't know. Maybe." He admitted as he watched her pour vodka into a cup of ice.

"Probably," Noah scoffed as he looked at the wolf. "Useless, really. Why would Warren even let him into the pack?"

Kee frowned at him as she squirted cranberry juice into the glass from the bar gun. "Don't be mean, Noah. You don't know what he's been through." She chided before walking over and setting the drink in front of the werecat.

"I'm being honest! It makes sense that his old pack didn't want him. I mean, it's basically like having a pet." He continued on with a sneer. "A wolf pack doesn't need a *wolf* pet."

"That's enough, Noah. Warren said he was given to the pack by the Alpha of LA County. We had to take him in, so just leave it," he looked at his girlfriend and tried to change the subject.

"Can we get two pints of the seasonal porter?"

"Sure," she said with a smile as she headed towards the taps.

Her well was on one side of the bar, the taps on the other. In the middle was an island of the bar's various liquor bottles. She got to the beer line and grabbed two cold pint glasses from the fridge next to it. As she poured the first one from the tap, she felt a cool air brush against her back. She looked over her shoulder and nearly dropped the other glass when she saw Lucas standing at the bar. His face was impassive, but the tight skin around his bright green eyes watching her told her he was angry.

Kee swallowed thickly and turned back to the beer, her shoulders stiff. She couldn't believe he was at her work. She hadn't spoken or seen him since the night he was in her apartment.

*Honestly, I'm not sure I want to see him. What do you say to someone who might have drained you dry?* Her mind drifted back to the text message she had never been able to read. *What had he said? Did it have something to do with why he's here now?*

She quickly focused back on the beer when she felt it overflow onto her hand. She dumped a little off the top and then started pouring the next one. She could feel Lucas' eyes staring at her, making the back of her neck itch. Glancing over at the other side of the bar, she frowned when she couldn't see Cain over the island of alcohol bottles. She wasn't sure what would happen if Cain saw Lucas without knowing what really transpired that night. But, then again, maybe it would be worse if he did know. Cain had always been protective, the jealousy had just been something new.

"Miss Quinn."

She jumped, sloshing the beer onto the floor. Her skin broke out in goosebumps as his deep voice sent a chill down her spine. She pushed the beer handle back, cutting off the tap, and cleared her throat twice before speaking. "I'm working."

"Clearly." The vampire responded, leaning forward to rest his elbows on the polished, wooden bar top.

She grabbed a pint glass in each hand but didn't turn around. "What do you want?" She asked quietly, trying not to draw a certain werewolf's attention towards them.

"We need to speak," Lucas stated simply. "Since you refuse to acknowledge any of my messages."

She finally turned around, meeting his eyes for a second before looking over in Cain's direction. "It's not a good time, Lucas."

"Make it one. I will be waiting outside." He informed her as he straightened. "Do not continue to leave me waiting."

That snapped something inside her. "Or, what?" She couldn't help but remark sarcastically, anger seeping into her tone. *Did he really think he could come in and boss me around after what he did? Hell no.* "Are you going to sink your fangs into me again?"

His eyes narrowed into a hard glare, his aura flaring with another cold wave of air that made her step back. "Do you wish to have this discussion here?" He had asked it quietly, but the tone sent another wave of chills down her spine.

"Is there a problem?"

*Fucking shit.* Kee cursed in her head as Cain rounded the side of the bar, his eyes dark with his wolf's presence. "No, Cain, there isn't." She said calmly as she looked at him from behind her bar top. He was sneering at Lucas, who in turn was looking impassively at him.

"You heard her, Mr Donovan," Lucas replied evenly before looking back at his employee. "I will be outside. Do not keep me waiting." He warned her before walking away from the bar, heading towards the side entrance that led to the smoking patio.

"Kee." Cain said softly, but his voice was rough.

"Cain, it's not what you think," she set the two glasses down on the counter before meeting his eyes. "I promise I will explain everything.

He just needs to talk to me for a minute since my phone is broken. It's probably just work related, okay?"

"*Probably.*" He repeated suspiciously.

"Cain, please." She begged him to understand. *But, how can I even ask that of him after how he had found me a few nights ago?*

"Go to your bloodsucker, Keira." He said stiffly before picking up the glasses and taking them over to his seat.

She cursed at Lucas' shit timing as she moved from behind the bar to storm out onto the outdoor smoking patio. She saw him leaning against the wall towards the back, watching her as she neared.

"Miss Quinn." He greeted pleasantly as if he hadn't just ruined her night.

She gave him a scowl. "How many times do I have to tell you to call me Kee?"

"More, it seems." He replied lightly.

She sighed and leaned back against the cold wall, crossing her arms over her chest as she glanced up at Lucas. He was wearing black slacks and a deep blue dress shirt, his hair neatly styled to the side. She met his emerald green eyes and realized he was staring back at her. She quickly looked away. He had never compelled her before, but she didn't want him to start now. "So, what do you want to talk about?"

"Why have you not returned my text messages?" The vampire questioned, eyes never leaving her face.

"I don't have my phone." She responded with a shrug. "So I didn't get them."

"You had your phone when I put you to bed." He stated casually. He tried to hold back his smirk when her cheeks reddened.

She flushed when she remembered waking up naked. "Bet you got an eyeful." She muttered sarcastically, not looking at him.

He gave a one shoulder shrug. "I did not expect you to shift back to your human form when you did. We were still lying in the bathtub."

Her cheeks were bright red now. "We wouldn't have been in that situation if you hadn't attacked me!" She accused.

Lucas sighed and stepped closer to her, almost trapping her against the wall. "I tried to warn you to get away," he said softly, almost earnestly. "But still, I did not mean to attack you. I underestimated my condition and endangered you by seeking shelter in your home."

Kee looked up, tilting her head back slightly so she could see his solemn expression. "I thought you were going to kill me." She murmured, recalling the fear she had felt with each hard pull of his mouth.

He lifted a hand to touch her cheek but stopped when she flinched, letting it fall back to his side in a fist. "I could never kill you, Keira."

She mentally berated herself for recoiling away from him. *I can't help it. It's a reflex.*

He saw her brows knit in confusion and quickly switched the topic. "What happened to your phone?"

She huffed at the change of topic and looked away from him when he took a step back. "It broke," she scoffed. "Maybe shattered is the better word."

"Shattered?" He echoed.

She sighed. "Cain and I got into a fight, and I knocked it off the nightstand."

Lucas tensed slightly, his eyes narrowing into an icy glare. "Did he hurt you?" His eyes glanced towards the door leading back into the bar, body tensing.

She blinked at the sudden hard tone in his voice and shook her head. "No, just scared me a little, I guess."

"Did he put his hands on you?" He pressed.

*Why does he care?* "It's not what you think. It was just his alpha side coming out." She shook her head again when he scowled. "Let it go, Lucas. He was jealous. He assumed that you and I had...*you know.*"

"Why would he assume that?" Not that the idea had never crossed his mind.

She gave him a disbelieving look, oblivious to his thoughts. "I was naked in bed with your scent all over me and a bite mark on my wrist. What other conclusion could he come to?"

"Hm," he changed the subject. "Did the cleaners do an adequate job?"

This time she was thankful for the change of subject. "Yeah, thank you for sending them." She had been surprised when the cleaners showed up at her door the night of her and Cain's fight, saying they were sent by a Mr Vranas. They had only been there for an hour, but had the whole apartment sparkling after they left.

He nodded once and the two fell into an awkward silence. He had the last few days to think about what he wanted to do with his employee. He wasn't done with her skills, not by a long shot, but he could not force her to stay. The fact that she hadn't answered him made him assume she was leaving her job, and that had bothered him. He would admit that he wanted another taste of her, but he refused to cross that line again. He didn't want the constant temptation, but she was also extremely valuable to him. That left him uncertain on how to continue forward. Especially now that she was talking to him and not running away.

Lucas looked at her again, taking in her reclined form against the brick wall. Her arms were crossed tightly across her chest, her eyes looking down at the spilled beer on her shoes. Her long hair was pulled back from her face in a high ponytail.

"Keira." When she jerked her head up to meet his gaze, he continued. "Where do we stand?"

She looked back down and shuffled her required, nonslip shoes along the concrete surface. "I don't know." She really didn't. Part of her was scared of him, but part of her wanted to continue working for him. Plus, it was hard to let go of someone who accepted you for who you were. She didn't have many to begin with.

He clenched his jaw. "Should I relieve you of your position?"

She exhaled in a heavy sigh. "I've been thinking about that," she admitted before looking at him once again. *Really, working for him is the main reason I can afford my apartment downtown, but I also like the freedom of being myself.* "I don't want to quit, but I've been thinking of how to make the best of the situation."

"Which is?"

"A raise." She gave him a small, teasing smile. "You took what wasn't offered, so I'm demanding the same."

He tilted his head slightly at her in disbelief. "A raise?" He was quiet for a moment before he let out a laugh. "Is that what you want?"

Her smile widened at his laugh. She had only heard it maybe a handful of times in the past two years. It was a nice sound. "Yeah, I think I deserve it."

His laugh settled down into a smirk. "Fine, Miss Quinn, I will give you a raise. Now, if there is nothing else, I will leave and let you get back to your other job. I will be in contact." He said as he began to walk towards the exit of the patio.

She pushed off from the wall and looked at his back. "I don't have a phone, though." She scoffed when he simply lifted a hand and waved it at her without turning around. She rolled her eyes, but a small smile still tilted up her lips as she turned and headed back inside the bar. She made it in time to see Cain and Noah getting up from their seats, glasses empty. All humor leaving her, she hurried over to her boyfriend and grabbed his hand in both of hers. "Cain."

He looked down at her with a clenched jaw. "I have to go."

She frowned. "I get off in twenty minutes. Meet me at my apartment, please? I will explain everything."

He glanced at the other two werewolves as they waited off to the side. "I have to take Noah home first, but Conrad will be with me if I come."

"That's fine." She said quickly, giving his hand a squeeze.

He stared down into her pleading eyes and sighed heavily as he caved. "Alright."

"Thank you," she tightened her hold on his hand again before letting go. "I love you."

"You, too." He mumbled reluctantly as he turned and headed out the door, his two pack mates behind him.

"Ay! What the hell are they paying you for? Get me another drink!" The werecat hissed at her, tapping his empty glass against the bar again. "You listening!?"

She rolled her eyes as she headed back behind the bar. "Yeah, yeah, I heard you!"

# _Six_

After work, Kee changed into leopard print pajama shorts and one of Cain's oversized shirts. She had just finished clipping up her hair in a loose bun when she heard three raps on the front door. She quickly walked down the hall and to the door, giving the werewolves a welcoming smile as she opened it. "Thank you for coming."

Cain nodded at her and walked into her apartment when she stepped aside, Conrad following close behind him. When she closed the door behind them, he looked at her attire and couldn't help the small smile that curled up his lips. "I was wondering where my red shirt went."

She widened her grey eyes and gave him a slight head tilt. "What red shirt?" She asked innocently as she tugged on the hem. "This is *my* shirt, and it's my favorite."

He rolled his eyes, but was powerless to stop his smile as it widened. So much for staying mad at her. "I guess that means I have no chance of getting it back."

Her face instantly deadpanned. "Not a chance," she commented before laughing and giving him a bright smile.

"You're lucky you're cute." He teased.

She stuck her tongue out at him and then turned her attention to the wolf standing uncertainly by the wall. "Conrad, do you want something to eat or drink?" When his amber eyes flicked towards her and then towards the ground, she let out a soft sigh. "Well, why don't you go relax on the couch? Cain and I will go talk in the bedroom."

Cain nodded at Conrad when he looked at him for approval. He watched as the wolf jumped onto the couch and then looked down at Kee, his expression turning serious once again. "Let's get this over with."

She frowned at his exasperated tone but agreed as they walked to her room in silence. She plopped down on her bed and felt her heart clench when he remained standing. She drew her knees to her chest and took a deep, nervous breath before telling him everything that happened a few nights ago.

"And then you woke me up." She murmured when she finished her story, resting her chin on her knees.

Cain was furious, his beast thrumming inside him like a second heartbeat. "How could he do that to you?" He bent down and angrily tugged at the laces on his work boots before kicking them off. He turned his attention back on her and felt his chest tighten at the vulnerable look in her eyes. "Kee..."

"I was scared," she admitted quietly and closed her eyes. She hid her face in her knees when the mattress dipped under his weight. He moved behind her and wrapped his arms around her shoulders, pulling her back against his chest. Having missed his presence, the warmth of him around her, she relaxed into him. His pine and earthy scent soothed her, made her feel safe. "I just felt so powerless, so *weak*. Then it happened again with you in the morning, and it was so frustrating." It reminded her of the time with her father.

*I thought I had grown stronger since then, but apparently not.* She thought miserably.

"I'm sorry," he told her softly as he reached up and unclipped her hair, letting it cascade over her shoulder. "For everything. Getting so jealous, losing my temper, for my wolf, *everything*. I never wanted to make you feel weak because you're everything but that. You're one of the strongest women I know. And definitely one of the most stubborn." When that earned him a soft laugh, he nuzzled the top of her hair in apology. "I'm sorry I doubted you."

She closed her eyes and tilted her head back against his shoulder. "I told you it wasn't what it seemed." She whispered as she basked in the feel of him, of the solidity of his person against hers. "But, I understand that it looked bad."

Keeping his arms around her, he took her with him as he fell back against the bed and rolled them to the side. He released her so he could caress her cheek, his blue eyes staring up into hers seriously. "I'm sorry I tried to make you submit to me," he glanced away, looking like a kicked dog. "I feel so guilty for even grabbing you like that. I never meant to do that, Kee. My alpha came out, but that's no excuse. I will never hurt, or scare you, again."

She gave him a small smile and put her hand on his, drawing his eyes back to hers. "Promise?"

"Yes." He cupped the back of her neck and pulled her closer so he could press their foreheads together. "I swear on my beast."

Her smile widened and she pressed a tender kiss to his lips, the new scruff on his face tickling her. She lightly ran her fingertips over the short pricks of hair. "Growing a beard?" She teased.

He grinned, his hand running down her back. "I wanted to try it. Do you like it?"

"So far." She responded and then giggled when he kissed her again while simultaneously grabbing her ass. "Don't be bad. Conrad is just down the hall."

"I wouldn't be surprised if he's used to hearing Warren and Nat go at it," he replied with a squeeze of her fleshy cheek before flipping them over so he was on top. "I haven't seen you in days, Kee. You're not getting out of this until we are thoroughly covered in each other's scent."

Cain made quick work of her shirt before he hooked his thumbs in her shorts and slid them, along with her panties, down her legs. He tossed the clothes aside and stared down at her naked form sprawled out before him. A growl of appreciation rumbled in his chest. His nostrils flared as the heady scent of her arousal quickly filled his nose, making his cock harden further. Gods, everything about her was delicious.

"What?" She asked softly, pressing her knees together self-consciously. "What are you looking at?"

"You," his eyes languidly traveled up her body until they met hers. "I'm enjoying the view."

A blush warmed her cheeks. "You've seen it before," she murmured, watching him as he tugged off his clothes and threw them on the floor to join hers.

"Doesn't matter," he replied as he slid his hands under her knees to pull them apart. "I love looking at you, and I'll never get tired of it." He promised as he settled between her thighs, rubbing the head of his erection up and down her folds, coating it in her slickness.

Her heart fluttered at his words, but before she could reply, he surged forward and buried himself deep within her heat. She sucked in a breath at the full feeling and let out a throaty moan as he shifted his hips.

Cain withdrew until just the head remained before thrusting hard back into her. He repeated the movement, over and over until he had a steady rhythm. When she tilted her head back with another moan, he bent over her to nip the column of her throat. His wolf rumbled in approval when she moved her hands to his shoulders, nails biting into his skin as she clung to him and moaned his name.

"You're mine," he growled against her neck, voice rough with the presence of his wolf. All he wanted to do was sink his canines into her creamy flesh and officially make her his. He wanted Kee as his mate and meeting the pack had been but the first step. Once he had Warren's approval, he would ask her. "Say it."

"Fuck!" She cried out as he lifted her hips, the new angle hitting that sweet spot inside her.

She squirmed as her pleasure mounted, legs beginning to tremble on either side of him. She tossed her head back against the pillow again, eyes squeezed shut as the wave built and built within her. She could feel her skin begin to heat, chest flushing with the incoming orgasm.

"Say you're mine," he repeated, slowing his thrusts.

"Cain!" Kee protested, her climax slipping away before it could teeter over.

He stilled his movements, hands releasing her hips to slide up to her waist. His lips brushed her ear. "Say it, Kee." He rumbled in her ear before biting the lobe.

"I'm yours," she huffed out, her tone on the edge of pleading.

Cain growled in triumph and grabbed her hips to flip her over onto her stomach. He jerked them back, forcing her to her hands and knees. Using his grip as leverage, he slipped back into her in one smooth thrust and began a relentless pace.

Kee moaned and gripped the comforter tightly in her fists. She dropped her head, hair falling in a curtain of dark gold around her face as she tried to rock back against him to meet his thrusts. His hands tightened on her hips, stopping her movements to remain in control. When he grunted and increased his speed, she rubbed her clit with her middle finger.

He groaned when she clamped down on him with a cry, pushing him over the edge to his own climax. He slammed into her a final time and came, coating her walls with his seed. Feeling completely spent, he slowly pulled out and flopped down on the bed next to her. He gave a lazy smile and wrapped an arm around her shoulders when she snuggled up to his side. "Love you," he mumbled.

She smiled and pressed a kiss to his chest. "Love you, too."

—

A persistent, loud knocking echoed throughout Kee's apartment the next morning, making her jerk awake. She groaned and tried to rub the sleep out of her eyes. She gave a tired laugh when she was pulled tighter against a naked chest. Her bare skin tingled as his scorching flesh pressed against hers and she hummed when she felt something firm press against her ass. She almost wiggled back against him but sighed when the knocking became louder.

"They're not going away." She whispered.

"Fuck them." Cain growled low, lust in his tone as he ran his hand down to her hip, pulling her firmer against him.

"I'll make sure to tell them you said that," she laughed as she rolled away from him and stood from the bed. She picked his red shirt up off the floor and slipped it on, the bottom hem falling to her upper thighs. "I'll be right back." She told him as she walked out of the bedroom.

She padded down the hallway and saw Conrad standing on her couch, his hackles raised as he stared at the door. "It's okay, Conrad." She tried to soothe him as he leapt off the cushion and followed her to the door. When the loud knocking came once again, she rolled her eyes and shouted, "I'm coming!"

"Miss Keira Quinn?" A man asked briskly once she pulled the door open. His face was blank, but irritation gleamed in his brown eyes.

"Yes, that's me." Her brow furrowed when his eyes scanned her appearance, trailing slowly down her body and then back up. *Pervert.* "Can I help you?" She asked uncomfortably while Conrad growled at the same time.

He instantly lifted his eyes to meet hers, his face unimpressed. He then held out a small, black box to her. "A delivery."

She lifted a brow at him, not taking the package. "Why not just leave it at the front desk? You didn't have to stand here and wake the whole floor up."

He frowned at her. "I was told to make sure it was delivered to you personally." When she still hesitated, he huffed. "Mr Vranas was *very* specific."

At the mention of Lucas, her eyebrows lifted in surprise. When he said he would be in touch, she didn't think he meant the next morning. She took the package from him. "There, tell him I got it."

"Will do." He stated flippantly before walking away from her door.

Kee watched him go before closing the door and locking it. She walked over to her black leather couch and sat down, Conrad cautiously following her. She smiled at him as she set the package on her glass coffee table. A white envelope nestled in red tissue paper greeted her when she opened the lid. Picking it up, she slid her finger under the sealed flap and took out a simple matte, black card. She flipped it open and read the message written in Lucas' neat penmanship.

*'Miss Quinn,*

*I have supplied you with a new cellular device so I can contact you more conveniently. Think of it as part of your raise. Please see to it that it is not broken. Also supplied is equipment you will need for our next meeting. I will contact you with more details later.*

*-L.V.*

*P.s. Take heed, it is ready to be used.'*

She rolled her eyes but couldn't help the smile that tugged at the corner of her lips. He didn't have to buy her a phone, but she would admit that she was happy she didn't have to spend the money to get a new one. She set the card down on the coffee table and pulled out the tissue paper from the box. A new black smartphone sat there waiting for her, the charger and a set of earphones next to it. It didn't come in the box it was originally packaged in, but she didn't care. She lifted it from the tissue and pressed the home screen, not surprised that it was already on and fully charged. He did say it was ready to be used, but she wasn't sure why she had to be careful.

She set her new phone to the side and removed the rest of the tissue paper, curious as to what the equipment could be. When the item was finally in view, her lips parted in shock. There, sitting innocently on top of the thin tissue paper, was a gun. She looked at Conrad, who tilted his head at her in question. She looked back down at the gun and knit her brows together.

*What in the hell was Lucas thinking? I have exactly zero experience with guns! What does he expect me to do with it? Am I supposed to kill someone?* She paled, the color draining from her face. What else could he want her to do with it? She shook her head and swallowed thickly. There was no way; he knew her better than that.

Hesitantly, she reached into the box and lifted the firearm from it with both hands, surprised by its weight. She saw Conrad back up from the corner of her eye but didn't put it down. She knew nothing about guns. She couldn't tell any of them apart, except for the obvious like a shotgun or a rifle. Everything else looked pretty similar to her. She wrapped one hand around the grip, keeping her finger away from the trigger. She inspected it inquisitively, turning it this way and that.

Curiously, she did what she saw in the movies, pulling back the top piece of it to see if it was as easy as it looked. She blinked when it clicked and snapped back into place. She went to put her finger on the trigger but stilled when she remembered Lucas' last sentence.

*He had meant the gun was ready, not the phone! Gods, I'm a fucking idiot!* She quickly put it an arm's length away.

"Kee? What are you doing?" Cain asked sleepily as he walked into the living room wearing just his boxers. He blinked when he saw her awkwardly holding a gun at arm's length. He quickly moved forward and carefully took it away from her. "What the hell? Where did you get this?"

"From a package Lucas sent me," she said as she tucked her hair behind her ear. "That's what all that pounding was. I guess it had to be delivered straight to me."

He set the gun back in the box as he sat down next to her and reached for the card on the coffee table. He scoffed as he finished reading the note before tossing it back down on the table. "What does he expect you to do with it?"

"I have no idea, Cain," she replied as she rubbed her arms. "I don't think I can kill someone."

"Has he ever asked you to do something like this before?"

She shook her head. "I guess I'll find out his reasoning when he contacts me." She showed him the first part of her package. "On a lighter note, he got me a new phone, too."

His face scrunched in annoyance. "Bastard beat me to it."

Kee lifted a slender brow at him. "Beat you to what?" She didn't bother to comment on his hostility towards Lucas. Cain had disliked the vampire before their fight and apparently hated him even more after.

"Getting you a phone. I was going to take you today to get one since I'm part of the reason yours broke." He ran his hand through his dark brown hair in frustration. "Now what am I supposed to do to make it up to you?"

"You don't have to make it up to me, Cain." She told him with a reassuring smile as she reached over and pressed a kiss to his cheek.

"I want to." He pressed, his dark blue eyes holding hers.

"So persistent. Fine, how about a case instead?" She offered with a smile. "That way it won't break again so easily." She laughed when he pouted at her. "Dinner too, then."

He sat up straighter at the mention of dinner. "Actually, Warren and Natalie asked us to join them for dinner tonight." When she tensed, he put his hand on her knee. "Don't freak out. They like you, Kee. They feel bad about what happened."

She pursed her lips and looked away from him, her eyes meeting Conrad's anxious ones. "I don't know, Cain. It didn't go very well last time. I don't like being put on the spot like that."

"I know, but Nat said Warren won't do that again. He was just doing his job as alpha, I don't think he meant any harm." He explained softly.

She sighed, still holding Conrad's gaze. "Will the whole pack be there?" She frowned when the wolf looked away.

"Most of them. It's a pack barbeque before tomorrow's full moon." He gave her knee a soft squeeze when she still didn't look at him. "We don't have to go if you don't want to."

She bit back her refusal when he all but whispered that last sentence. She knew he wanted to go, knew his pack meant everything to him. With another heavy sigh, she gave in and looked at him. "Fine, but no fighting afterwards."

He smiled brilliantly at her, flashing her white teeth. "Deal." He relished the sound of her laugh as he pulled her closer.

She snuggled into his side and he wrapped an arm around her, his thumb rubbing small circles on her shoulder. She was happy they had made up, but she was apprehensive about meeting with his pack again. Did he tell them that she had supposedly cheated on him? What would they think of her if that was the case?

"We should probably put that away before we leave." He commented, looking at the black box on the coffee table.

Kee sat up, grabbed the box and slid it under the couch. "We'll deal with it later." She then stood up and put her hands on her hips, turning towards the boys with a wide smile. "How about some coffee and breakfast?"

# _Seven_

"Kee! I'm so happy you came!" Natalie cooed as she saw Cain enter the living room with Kee and Conrad trailing behind him.

It was a large, two story house situated in the hills of Burbank, near the edge of La Tuna Canyon Park. Since Warren was the alpha of the LA pack, she didn't understand why he lived in the next city over until Cain explained that the city of Burbank fell under the LA pack territory. Plus, the hills provided ample running and hunting space.

The house itself was pretty, the inside was professionally decorated in rich, dark browns and creams. The floor was a polished dark wood, matching that of the coffee table and entertainment center. The couches and curtains were cream, the walls just a shade or two lighter. It was welcoming, yet stiff, not quite having that homey vibe.

"Thank you for inviting me, Natalie." Kee said, trying to smile naturally. She chose to wear black leggings, knee high boots, and a form fitting, lavender button up that reached to the tops of her thighs. She had worn something comfortable, yet cute, trying to look good for Cain and his pack.

_Damn, I should have dressed up._

The woman before her screamed wolf queen. Even if she hadn't known she was Warren's mate, she would have bet Natalie was an alpha's woman. She exuded confidence. From her relaxed posture to the deep cleavage dip in her dark red dress. Her light blonde hair fell in perfect, loose waves to the middle of her back, her hazel eyes accented with natural hues of eyeshadow.

"Of course, my dear." She cupped Kee's cheeks in her hands and rubbed their noses together in an intimate greeting that made Kee feel awkward. "Warren wanted you to come so he could do a little bit of groveling."

"I do *not* grovel," came the smooth voice of the alpha. He and Cain clasped forearms in greeting before he approached the two girls. When Nat stepped away, he took her place, holding the newcomer's face in his hands. "But, I *do* apologize."

Kee tensed, her body going rigid as the alpha nuzzled her forehead. She knew werewolves were physical creatures, showing emotion and such through contact, but it was still something that made her uncomfortable. Ever since she was beat as a child, she didn't like people touching her. It had taken her a while to get used to it with Cain, and now she craved his touches. But people she didn't know being so familiar with her pushed her comfort zone.

"I-it's fine." She stammered as she looked to the side, not meeting the alpha's gaze.

"I would never want to cause disruption in my beta's relationship." He told her seriously. "You are important to Cain, so you are important to me. To *us*."

Warren pulled away from her but moved his hand to the small of her back, leading her towards the couches where four other werewolves sat. "Kee, allow me to introduce the two other wolves who have status in my pack." He gestured towards a wolf with blonde hair and light green eyes. "This is Mason. He's the pack representative when it comes to matters outside the pack. He makes sure I know what is happening with the other monsters in town."

"It is a pleasure to meet you." Mason stated with a warm smile as he reached out to shake her hand. He then gestured to a man with tawny bronze skin, his light brown eyes matching the hair that fell to his shoulders. "This is my mate Brandon."

"Can't get Cain to shut up about you. We're sorry we couldn't meet you with the pack at Shifters, we were attending a meeting." Brandon explained, dropping his arm along the back of the couch behind his mate after shaking her hand as well.

She didn't bother to ask about the meeting; it wasn't her business. "It's very nice to meet you both." She responded before Warren turned her attention towards the other couch. A man with short cropped black hair sat next to a woman with dark brown hair cut in an A-line. Both of them had different shades of blue eyes, the man had ice blue while the woman had more of an aqua. They were both very striking, beautiful people.

"This is my younger brother Wyatt, and his intended mate Katie." Warren introduced. "Wyatt handles all of my business outside of the pack."

"Like, your dirty work?" Kee blurted before she could stop it.

Warren and Wyatt let out identical laughs. "You could say that," the younger brother said as he leaned back against the couch. "But that's not all."

"Don't let his tough act fool you, Kee; he's a puppy inside." Katie chimed in with a soft laugh. She stuck her tongue out at her boyfriend when he gave her a half-hearted glare.

Kee laughed. "That's like Cain. He acts hard, but one scratch behind those ears and he's butter."

"Hey!" The beta protested, causing the two girls to giggle, Nat joining in as well.

*Maybe this dinner wouldn't be so bad after all.* Kee thought optimistically.

"Well, why don't we all go outside? I need to make sure the pack isn't destroying my backyard with their version of football." Natalie said with a roll of her eyes. "Really, I just had the gardeners trim up my rose bushes. If they're ruined, I'll hurt them."

Kee started to laugh, but cut it off in her throat when she realized Natalie looked serious. *Has she attacked members of the pack before for something so trivial?* She glanced over at Conrad, who was staring back at her intently. She gave him a smile, but he looked away and followed the others to the back door.

"I saw you at Shifters," Katie stated as she came up to Kee's side, looping their arms together as they walked outside. "I wanted to talk to you, but then you were gone."

Kee was thankful that she didn't mention the embarrassing exchange between her and Warren. She opened her mouth to reply to Katie but was stunned into silence when they walked out the door. The backyard was practically the foothills, the shrubbery and trees that decorated the hills of the mountain sloping down towards their house. A half-acre was cleared of trees and bushes for the actual backyard, giving the house a wide area of open grass.

She was snapped out of awe when Katie laughed next to her. "Pretty, isn't it?"

"Gorgeous." She agreed, almost breathless.

"It's perfect for the pack. That's why this house is the alpha's house no matter who it is." Katie said with a smile.

"What do you mean?"

"When a new wolf becomes alpha, they move in here. Sometimes the retiring alpha will take the new alpha's old house, but most of the time they don't live after the fight for alpha." She shrugged and then continued her story. "So, when the full moon comes, we shift here and run through the La Tuna Park. There aren't really any neighboring houses. The ones that are here are also owned by wereanimals so they understand not to interfere."

"That makes shifting and hunting easy." Kee commented.

Katie perked up and turned an excited smile to the new girl. "Will you be joining us tomorrow for the full moon shift?" Pack runs and hunts were big events for werewolves. Not only did they deepen the bond between each member, but also allowed their inner beasts to let loose.

Kee tried to stop from tensing. "No, I'm sorry; I have to work. One of the downsides of working at Shifters, you can't have all your staff take off the same night." She hastily added. "So, you know, the ones that can resist the shift have to work."

Katie pouted. "That's not fair, but I get it. Well, hopefully next month!"

She smiled noncommittedly, "Hopefully."

She let Katie drag her over to the picnic table where a few other girls sat, talking amongst themselves as they sipped on their drinks. They hushed when they approached, and Kee didn't miss the particular unfriendly look from someone on the opposite side of the table.

"Girls, for those of you who weren't at Shifters, meet Keira, our beta's chosen female!" Katie gushed with genuine enthusiasm as she sat down, letting Kee sit on the outside next to her.

"Please, call me Kee." She insisted with a small smile as the other women introduced themselves with names she would never remember. "It's nice to meet all of you."

"It would have been *nice* if you didn't run away last time."

The shapeshifter glanced over at the girl at the end of the table again. She was taller than her, maybe five nine, and had auburn colored hair that fell in natural curls to her shoulders. Her eyes were a mix between blue and green and set in a hard glare.

Kee cleared her throat once as the other women at the table tensed. "Yes, it would have been, but it happened."

"Clearly."

"I'm sorry—," She paused, trying to remember the wolf's name.

"Alyssa." She growled out.

"Alyssa," she repeated before continuing. "My past is a sensitive subject and I wasn't prepared to talk about it. I was caught off guard."

She scoffed, tossing her curls over her shoulder like a child. "Real wolves don't run away from confrontation."

*I'm not a real wolf.* Kee had to literally bite her tongue to stop herself from saying it aloud. Instead, she shrugged and tried to avoid further argument. "You're entitled to your opinion, but I'm sorry you feel that way."

Alyssa snarled as she stood, hands slamming down on the table. "You call yourself a wolf? You're not even trying to argue with me! I'm challenging you, but you're so fucking passive! You're not good enough for Cain!"

Kee felt tensions rise at the table, but no one stepped in to stop her. Alyssa's wolf must be more dominant than theirs. *Interesting.*

"And, where the fuck did you even come from? Why did he choose you and not one of his own pack members? What did you do to him? What—" She was cut off when a delicate hand fell on her shoulder, an angry aura pulsing almost visibly around the table.

Kee watched as all the women at the table dipped their heads down, looking away from Natalie as she pushed her energy down on Alyssa. She heard murmured words between Nat and Alyssa but didn't pay attention to them, nor did she look up when the fuming wolf stormed towards the woods. Instead, she looked over at the oblivious men across the yard. She couldn't help but smile when she saw Cain pull his shirt off along with half of the other wolves, the two groups splitting up to face off against each other.

Her eyes traced her man's tanned torso. She first took in the tribal wolf head tattoo on his left pectoral and then traced the tribal marks with her eyes as they twisted up over his shoulder and then spilled down his arm to form intricate Celtic braids and knots. She dragged her eyes back to his torso and followed each dip and contour of his abs. He wasn't overly muscular like Noah, but he was defined enough to show he had a six pack when he flexed. She hummed in her throat when her eyes fell to the lines that dipped down from his hip bones and disappeared under the waistband of his jeans, making an incomplete 'v' shape.

"Kee, *Kee!*"

She blinked and turned to look at the giggling girls at the picnic table. "Huh?" She realized Natalie was handing her a wine glass, and from the amused look on her face, she assumed she had been there for a second. She blushed and accepted the glass. "Thank you. Sorry, I spaced out for a second."

"Don't apologize. I love the way you look at him," Nat told her with delight. "It reminds me of how someone would look at art."

"He *is* art." She mumbled, cheeks hot as the women laughed once again. She took a gulp of the wine, trying to swallow away her embarrassment.

Katie sighed happily. "That is proof enough that you're perfect for him; I don't care what Alyssa says."

A genuine smile finally curled up her lips. "That means a lot to me, thank you."

Kee looked back at the men when growls echoed in clearing. Cain's team had the football, the wolves with shirts trying to intercept them and stop them from passing the ball. She watched as Noah ran across the field, his head turned so he could look behind him as he watched for the ball. At the same time, she saw Conrad getting up from his grassy spot on the sidelines, his eyes on Noah as the other wolf ran in his direction.

"Cain! Pass it!" Noah shouted, waving his arms.

Kee watched as Cain was tackled right as he threw it, the ball going off course. Her attention instantly went back to Conrad, who had purposefully moved out of Noah's way the first time. But that was before Cain threw the ball. She stood up and put her wine glass down on the table as she waited for the inevitable crash. Seconds later, she winced as Noah ran right into Conrad, the force flinging him over the furry back and straight into the grass. She was on her feet and moving before she knew what she was doing.

"What the fuck, mutt?" Noah snarled as he picked himself up off the ground, wiping dirt and pieces of grass from his face. Conrad looked away in submission, ears flat against his head and tail tucked between his legs. "Why are you in everyone's way?!" He shouted, dark brown eyes taking on the gleam of his inner wolf's.

"Leave him alone, Noah!" Kee shouted as she raced over to them, planting herself in front of Conrad so she faced Cain's best friend. She felt the familiar cold wave of adrenaline begin to creep into her veins when she realized what she was doing. She was protecting Conrad, but Noah was bigger and much stronger than her. She was scared of Noah, but she wouldn't allow herself to back down without a fight. Conrad didn't deserve to be punished for something he tried to avoid.

"Get out of the way, Kee. This doesn't concern you." He growled, predatory eyes now on the person who was stopping him from his prey.

"No," she said, putting her shaking hands on her hips as she stared at him, challenging him. Every member of the pack stared intently at the trio, curious to what would happen. For once, she didn't care that all eyes were on her. She finally realized why Conrad acted the way he did, and it correlated way too closely to her own pain. "It was your fault for running out of bounds. *You* ran into him. He doesn't deserve to be scolded because you weren't looking where you were going."

Noah's lip lifted in a snarl before he shot out to grab the scruff of Conrad's neck, making the wolf yelp. He had moved too fast for her to stop him, but she quickly put her hand on his wrist when he tried to pull Conrad out from behind her. He growled at her. "Let me go, or I will break your tiny hand, Kee."

She saw Cain start to move towards them, but Warren had put a hand on his shoulder, shaking his head. She didn't know what it meant, but she didn't want to rely on Cain's help. She had decided to protect Conrad from Noah and she intended to, despite her anxiety. "Let him go, and then I'll let you go."

"Move, Kee! I don't care if you're Cain's bitch; I'll hurt you!"

Grey eyes hardened as she straightened her spine defiantly. "You can try." She saw his free hand start to move and her adrenaline had her acting before she could process it. The martial arts training from when she was little kicked in as if it were muscle memory. Her right hand went up, palm faced outwards with her four fingers tight together and thumb out to the side. In a swift, sure movement, she struck. She hit him square in the nose, breaking it, and then twisted her palm to the left with a push so it would dislocate.

Noah yelped in pain and quickly released Conrad so he could cover his nose as blood spurted from it. She watched him fall to his knees in front of her, but she stayed in a defensive position in front of Conrad. Her adrenaline still coursing through her veins, her heart-beat hammering almost painfully in her chest. It wasn't until she felt Conrad rub his head against her arm that she tore her eyes away from Noah. She lowered her hands from the defensive stance and placed one on his head, smoothing out the fur between his ears. He didn't flinch or move away like she thought he would but leaned into her hand instead, keeping his gaze locked with hers. They only eye broke contact when Cain came up to them and pulled her into a tight hug.

"Kee," Cain rumbled in pride as his hands slid down to her ass and lifted her. "You still surprise me." When she automatically wrapped her legs around his waist, he gave her a fierce, hungry kiss.

She cupped the back of his neck as she kissed him back, returning his enthusiasm. She pulled back slightly to see the wolf's gleam in his eyes. "Why are you all riled up?" She asked with a smile.

"Because you just challenged a wolf while defending another," he said proudly. "You proved your strength to my pack and established dominance." He lowered his tone, his lips moving close to her ear. "*We* just want to take you right here on the grass in front of everyone."

She knew he was referring to him and his beast. She felt a hot wave of need rush through her, but at the mention of everyone, she looked over his shoulder to see the entire pack staring at them with mixed expressions. Longing, hunger, and respect were just a few of them. She flushed and tore her eyes from them. She pressed a quick kiss to Cain's lips. "Tonight." She promised.

He growled in both disappointment and eagerness. He slowly released her, making sure her body slid down his bare chest and the erection straining under his jeans. "Tonight." He agreed with a deep rumble that made her thighs clench.

She shyly tucked a strand of hair behind her ear when he looked at her for a few seconds longer before bending down to tend to Noah. She resisted the urge to step back when Cain helped his friend stand, Noah giving her the dirtiest look he could muster. She swallowed a lump in her throat, but otherwise held her ground as he glared at her. When Cain finally hauled him away towards the house, she relaxed.

She looked down at Conrad again when he nudged her arm. "You okay?" When he nodded, she smiled at him. "Good." She patted his head and then walked back over to the picnic table, the wolf remaining by her side for the rest of the evening.

After dinner, Kee sat in the living room with Natalie and Katie,

Conrad lying by at her feet. Kee was having a great time, which was a surprise. She somewhat expected a fiasco like last time, especially after the incident with Noah, but the night had gone rather smoothly. She had enjoyed the company and didn't hesitate in accepting when Natalie offered her another glass of wine after everyone else left.

"Natalie, if I may ask, how long have you and Warren been together?" Kee asked, taking a small sip of her wine as they sat on the pristine, cream leather couches.

The woman smiled tenderly. "Thirty-five years. I met him when I was seventeen. I was still in high school, but he graduated six years before me."

Kee did quick mental math. Natalie was fifty-two? Not that it was old, but she didn't look a day over twenty-one. Sometimes she forgot that preternaturals didn't age like humans did. "How did it all happen?" She asked, cradling her wine glass in both hands.

"Well, I met him at an LA County pack meeting. All the alpha's in the county came together to discuss legislation. My dad was from the Glendale pack and brought me along. I think he was secretly trying to scope out potential mates for me." At Kee's horrified look, she laughed. "This was before the Monster Movement, Kee. We were still in hiding and had a very strict way of living. Alpha's had the right to choose a mate for their female pups."

"Is that how it is now?" She questioned with a frown.

She gave an elegant shrug. "I'm sure there are some pack alphas that are stuck in the old ways, but most have changed with the times." She clarified and then continued her story. "Anyways, at the time, the Alpha of LA County was also the LA pack's alpha, so we all went to him. Warren was part of the LA pack and my inner wolf was instantly drawn to him, but he had never paid any attention to me. Or, so I thought." she chuckled, pushing a blonde wave over her shoulder.

"This is my favorite part of the story." Katie grinned.

Nat smiled. "A year or so later, to alleviate some of the tension between packs and encourage bonding, the alphas decided to plan a trip to Glamis for a run. The LA alpha chose a few wolves to overlook the trip, and Warren was one of them."

"The alpha must have really trusted him." Katie commented as she took a large swig of her merlot.

She nodded. "I think it was pretty apparent that Warren was meant to be an alpha from early on. My wolf certainly knew," she paused to take a sip from her glass. "In Glamis, we shifted and ran, enjoying the cool sand between our paws." They sighed longingly, causing Kee to nod awkwardly since she didn't know the feeling. "After we shifted back, some of the younger decided to take the party to the next level by bringing alcohol."

"Of course." Katie scoffed as she refilled her glass for the fourth time.

"Well, they started acting up, their hormones and beasts getting out of control with their alcohol intake. They started harassing the few girls that were there, me being one of them. I made it very apparent I wanted nothing to do with one guy in particular, but he wouldn't take no for an answer. He grabbed me, and I started swinging and growling, trying to get him to let go. I gave him a black eye, but that just angered him, made him possessive. He took me to the ground, but as soon as my back hit the sand, he was gone. Warren had him pinned to the sand, snarling until the boy submitted. When he finally let go, the boy ran away almost sobbing." She smiled at the memory before taking another sip.

Kee blinked as she swallowed some of her moscato, always preferring sweeter wine rather than the bitter reds. "What happened after that?"

"I told him I didn't need his help." She answered with a laugh. "He seemed taken aback by my haughtiness, but he scoffed and said he did it for himself because he was bored. I knew he was lying, but it still made me smile. The rest of the night he stayed by my side and eventually asked me to dinner. I accepted, and a week later we went out. It was then that he told me he had noticed me the year before but never had the chance to approach me. With my father's approval, I joined the LA pack to be with him, and we've been together ever since."

"That's really cute." Kee cooed.

"What about you, Kee? How did you and our beta meet? He said he met you at Shifters, but men suck when it comes to details." Katie slurred, pouring herself what was left in the merlot bottle.

Kee told them of how she and Cain had met, smiling fondly at the memory. "It's been a little over a year since then."

"That was probably a first for Cain," Nat teased. "Girls always want in his pants so they play the sweet, seductive role, but he doesn't like girls like that. He likes girls that will challenge him, not submit so easily to him."

She laughed. "Yeah, he told me the second time we met that my shyness had turned him off," she smiled as Cain, Warren and Wyatt filtered back into the living room from the backyard. "So, I'm glad I told him to fuck off and got a date out of it."

"And she's been mine since." Cain added as he came up beside her, pressing a kiss to her temple.

"You're so cute!" Katie gushed with a heavy slur. She then frowned when Wyatt took her glass out of her hands, setting it down on the coffee table. "Hey!"

"Come on, drunkie. Let's get you home." He said with an exasperated tone. When she protested, he easily picked her up and slung her over his shoulder. "I'll see you later, brother."

"Yes, I will be in contact regarding Mason's early departure. I may need you to do something for me." Warren told him as he patted his shoulder. When Wyatt nodded and left the room with his grumbling girlfriend, he turned towards Cain and Kee. "Will you also be leaving?"

"Yeah, I have to work tomorrow morning." He replied stoically, not looking at his alpha.

He nodded once, his ice blue eyes sliding over to look at Kee. "Alright, just make sure you relay to your woman what I told you."

"Relay what to me?" She looked at Cain and frowned. He had set a carefully blank expression on his face, but she could see the skin of his eyes were tight with anger. "Cain?"

He took her small hand in his, giving it a squeeze. "I'll tell her." He said but didn't look at either one of them. "But I already told you what the answer would be."

Warren's expression turned cold. "And you know what I said in response."

Nat glanced between the two as the tension in the room mounted. "Warren, what is going on?" She demanded, not liking the aggression growing between the alpha and beta.

He straightened his spine, his shoulders pushing back as he looked down at his mate. "Kee's initiation into the pack."

Kee watched Natalie carefully as she looked between the two men. First confusion reflected in her hazel eyes as she stared at her mate. Then, as if something clicked in place, understanding passed across her face before fury replaced it. "Nat? What is it?" Kee asked, her tone hesitant.

"*Natalie,*" Warren said sharply, making the woman close her mouth before any words could escape. He looked at Cain once again, his aura expanding. "What I said is final."

Cain failed in keeping the snarl from his face. "I heard you," he growled low before storming out of the room, pulling Kee in tow with Conrad following close behind. He didn't slow his pace until they were out of the house and climbing into his white Ford truck.

"Cain, what is going on?" She demanded once they were in the truck. She frowned when he just sat in the driver's seat clutching the steering wheel so tightly his knuckles turned white. She reached over and put her hand on his shoulder. "Cain?"

He took a deep breath to try and calm himself. "Not now, Kee. Please, I'll tell you later. I just need to cool off right now."

She squeezed his shoulder before pulling her hand back to set it in her lap. She didn't say anything else, choosing to look out the window instead as he began to drive her back to her apartment. Her brow furrowed as she stared out at the scenery flying by, her mind reeling with the little bits of information she had. Why would Cain be so angry about her initiation? Also, was that what she wanted? To be part of the pack? She didn't think so. As a shapeshifter, she would be at constant risk. It just wouldn't work.

*But, how do I tell Cain that?*

# *Eight*

Kee sat on her couch, a mug of coffee cradled in her hands. A frown pulled down the corners of her lips as she thought about the pack picnic yesterday. Rather, what happened at the end. Cain had dropped her off and almost left without kissing her goodbye. Before dating Cain she wouldn't have thought twice about it, but the were-wolf had made it a point to kiss her every time they parted ways. Now, she expected it. So, for him to almost forget made it apparent to just how upset he was about her initiation.

*What could Warren have possibly said?*

She sighed heavily and looked over at her companion as he whined at her. She forced a smile and reached out to pet him, still surprised when he let her. He closed his eyes and leaned into her touch. Her smile faltered when she remembered how Conrad refused to leave last night with Cain. The beta had tried to grab his scruff, but Kee interjected, telling him it was fine and he was welcome to stay. Cain hadn't been happy but didn't fight her on it. He was still too angry to even try to speak to her.

"I hope Noah doesn't try to come after you when you go back to the pack." She told him softly. She frowned when his eyes snapped open and looked up at her. His amber eyes gleamed with an intensity that made her look away. She felt him shift on the couch and crawl closer to her, his large paws resting on her legs. When she glanced back at him, he put his head on her lap, eyes holding hers. *Is he giving me the puppy dog stare?* "What's wrong, Con?"

He blinked at the nickname and tilted his head a little, making her laugh. Her attention was drawn to her phone when the text tone went off. She reached for it, her heart skipping a beat when she saw it was from Cain. He wrote that he was going over to Warren's after work for the pack run and that he would talk to her tomorrow morning. She wrote him back telling him to be safe and that she loved him, but her heart was heavy with disappointment. She put the phone back down on her coffee table and ran her hand through Conrad's thick fur to calm her nerves.

"Are you going to shift for the full moon?" She asked, trying to take her mind off Cain. When he blinked up at her, she let out a soft laugh. "I guess if you're already in your wolf form, then you don't need to." She drained the rest of her coffee and set it on the table next to her phone. "Since I don't have to work until tomorrow, do you want to eat some breakfast and watch movies all day?"

She laughed when he leapt off her lap in agreement. She stood and grabbed her cup before walking into the kitchen. After setting the cup in the sink, she went to the fridge and scanned the shelves. The wolf came up next to her, his head at her hip as she pulled the eggs and bacon out and set them on the counter. Conrad just stared at her, head slightly tilted as he studied her. After a few seconds, he turned and walked out of the kitchen.

"Conrad?" She called, but he had already disappeared around the corner of her hallway. She frowned when he didn't come back. Fetching a frying pan out of her cabinets, she put it on the stove and turned on the heat. She then got out a large bowl and began cracking the eggs on the rim.

"Can I help?" Came a soft, masculine voice.

She let out a startled scream, dropping the egg on the counter as she jumped. She spun around to see an unfamiliar man standing by her table. Golden blonde hair with natural light brown highlights spilled over one bare shoulder, the ends resting right below his chest. He was half naked, one of her towels wrapped around his slender waist to cover the lower half of him. His five-eight form was fit, strong, but not in the obvious way. Amber eyes stared at her with uncertainty before looking away.

"C-Conrad?" His name came out in a breathy exhale, but when those familiar eyes met hers once again, she knew there was no question. "Oh, my gods, Conrad!" To say she was stunned was an understatement. Cain and Noah assumed he was stuck in his wolf form, so she didn't expect to ever see him as a human.

"Yes?" He stiffened when she came up to him and flinched when her hands reached out to touch his face. When he felt her soft hands cup his cheeks, he relaxed his muscles and looked down at her as she studied him.

"I'm so happy," she cooed when a nervous look scrunched his face. She gave him an encouraging smile when they made eye contact again. "They said you were stuck as a wolf."

He cleared his throat before responding, trying to warm up his vocal cords from lack of use. "No," he replied, his voice rough. "I just prefer my wolf form."

"Why?" She asked.

His brows knit together, putting his hands on hers to remove them from his face. "Do I have to answer?"

Kee blinked at him, drawing her hands back. "Of course you don't.

You can do whatever you want to do, Conrad. Why would you ask me that?"

The werewolf remained quiet for a moment, searching for the right words. "Alphas can demand what they want." He finally told her in a hesitant tone.

She stared at him, trying to make sure she really heard him right. "Alphas can, yes, but not me." She said slowly. "I'm not your alpha."

He held her gaze. "What if I want you to be?"

She took a deep breath and swallowed thickly. Where had this come from? "Conrad, I can't be," she started, breaking eye contact first this time. "Why would you even say that? You have Warren."

*And I'm not a wolf.*

Conrad reached down and grabbed her hand in both of his. "Because you are worthy. I didn't see Warren as my alpha. I was given to the pack because my own didn't want me. An alpha who lets a member of their pack get constantly bullied is nothing to me." He squeezed her hand. "But from the first time I saw you, you offered nothing but compassion. When you saw me under the table, you were upset for me. The second time, you were kind to me and didn't treat me any differently. You protected me from Noah and then didn't let Cain drag me away. You are the person I want to follow."

Her bottom jaw dropped open at the vehement emotions shining in his eyes. "Conrad, I'm so glad that I helped you, and I would do it again. But you don't understand, I *can't* be your alpha. I'm dating Cain, who's next in line to be alpha. Wouldn't that be a challenge to Warren?"

He gave a one shoulder shrug. "I don't care about Warren."

"But *I* care about Cain." She retorted as she tugged her hand from his. "Or, do you not care about him either?"

His eyes softened. "I do. He's also been nice, but he's more of a babysitter. He hasn't protected me like you have."

"He will if he needs to," she said. "Cain is a good guy."

"Cain isn't in charge of the pack; Warren is."

"Which is why I can't be your alpha. I'm not even—" she quickly caught herself before she blurted the truth, "part of the pack."

"You're a lone wolf, and I choose to follow you." He said stubbornly. "When you join the pack, I will still answer to you."

She rubbed the bridge of her nose. "Conrad, you don't get it. There are other factors to this that I can't tell you." She walked back over to the counter and started picking up pieces of the eggshell. "I'm very flattered, but I can't be your alpha."

He went to the sink and grabbed the sponge, getting it wet before walking over to help her clean up the mess on the counter. "I don't care," he mumbled defiantly. "I'm staying."

Startled, Kee looked up at him and saw the determination in his eyes. "What, you want to stay here?"

"If you will let me. I can help around the apartment." He offered without looking at her, his brow set in a firm line. "I don't want to go back to the pack."

She turned back to the stove, letting Conrad walk away so he could rinse out the sponge as she let his words sink in. She put the strips of bacon in the pan, letting them cook as she thought. She would admit that she didn't want Conrad to go back to Warren's house. She was nervous that Noah would hurt him. Hell, she was scared Noah was going to hurt *her*. Plus, he had insinuated that he was bullied by the other wolves, not just Noah. Not only that, but his old alpha had literally given him away. Her heart hurt for the rejection he must feel.

But, her life was already complicated as it was. She worked for the Lord of Los Angeles County as his spy, using her shapeshifting skills. She was working at a bar, posing as a werewolf, and was dating the beta of a wolf pack. Could she really take a wolf into her care and be strong enough for him to be his alpha? She could barely be strong enough for herself.

She jumped slightly when a spatula came into her view, lifting the crispy bacon from the frying pan. She stepped to the side when he took the pan from the stove and dumped the grease down the sink. He then returned it to the stove and poured in the whisked eggs. "Cain taught me to not wash all the grease out." She commented quietly as she watched him.

"It gives the eggs an extra flavor." He replied, moving the eggs around the pan as they cooked.

She nodded in agreement and leaned against the counter, crossing her arms over her chest as she studied his profile. She shouldn't let him stay. She really, really shouldn't. Especially now that he had demonstrated his human form. It wasn't fair to Cain to let another man into her home. Although, wasn't that how a lot of packs worked? But she wasn't a wolf, so did it really matter? She was sure she could talk to Cain about Conrad's safety, but she had seen how animalistic and cruel the wolves could be.

*What the hell do I do?*

"Utensils?" He asked as he divided the eggs and bacon onto plates and set them on the table.

She jumped slightly as she was startled from her thoughts. "Drawer to the left of the sink." She answered distractedly. When he turned to get the utensils, she realized she still hadn't answered him. She then bit the inside of her lip and sat down across from him as he took a seat at her table.

Conrad silently ate his breakfast, not looking up at her. She pushed her eggs around on her plate as she contemplated her choices. She could let him stay with her so he could be safe and comfortable. He could do some housework and maybe run errands for her when she was busy with work. However, she didn't want to upset Cain with a guy living in her apartment. Also, there was the problem of her being a shapeshifter and Conrad not knowing. What if he found out and left? What if he told the pack?

With a heavy sigh she set her fork down and cleared her throat. When he looked up at her, she licked her lips nervously. "Conrad, you said you see me as your alpha, right?"

He set down his fork as well, his amber eyes meeting hers seriously. "Yes."

Her brow furrowed as she prepared for what she was going to say. "I can't accept this role unless I know I can trust you. And let me warn you, I do not trust people easily."

Instead of inquiring why, he asked, "How can I gain your trust?"

"By keeping a secret to yourself. It's important to me and very, *very* few people know it."

He tilted his head at her, his hair falling over his shoulder again. "Who would I tell?"

She shrugged. "The pack? I don't know."

"I don't want to go back to the pack, Kee." He told her firmly, eyes narrowing. "So why would I tell them anything about you?"

It was the first time he had said her name since he shifted, and it nabbed her attention. "Because you won't like what I'm going to say. You might even run back to them once you hear it." She flinched when he suddenly scowled at her. "Don't give me that look, Conrad. You have no idea what I'm going to say."

"Don't undermine my loyalty." He growled.

"Don't growl at me," she snapped. She then cursed when he obeyed, his gaze dropping down at his plate. *Fuck*. Well, this would be the test to see how serious he was. He would either accept it, attack her, or simply leave. If he did anything but the first, she wasn't sure what she would do. Would Cain be able to handle it? Or would she have to ask Lucas for a favor with damage control?

She could already see his disapproving frown.

Kee rubbed her temples and then pressed a hand to her brow line. She just had to say it. Blurt it out. There was no use stressing over it until it happened. "I'm a shapeshifter." She mumbled.

"What?"

She clenched her jaw and raised her voice as panic welled in her. "I'm a shapeshifter!" She lowered her hand and met his surprised expression. "I'm not a werewolf. I'm not were*anything*. I can change myself into *any* animal." Her stomach tightened with nerves when he just stared at her. Well, she had divulged her truth and now he would leave. Why did she do that? Why did she think he would be different like Cain and Lucas?

"And?"

She blinked in surprise. Now it was her turn to ask, "What?"

"You're a shapeshifter. So what?" He asked as he held her stunned stare. "Am I surprised? Honestly, yes, but you have shown me kindness when my own kind hasn't. I told you that I chose to follow you, and that doesn't change just because you're not a wolf."

Her eyes stung at his words. "I can't be your alpha, Con."

He snorted. "You are an alpha to me, and I'm a wolf. That's all that matters."

Her bottom lip trembled, but she held in her tears. "You really mean that, don't you?"

Conrad gave her a reassuring smile. "I do. And I'm sorry, but I have to ask, does Cain know?"

She nodded. "He does. So does Lucas."

"As in the vampire? You mentioned him earlier."

"Yeah, I work for him. So if you're going to be staying with me, you're going to have to get used to him being around." She told him as she picked up her fork and turned her attention to her breakfast. "Lucas is just as important to me as Cain."

He couldn't help but grin. "So, that means I can stay."

"Yes, but you're going to need some clothes. I can't have you walking around in a towel." She smirked at him through a bite of egg.

"I think I can handle that." He replied with another smile.

# *Nine*

A slight shift in temperature was all Charles needed to know that he had a visitor. He looked up at the door when it opened, the pretty brunette shooting him a warming smile. "You have a visitor, Charlie."

He nodded at his human girlfriend and gave her a small smile. "Thank you, Tabitha."

She stepped aside to let the taller man walk past her. He had long brown hair tied back in a low ponytail and eyes as red as rubies. She had never seen him before, but she assumed he was one of Charlie's vampire friends. She smiled down at a white cat when it rubbed against her ankle on its way into the room and turned her attention back to the vampires. "Can I get you guys anything?" She offered politely.

Charles, seeing the fellow vampire eye the puncture wounds on Tabitha's neck, quickly responded, "No, we're fine. I'll see you in a little."

"Okay! Have fun!" She chimed, closing the door behind her as she left.

Charles waited a few seconds before standing and looking at

his visitor as he ventured further into the room. "Damien, I wasn't expecting you."

"Clearly, but that was intended," he responded with a smirk. He glanced around the office as he walked, taking in the modern decor and little knickknacks on the desk and bookshelves. "How very *mundane*."

Charles cleared his throat. "Yes, well, Tabitha decorated it."

"Cute," he commented bluntly. "Anyways, I am sure you are wondering why I am here."

"Not to be rude, but yes, I am. I thought we were done after...you know."

"That is what brings me here, Charles. I need to make sure you clearly understand how important it is that you do not to tell anyone. We don't want the other lord knowing, do we?" He asked casually as he slid a gloved finger across a hanging frame that contained a picture of the couple. He rubbed his pointer finger and thumb together, staring down at the dust dispassionately.

"What do you think he will do if he finds out?" The pale man asked as he leaned against the desk in his home office, his hands gripping the edge of the polished wood nervously.

"He can't do anything unless he has proof." He replied smugly. His crimson eyes shifted towards the sofa as a movement caught his eye. He scowled as he watched a white cat stretch along on the cushion, its little claws stabbing into the fabric.

Charlie followed his gaze and shrugged a single shoulder. "My human is always bringing in strays. I deny her so much; may as well allow her something." He explained needlessly.

He scoffed. "Humans are only good for blood."

"Damien, not everyone thinks that way. They're more than meals."

A sharp, humorless laugh escaped him. "Now you sound like *him*. You going to join his side, too?"

His brows furrowed. "Don't insult me, Damien. Just because I believe humans are more than meals doesn't mean I'm suddenly going to worship the ground he walks on. He may have beaten Alexander, but I have chosen my side." He defended. He lowered his voice to a hush. "Did I not prove that last night?"

Damien stared at him for a moment before he smirked. "That's good to hear, Charles," he cooed as he stalked towards him. "And yes, you did prove yourself last night. Thank you for your help." His smile turned kind as he stood in front of him. "Our lord thanks you even more."

His face flushed, his pale cheeks taking on a soft hue of pink as the blood he drank earlier rushed to them. "Anything for Alexander."

"Anything?" He asked in a sing-song tone.

The man's brow furrowed once again in apprehension. "Yes, of course."

"Good, then you will understand this." Before the vampire could ask questions, Damien thrust his hand into the man's chest. When he jerked it back out, Charles' heart was a bloody heap in his palm. "My apologies, Charles, but the less witnesses the better." Without any effort, he crushed the organ in his fist.

After the body dropped, he tossed the pulverized heart aside and proceeded to step on Charles' head. Bloody bits of flesh spewed out with each hard, forceful stomp. Blood seeped down into the carpet, little pieces of crushed skull sitting on top of it like confetti. When Damien was satisfied that both heart and brain had been damaged beyond repair, he bent down and wiped his glove off on Charles' shirt.

He glanced at the cat as it came up to his side and scratched it behind the ears leaving a large smear of blood on the white fur.

"You can keep a little secret, right?" He laughed when the cat mewed and rose to his full height. "Good. Now, where did that walking meal go?"

—

Kee stumbled into the sliding back door of her apartment, not bothering to try and close it with her tiny white paws. She kept the back door slightly ajar when she worked surveillance so she didn't have to worry about people finding out about her secret when she came home.

"Welcome back." Conrad's voice came from above her.

She looked up at him as he slid the door shut behind her and offered a thankful meow. She waited until he pulled the curtain shut before beginning to shift back to her human form. She tried to bite back the painful yowl that escaped her lips as her limbs began to stretch out with loud cracks and pops.

He frowned at her obvious discomfort as she began to morph back into her humanoid form. "Do you need help?" He asked, following her down the hall as she tripped.

"No." She answered with a voice mixed between a hiss and cry. When her legs were back to normal, she staggered into the bathroom and braced herself against the counter, taking deep breaths as her body continued to readjust itself back into its normal height. A violent tremor went through her as the fur disappeared, causing her knees to buckle. She felt arms encircle her, keeping her from collapsing to the floor. When another wave of stretching and pain hit her, she pushed Conrad away and leaned against the counter, arms quivering.

"You smell like blood." Conrad stated as he studied at her, not knowing what to do. "Are you hurt?"

She glanced up at the mirror in time to see the white bleed from her hair, leaving it her natural dark blonde. She scowled when she saw dried smears of blood on and around her ears from where Damien had touched her. "It's not mine." She croaked.

"Oh. Do you need me to get you anything?" He offered, easily ignoring that she was naked in front of him. He was a werewolf, being around naked people was practically second nature to him.

She shook her head after another tremor ran through her body. "No, I just want to shower. I'll see you in a bit." When he dutifully left, she started the shower and stepped in. She leaned against the cool tile, eyes closed tightly as she waited for the tingling sensation and numbness in her fingers to subside. No matter how many times she shifted into another form, even one she had done a hundred times, she couldn't get used to the discomfort that came afterwards.

Once she regained the feeling in all her limbs, she scrubbed herself clean, paying extra attention to the skin around her ears. Satisfied that every speck of blood was off her, she stepped out of the shower and dried off. With her hair twisted into a towel, she walked into her bedroom and changed into a pair of yoga pants and tank top that hugged her torso.

After dressing in her comfortable sleepwear, she walked down the hall to the kitchen and grabbed a water bottle from the plain white fridge. As she shut the door, she frowned at the picture of her and Cain hanging from a magnet, the two of them smiling happily as they hugged each other. With a heavy heart, she made her way to the living room and sat down next to Conrad on the couch.

"Feel better?" He questioned.

"Yeah, sorry. I don't like to be touched when I'm shifting. It's too much of an overload for my senses." She explained to him as she twisted off the cap from her bottle and took a tentative sip.

"Now I know for next time." He commented.

She gave him a disbelieving smile. "You're taking this all pretty well." She laughed. "Even Cain was freaked out the first time he saw me shift."

It had only been two days, but living with Conrad was easy. They talked every time they were in the same room, telling little bits of information to each other. She had learned that he was also twenty-five, just a few months younger than her, disliked mushrooms, and had a sweet tooth.

Conrad shrugged and pushed back his hair. "It's a little weird. Especially when I saw how much pain you were in. That doesn't happen with us," his amber eyes met hers. "But this is who you are, and I accept it."

She flushed at the sincerity in his eyes. It reminded her somewhat of when Lucas had found her the first time.

She had been in her favorite black and white cat skin, being chased by two drunk werefoxes downtown. She had run to the back of Byte and shifted from a cat to a Rottweiler before they turned the corner. She growled low at them and bared her teeth. The foxes, forgetting about the cat they were chasing, looked at the new target with a laugh. They went in to strike, but a man stepped in front of her. He had told them to leave his property or die. He had stated it so casually, so factually, that the foxes didn't immediately move, as if confused. It took one flare of power from Lucas to send them running.

She could remember as clear as day when he turned to her, those striking green eyes calm and clear of any disgust. His hands were casually in his pockets as he said, *"I have yet to meet a true shapeshifter. I assumed there were none left."*

Kee had been terrified. Not only because of the overwhelming power she had felt from him, but because he found out the truth about her. She had backed up, hackles raised as she growled. When he simply asked her if she would work for him using her talents in response, she had been dumbfounded. He had never, not even once, judged her or looked at her as if she shouldn't be alive.

She had worked for him ever since.

Kee cleared her throat and took another drink of water before changing the subject. "What did you do tonight?"

"I grabbed some more clothes from Warren's house." He laughed when she gave him a worried look. "Relax, I waited until Warren and Natalie left for their date. I told you my old pack sent a box of my things when they handed me over to the LA pack, so I'm slowly taking more and more things and bringing it here."

Her eyes softened as she looked at him. "One day, I hope you'll feel comfortable enough to tell me what happened to your pack." She said as she looked at him.

"Maybe one day," he replied evasively. "Have you heard from Cain?"

She pursed her lips together. "Yeah, he said we'll talk tomorrow." All day she had been brooding over what Warren could have possibly said to her boyfriend to make him avoid her.

"Isn't that what he said the last two nights?" When her face fell, he changed the subject. "How was your job?"

She sighed softly when he changed the subject and took another swig. "I can't really talk about it unless Lucas is here."

"And here I am." His deep, rich voice came from behind the couch.

She choked on the water in shock, Conrad reaching out to pat her on the back. She inhaled greedily after her coughing fit and turned furious eyes on the vampire. "Damn it, Lucas!" She exclaimed, clutching the water bottle to her racing heart. "Can't you knock? You're going to give me a fucking heart attack one day!"

"Language, Miss Quinn." Amused, bright green eyes peered at her through thick black lashes as he rested his elbows on the back of the couch and leaned towards her. "What fun is knocking?" He cocked his head a little bit before his eyes shifted to Conrad. "And, who is this?"

The wolf shrunk back slightly when the vampire suddenly stared at him, his eyes intense. He let out a low growl and glanced at Kee for help. He had little experience with vampires. Yes, he had seen them occasionally when he was with his other pack, but he never really interacted with them.

Kee put her hand on Lucas' cool cheek and guided his head back towards her direction. "His name is Conrad and you'll leave him alone."

The lord lifted a brow at her protective tone. "A pet, hm?" He questioned with a bemused expression. He turned his face in her palm and nipped at her skin, making her draw it back. "How does your other wolf feel about your pet?"

"Conrad's not my pet," she defended with a frown. "I just don't trust the pack to not hurt him. If that means him staying with me then so be it." She stated quietly before taking a sip of water.

"You did not answer the question." He pointed out, his smirk widening. He swept his eyes along her person, taking in the tight tank top that hugged her slender frame. With her choice in bottoms, he was able to appreciate the shape of her long legs. He clenched his jaw slightly when felt Conrad staring at him. He abruptly cut off his wandering thoughts. "Trouble in paradise?" He teased her.

"Maybe, I don't know. I'll find out more tomorrow, I guess." Kee told him before changing the direction of the conversation. "And you're right, Damien was involved in the murder last night. The man he killed tonight helped him." She informed him. The muscle in his jaw flexed ever so slightly.

Instantly his mood shifted, tension running through his body. "What was said?" Lucas asked sharply, his tone cold.

She told him exactly what had happened when she spied on the two vampires from the couch. "He ripped his heart right out of his chest and crushed it. Then he kicked in his head until his brains spewed out. When I left, he was looking for Charles' human. I'm pretty sure he killed her so there wouldn't be anyone around to say what happened."

She turned on the couch to look at him when he remained silent. She let herself take in his appearance for the night. He was dressed in black slacks with a red button up shirt, the top two buttons undone to show a slice of pale skin. She always saw him in his business-casual attire and she wondered what he would look like in normal clothes. *Does he even own any?*

"Keira."

She jumped when she was suddenly addressed. She met his serious gaze and frowned. "Yes?"

"Did they admit to killing my subordinate?" He repeated calmly.

"Not verbatim, but it was implied." She blinked when he suddenly leaned in closer to her, their faces inches apart. She heard Conrad growl in warning but ignored him. She tightened her grip on the water bottle, the plastic crinkling in her hand. Memories of him licking her palm replayed in her mind. Damn it, why was she both excited and terrified by his closeness? "Y-yes?"

"I need a confession, Miss Quinn; that is the only way I can move forward." He told her as he stared down at her. He could hear the pounding of her pulse, the lively beat making his own dead heart flutter with an uncertain eagerness.

"As you know, I prefer *Kee*." She swallowed thickly and put a hand under his chin, trying to push him slightly away from her. "I'm doing what I can, Lucas, so don't try to intimidate me. Do you have any idea why Alexander would want to have your person killed?"

The vampire lifted his head away from her hand and stepped back from her. He crossed his arms over his chest and leaned against the back of her couch. "He does not like that I beat him. He still thinks he is superior to me so he is picking off my people to prove it."

"You won the fight though." Kee replied as she looked up at him.

"I showed mercy when I should not have." He commented quietly as he stared up at the ceiling, lips pulled down in a frown.

She took a slow sip before looking down at the bottle. "Do you wish you had killed him?"

"Yes." There was no hesitation.

"You did it to save his followers, so your coven wouldn't wipe them out." She stated, glancing at him from the corner of her eye. "But, now your subordinates are suffering." She saw his lip curl up in an animalistic snarl, a pearl white fang gleaming at her.

"Yes, Miss Quinn, thank you for the reminder." His voice was like ice and it sent chills down her spine.

She blinked when he pushed away from the couch, his back to her. Guilt pinched her stomach. "Lucas, I didn't mean—"

"We are finished with business for tonight." Lucas replied as he pulled a folded envelope out from his back pocket and set it on the edge of the couch. "I will call when I need your services again." With that, he was gone.

Kee frowned at the spot he had been in seconds before. She didn't mean to make him feel bad and guilt nagged at her. She looked over at Conrad, who gave her a small shrug. "I didn't mean to upset him." She told him softly.

"So tell him that next time you see him." He told her simply.

"Yeah." She mumbled as she pulled her knees under her on the couch. She couldn't believe she had made Lucas mad. She should have realized that it was a sore subject for him. Did she hurt his feelings, too? Why did her heart sink at the thought of it?

# *Ten*

Kee sat on her couch the next night, snuggled up with a red fleece blanket. It was early in the evening, the sun just barely done setting. Conrad was in his wolf form, snuggled up to her side with his head in her lap. She had put on one of her favorite movies and was glad that Conrad hadn't protested to the musical. Cain would be coming over soon, but he wasn't a fan of musicals. He had made that clear in the early stages of their relationship. He preferred action or horror movies, which she didn't mind, but a change was needed every once in a while.

Hearing her phone ring, she reached for it, thinking it was Cain. She tensed when she saw a different name displayed on her screen. She tapped the green button and pressed the cool glass to the side of her face. "Mr Vranas." She greeted him lightly, her stomach bunched in nerves from how they had parted last night.

"*Miss Quinn,*" came his deep voice, an edge of humor in it at her greeting. "*Are you available this evening?*"

The knot in her stomach loosened when he didn't seem angry. "For work?" She asked and then rolled her eyes. *What else would he be calling for, Kee?*

"*Of sorts,*" he paused for a few seconds. "*Is that The Phantom of the Opera?*"

"Yeah, sorry, I'll pause it." She replied as she hit the button on her remote, freezing the scene where Christine and Raoul are out in the snow signing her favorite song.

"*The Broadway is much better than the movie.*" Lucas commented. "*Especially Phantom, it follows the book.*"

She could picture him at the theatre, looking stupidly perfect in a black tailored suit. "I wouldn't know, I haven't seen either of them."

"*Hm, how unfortunate. Anyways, were you free tonight?*"

"Yes, I'm off tonight. I've just been waiting for Cain to come over so we can talk." She told him softly. They were supposed to talk about what happened at Warren's, but she also wanted to tell him about her feelings on joining a pack. She sighed. She really didn't want to fight with him again after not seeing each other in three days.

"*Did you two makeup?*"

*He sounds tense.* "If you mean from the first fight, then yes. But, now it's something else that we need to talk about." She admitted, running her hand into her hair, pushing it back from her face.

"*What happened this time? A different vampire bite you?*" Suddenly his voice changed to a tease, as if he hadn't been on edge a few seconds earlier.

Kee let out a soft chuckle. "No, but it has something to do with his alpha and my initiation into the pack." She mumbled the last part, picking at the fuzz on the blanket.

"*Initiation?*" The vampire echoed with a hint of surprise. "*Should I congratulate you?*"

"No," she blurted out. "I don't want to be part of the pack, but I don't know how to tell Cain that." Conrad turned his amber eyes up towards her in question, and she pet the top of his head.

"*I suggest being honest,*" he then switched the topic back to work.

"*Can you meet me in Inglewood at eight tonight?*"

"Inglewood? That shouldn't be an issue. Can you text me the address?" She asked.

"*But of course.*" She could practically hear the smile on his face. "*See you then, Miss Quinn.*"

"Till then, Mr Vranas." She ended the call and looked up when she heard her front door open. She smiled at Cain and waited for Conrad to sit up before she stood from the couch. They met halfway across her living room, Cain folding her into his arms with a heavy sigh. "Bad day at work?" She cooed, rubbing his back.

"Kind of, but it's already better," he rumbled as he hugged her tightly. "Gods, I missed you." He had truly missed her, but he was apprehensive about telling her the truth of her initiation.

"I missed you, too." She smiled before pulling back just enough to press her lips against his. He sighed contently and kissed her back, nuzzling their noses together when they pulled away. "Why don't you go relax on the couch?"

The werewolf glanced over at the television and frowned. "Can we change this shit?"

She rolled her eyes. "It's not shit," she huffed. "Just because you don't like it doesn't mean no one else does." She walked over to the couch with him and snatched the remote out of his hand when he went to change it.

"Come on, Kee." He whined, giving her a pout as he flopped onto the cushions. He patted Conrad's side when the wolf tilted his head at him.

"Cain, we always watch what you want." She pointed out. "You came over to my house, not the other way around."

"I came over because we have to talk about the other night." He grumbled as he leaned his head back against the pillows. His face had gone serious, his lips pressed together in a hard line.

"Then we won't watch anything." She turned off the movie and sat down next to him. They sat in an awkward silence that seemed to stretch on for hours. "So, what happened with Warren?" She pushed when she couldn't take the tension anymore.

A growl rumbled in his chest. He thought he had gotten most of his anger out during the full moon run and the nights that followed, but clearly the tendrils of it still remained. "He wants you to be a part of the pack." He watched as Conrad jumped off the couch and went to where Kee sat, sitting down by her feet and looking at him.

Kee already knew that, but she didn't expect his dejected reaction. She frowned at him. "I thought you wanted me to be a part of your pack."

*If he changed his mind about me joining the pack, maybe that would be a blessing in disguise. Maybe I won't have to let him down.*

"Of course I do," he defended with a heavy sigh. He ran his hand into his hair and then down his face. "But it's the initiation that he wants for you that is the issue."

*Well, there went that escape route.* She absent mindedly reached out and stroked the soft fur on Conrad's head. "Why? What does he want me to do?"

He remained silent for a few seconds, brow furrowed as he searched for the right words to say. "Well, he's the alpha. In the past, alphas owned everything within the pack. What was yours, was his. So, it was pretty often for females to fuck the alpha whenever it pleased him."

She scrunched up her nose in distaste. "Sounds barbaric."

It was his turn to frown at her. "It's *animalistic*," he corrected. "That was just how it was in the past. We've come a long way since our ancestors, Kee."

"Then why are you bringing it up?" She asked. Her stomach dropped when he looked away from her. Apprehension crept over her as the pieces of what he said slid into place. *No. No, there was no way.* "Cain." She called his name and it came out as a strange mix of a demand and a plea. He couldn't possibly be saying what she thought he was. "*Cain.*"

He cracked his knuckles nervously, the popping sounds almost deafening in the tense silence. "He wants you to have sex with him for your initiation." He glanced at her face, grimacing at how blank it had suddenly gone. "It's not uncommon," he explained quickly, looking away from her again. "If the alpha finds the girl appealing, most of the time their initiation is to have sex with him. Think of it as a compliment."

Her patience had been rapidly draining the longer she listened to him, but her control snapped at his last sentence. She leapt up from the couch and all but shrieked, "A compliment?!" She saw him wince at the volume and heard Conrad whine. "You expect me to feel *flattered*?!"

"He thinks you're beautiful, Kee." He pointed out. "Plus, you took on Noah and won. You showed strength and dominance that's not common in other female wolves."

"He doesn't think I'm beautiful, he wants to *dominate* me, Cain! He thinks I'm a possession! A toy that he wants a turn playing with!" She was furious. "And, what, you're okay with him *borrowing* me from you?! With him fucking me?!"

He swiftly stood up and put his hands on her shoulders, as if afraid he would lose her if he let go. "Of course I'm not!" He shouted as he looked down into her furious grey eyes. He tightened his hold. "The mere thought of him touching you *infuriates* me!" He took a deep breath to calm himself. "Trust me, Kee, it makes my beast thirst for his blood and my claws ache to tear into his flesh. Believe me."

She stared up into his conflicted eyes, trying to cool her own anger like he had. "Then why would you even consider this as an option?"

He sighed heavily and closed his eyes tightly. "Because I don't have a say in the matter," he murmured angrily, an echo of defeat within his tone. He was the beta, not the alpha. "I asked him to pick something else, *anything* else, but he refused. His word is law, Kee."

She knocked his hands from her shoulders and stepped back. "Not my law." She stated, eyes narrowed into a hard glare. This was why she hated packs.

They ruined relationships.

Ruined families.

Ruined lives.

Cain's brow knitted together as he looked down at her again. "They will be when you join the pack."

She took a deep breath and let it out, trying to steady her nerves for what she was going to say. She balled her hands into tight fists, her knuckles turning white as she took Lucas' advice. "I don't want to be part of your pack." She said it softly, but saw him recoil as if her words had physically struck him. His eyes widened in shock before they hooded with hurt. "Cain, you have to understand how I feel about this."

"You would throw away everything we have together for one night, one moment that means nothing?" He whispered harshly, hurt making him defensive. Did he want Warren to touch Kee at all? No, of course not. She was his. *His* future mate. But, if she had to deal with one rut with his alpha in order for them to be together, he would accept it.

She ran her hands through her hair in frustration. "So, I have to fuck your alpha for us to have a future together?" She questioned incredulously. "And my initiation was just what solidified my decision, Cain. I've been having torn thoughts about joining your pack for a while now." She felt her heart clench at the obvious agony those words caused him.

*I didn't want it to end up like this.*

"Why didn't you tell me?" He asked miserably.

"Because your pack means everything to you." She reminded him softly, trying to be careful. Not because she was afraid of him, no, but because she feared she would wound him further. Cain had been her comfort and security for the last year and the last thing she wanted was to hurt him. And yet, she knew she ended up doing it anyways.

"Which is why I want you to join it." He told her as he stepped towards her.

She gently took his hand in hers, stopping it from cradling her cheek. She gently traced circles into his palm with her thumb. "I'm not a werewolf, Cain."

The silence after her whispered statement was suffocating.

"I don't care that you're a shapeshifter, Kee." He breathed, his fingers entwining with hers.

"I can't keep pretending to be something I'm not. I can't keep lying to your family." She watched as his large hand practically engulfed her smaller one. "If I sleep with Warren and become part of your pack, I'll have to keep lying to them. What happens if they find out I'm not really one of you? What if we have a baby and—" She choked up. "And it isn't a wolf?"

He didn't say anything at first, instead letting her words sink in. Finally he whispered, "I'd protect you, Kee."

He knew it would go badly. They both did. She closed her eyes tightly as they watered. Damn it, she did *not* want to cry. She met his gaze as she tried to blink the tears from her eyes. "How can you when Warren's word is law?" When his face crumpled in defeat, she couldn't help the tears that rolled down her cheeks.

He tried to stop the whine that threatened to escape his throat. She never cried, so seeing those tears made him understand that this was just as hard for her. He used his free hand to wipe a tear from her cheek, his thumb stroking her skin tenderly. "I love you." He told her, unable to find any other words. What else could he say after she used his own words against him?

She smiled sadly and pulled away from him, rubbing her palms against her eyes to dry them. "I have to go to work." She muttered as she turned from him, Conrad instantly at her heels. She walked to the entryway and pulled on the grey hoodie hanging by the door. She then slipped on a pair of Vans before grabbing her keys from the hook. She opened the door and paused briefly as she felt his eyes on her. "I think it's best if you're not here when I come home." She mumbled without turning to look at him.

"We both have a lot to think about." He murmured back.

She nodded once before walking out the door, letting it close firmly behind her and Conrad.

# *Eleven*

Lucas watched as his employee's white sedan pulled into the parking lot. He waited for her to get out of her car before approaching. A black eyebrow raised when her pet stepped out of the passenger side.

*When has she ever brought someone with her to a meeting?* As he neared them, his questions died on his tongue when he saw her carefully placed blank face. She seemed calm, but her aura was disturbed, her body tense under her dark grey sweatshirt. There was also the fact that her eyes were tinged red and glassy.

"Miss Quinn?" He asked softly as he stood in front of her, drawing her eyes to his.

"Hm?" Kee looked up at the vampire's emerald pools and quickly looked away from his questioning gaze. Apparently, she hadn't hid her emotions as well as she thought she did. It was embarrassing enough that she cried in front of Conrad on the way there, she didn't want Lucas to see it too. "I'm fine."

"You have been crying." He pointed out gently.

"I'm fine!" She snapped. When he blinked at her, she looked away and took a deep, shaky breath. She swallowed the rush of emotions and ran her hand down her face. "I'm sorry, you didn't deserve to be yelled at like that. It's just been a really rough past couple of days."

"It is of no consequence. Should we reschedule this for another time?" He offered. He glanced at the man who was an inch or two taller than Keira and saw the tension in his jaw. Either the wolf was warning him not to press the issue or he just flat out didn't like him. Perhaps both. He nodded when she shook her head. "Then let us get to it."

Kee nodded, thankful that he didn't pry or baby her. She felt him put his hand on the small of her back, ushering her towards the front door of the building with Conrad on her other side. Her brows knitted together when she read the lettering on the glass. "Gun range?"

He smirked down at her when she tilted her head up to look at him. "I take it that you did not look up the location."

She pursed her lips together. "No, I just put the address in my phone," she murmured before she was suddenly reminded of his package. She turned and punched him in the arm, irritation slipping away her other poorly sealed away emotions. "And what the hell was up with your package, Lucas? A loaded gun? Really!"

He couldn't help but laugh at her outburst. "I take it you did not bring it with you, then? Also, it is not truly loaded. The magazine is full, but there isn't a bullet in the chamber. Plus, the safety is on." When she deadpanned at him, he laughed once again.

His laugh swept over her skin like a wave of warmth. *Fuck, I love his laugh. It makes it hard to stay mad at him.* "There are still bullets in it!" She protested.

His laugh faded, but he was still smiling, the tips of his fangs showing. She haughtily crossed her arms when he opened the door for her. "I don't even know how to shoot a gun." She huffed as she stepped into the building, Conrad a few steps behind her.

"Which is exactly why we are here." He pointed out as he stepped around the wolf and took Keira towards the display case that served as a countertop. The two men behind the counter bowed their heads to him. "Was there any issue with my reservation?"

"No, sir," one immediately replied. "We blocked out the whole range for the next hour for you."

"Excellent," Lucas praised them. "Did you also prepare the two guns?"

"Yes, Lord Lucas." The other male replied as he put two guns onto the glass countertop. "A 9mm and a .45."

"Very good," he told them and then glanced at the wolf once again. "Would you like one as well, Mr Wolf?"

"It's Conrad, Conrad Novak." He replied, his honey gaze looking at the glass countertop.

"Mr Novak, the question still stands." He pointed out as he gestured towards the guns.

"I know how to shoot a gun," he answered tensely. "But I don't like them."

"Very well," Lucas dismissed him and turned to Keira. He picked up the 9mm, wrapping three fingers around the handle while his pointer finger rested lightly along the barrel. "This is the exact model I bought you," he explained. "This is how you hold it when you are loading it or not going to shoot it." When she nodded, he pressed a small lip that sprang out the bottom. "This is a magazine, which holds your bullets. It is empty right now, but it holds ten. When you slide it back in, you pull back this top piece to load the bullet into the chamber."

She watched, completely fascinated. "Wait, the top thingy loads it when you slide it back?"

"Yes."

"Fuck, then I think I actually loaded mine at home." She felt her cheeks burn in embarrassment when he laughed at her again.

"Good thing the safety is on." He mused and then smirked at her. "Your turn."

She watched as he put the gun back together before handing it to her. She felt a small wave of nervousness as she looked at the offered gun. She gingerly took it from him and immediately changed her hold when he reprimanded her. With his verbal instructions, she then popped out the magazine and pulled back the top slide. She put it all back together and then looked up at him. "How's that?"

"Good. Now, we practice shooting." Lucas gave her a quick instruction on how to load bullets and how to aim with the sight. He handed her a pair of goggles and then grabbed two sets of padded earphones. The vampires behind the counter handed him a short, rectangular bucket with extra ammunition. He placed their guns in it and looked at her. "Will you grab two target sheets from the shelf next to Mr Novak?"

Kee walked over to the small set of shelves and looked up at Conrad as he awkwardly stood by them. "Will you be okay out here, Con?"

He looked down at her concerned expression. "I'll manage." He gave her a small smile when she frowned at him. "I'll be here when you're done. Good luck."

"Thanks." She told him before grabbing two large paper sheets with targets on them.

She waved at Conrad before following Lucas through a heavy metal door. It led them to a long concrete room that was twice as deep. All fifteen stalls were empty and she followed him to the eighth one. When instructed, she hung up one of the targets on the metal wire and Lucas held the switch down to send it out into the range.

Lucas grabbed a set of the earphones and placed them firmly over her ears, giving her a reassuring smile when she blinked up at him. He gestured her to step back and then took a stance in front of the ledge overlooking the range. Kee watched as he confidently lifted his gun and fired into the target without hesitation. Ten clear shots rang out and she managed to only jump on the first three.

When his clip was empty, he sprang it out and set it aside along with the gun. He changed out the target papers and then held a pale hand out to her. Her stomach bunched in nerves as she slid her hand into his, letting him guide her to the window.

"Load your gun," he instructed, watching carefully as she slid the magazine into the bottom of the grip and cocked back the slide. "Perfect." He then turned her so she was in front of the small ledge and stood close behind her.

She flushed when his hands went to her hips, angling them so she was facing completely forward. She felt his leg slip between hers and her stomach did a funny flip. Feeling his knee nudge both of hers, she parted them until they were shoulder-width apart. She shuddered when his cool hands trailed up her sides and to her shoulders. They then traced down her arms until his hands were holding hers around the gun.

"Keep your arms still, but not locked," he said, bending so his lips were close to her ear. He resisted the urge to smirk when she shuddered. "When you aim, remember to use the sight with both eyes." His hands dropped back to her hips, his chest almost molded against her back. She fit perfectly against him. "Imagine the target is your frustration." He heard her swallow and lowered his tone to a whisper. "You may tell me you are fine, but I know you better than that. Use this to take out your emotions," he purred in her ear. "Let it go, Keira."

A tremor ran through her at his whispered command and she almost pulled the trigger out of reflex. The feeling of his body so close to hers was distracting, but she forced herself to focus on her target. She stared at the black silhouette and frowned as she channeled her feelings into it. It was her anger at Warren and her frustration with the pack. It was her hurt and betrayal with Cain.

It was her bitterness for being what she was.

She pulled the trigger with a quick, sure pull of her finger. She wasn't ready for the recoil, but it only jarred her a little, especially with Lucas' hands still on her hips. She didn't stop to inspect her shot, she kept firing; pouring her anger and remorse into each jerk of her finger.

Why couldn't Cain stand up for them? How could he so easily accept someone else screwing her? Why did she have to be a pack member to have a future with Cain? Why was Warren such an animal? Why couldn't she have inherited her parents' wolf gene? Why did she have to be cursed as a shapeshifter? And why couldn't people accept it? Why was it so bad to be one? What was the point of being born if her only purpose was to be hated?

She didn't realize her magazine had run out of bullets. She had just kept pulling the trigger until Lucas' hands cupped hers. She pried her fingers off the grip and allowed him to take it from her. She hastily stepped away before turning and brushing past him. She plopped down on a bench lining the wall and ripped her earmuffs and goggles from her head. She tossed them to the ground and buried her face in her trembling hands.

Lucas squatted in front of her and carefully watched her. He had felt the surge of emotions while she shot and sensed them quieting as she sat in front of him. He gently put his hands on her knees, noticing that her muscles tensed beneath his touch. "Do you feel better?" He asked.

She shook her head, keeping her face in her hands. She took a deep breath and then two more. She really didn't want to cry. She *hated* crying. Minutes passed by as she tried to collect herself. She was thankful that Lucas didn't pry, just kept his hands on her knees in his own way of offering her support.

*Why can't everyone else be like Lucas?* He never judged her based on what she was. Never sneered at her in disgust. Never hit her for being something he didn't want her to be. Never disciplined her for being different.

When she finally pulled her hands from her face, she met his questioning gaze. "Why don't you hate me, Lucas?"

He blinked at the question before his face softened. "Why would I hate you?" Once again, she had tucked her emotions away, her eyes dry from any tears but still a tinged pink.

"Because I'm a shapeshifter," she spat coldly. "I'm an anomaly, a freak, a *curse*."

*This is unexpected.* He knew how people felt about the rare breed of shapeshifters, but he had never known how she felt about herself. He wasn't pleased. *She does not know what it truly means to be a curse.*

"Are you having a pity party, Miss Quinn?" He mocked, tilting his head. The vehemence of the glare he received probably would have made anyone else shrink back. He could taste her anger on his tongue, but it simply interested him.

"Fuck you." She growled as she jumped to her feet and stormed past him, her thigh bumping his shoulder.

*Pity party? Fuck that.* She just wanted an answer to a question that had been plaguing her since they first ran into each other.

The vampire was on her in a flash, pinning her back to the wall. "Do not turn your back on me, Keira," he warned, his tone low and dangerous. As fascinated as he was, he would not be disrespected. It was true she never treated him as the reigning vampire lord of LA County, and normally he liked that, but not when he was insulted. "It is clear you are upset, but I will not put up with you pouting like a child." When she tried to struggle away from him, he captured both her wrists and pinned them above her head.

"I just asked you a question," she bit out through ground teeth. "You didn't have to insult me!"

"And yet you did the same thing." He pointed out, lowering his face to hers. "Something happened with your wolf, obviously, but you will not continue to take it out on me."

Kee scowled up at him. "I was asking a serious question and you belittled me. You don't understand how it feels to be so completely different from everyone else. To be hunted by people who are supposed to be your family, to be beaten by your own father because you're not what you're supposed to be!" Her hands balled into fists, the painful memories flashing before her.

*Damn him. And, fuck Cain and Warren for sending me back down this stupid path!*

"You wish to play this 'woe is me' game, Keira? Let us play." He dropped one of his hands so he could grab her chin, ignoring her free hand when it instantly latched around his wrist. "Do not speak to me about not understanding how it is to be an anomaly. I was different from my fellow Greeks before I was turned. I was starved, branded, and abused for being cursed by one of the Gods my people used to worship."

Despite her anger, Kee stared up at him in surprise, not saying a single word. She had heard rumors of Lucas' nickname, but didn't know what it meant. She had tried bringing it up to him once, but he had immediately shut her down, telling her it wasn't any of her business. Now he was telling the truth of his past and she wanted to know all of it. He had never opened up to her on a personal level and she found herself captivated by his tale.

"My parents were poor farmers. I helped as much as I could, spending long days in the fields, but it was not enough. I was fourteen when I found out about my so-called curse. Fearing what it meant for our wavering farm, my father sold me to a wealthy family as a servant. My new owners did not believe my father until I accidently set fire to the laundry. After that, they fed me once every three days, allowing me a cup of water every day just to keep me alive to appease Apollo.

"You see, my people stopped worshipping the many Gods centuries prior, having turned to the Christian one instead. Still, a boy wielding fire was undeniable. They wouldn't kill me because they feared the Gods of the sun would seek retribution. Odd how people will suddenly start believing in their forgotten Gods once they have proof of them."

He slid his hand from her chin to her neck, his eyes locked with hers. "They repeatedly cut into my flesh with a knife and then burned it shut, branding me forever with a symbol of my curse. They would demand I show them my fire, demand I burn something, but I could not control it. When I couldn't produce a flame, they would beat me within an inch of my life. For three years this continued.

"Then one day, I snapped. I was bleeding from my nose and mouth, my eye swollen shut. I had wiped the blood from my face, and when I saw the foot coming at me, I said no more. I held up my hand to block it, and out came my cursed golden fire. It burned the master's third son to nothing more than a charred pile of flesh and bones within minutes. The rest of the children had run away screaming and I knew I had to run as well. Fear of Apollo or not, my master would kill me. So I ran and ran until my legs gave out."

Kee saw that his eyes had become distant as he told her his story. She tugged on her other wrist and was surprised when he let it go. Seeing his face look so solemn, it wasn't right. Lucas was always confident and witty. He could be a frustrating, sarcastic asshole, and sometimes a terrifying monster, but sad was something that should never be associated with him.

She hesitantly reached out and gently cradled his face in her hands, trying to ease the pain that still lingered from his past. "Then what happened?" She encouraged softly.

His eyes cleared as she touched him and he refocused on her

face. "That is when my maker found me. She kept me alive for six more years, training me to use my power before she turned me into a vampire. It was not much better, my time with her, but at least she fed me and taught me things." He searched her eyes for pity but found none. He only found empathy, a shared pain between them. He lowered his voice and leaned in closer. "Do you understand now, Keira?"

"Yes," she whispered, staring up at him. "I'm sorry; I didn't know. I didn't mean to be selfish."

He sighed softly as she stroked his cheekbone with her thumb. "You are not selfish, just uninformed. I do not know of your past, only what you just told me, but I know you are strong enough to overcome that. Your wolf set you off and it simply brought back bad feelings. Do not let them consume you."

She nodded once. He was right, but she didn't want to talk about it anymore. "So, you're a pyrokinetic," she commented with a small smile as she changed the subject back to him. "That's why they call you the Curse of Apollo."

She hadn't removed her hands from his face, and he wasn't about to remind her. He enjoyed her soft touch. "Yes, but back then it was unheard of. Terrifyingly different, I suppose."

Her smile widened. "You're just a boy who can control fire."

His smirk matched hers. "And you are just a girl who can be anything."

Her heart fluttered at his simple, yet meaningful words. The comfortable silence between them shifted to something more tense and heated. Almost needy. He was so close to her that she could see the small flakes of amber that decorated the green around his pupils. He still had a light hold on her neck, her hands still cradling his face. All she had to do was move in slightly and their lips would meet. As if reading her mind, he dipped his head down to close those last few inches between them.

He touched his lips to hers and was pleased when she respond-ed in kind. Her lips were soft, warm, exactly how he imagined they would feel. He pushed his body into hers, trapping her firmly against the wall. When she made a small noise in her throat that was far from protest, he pressed his lips harder against hers. Her fingers flexed slightly against his cheeks before she opened her mouth to him. He eagerly accepted her invitation, his tongue slipping in to taste her.

She released a soft moan as their tongues met and slid against one another. She then sucked in a startled breath when she felt something sharp nick the side of her lip. She barely tasted her own blood before he was gone. He kept her away from him with the hold on her neck, his face turned away as he covered his mouth with his other hand.

She blinked at him as she realized what happened. "Lucas—"

"My apologies, Miss Quinn." He quickly cut her off, moving his hand away from his mouth so he could speak. He swallowed thickly and cursed his carelessness. Damn, even a small taste of her blood had his body on fire. When he felt her small hands clamp on his wrist, he glanced at her and realized he was still holding her neck captive. He abruptly released her and stepped a safe distance away. "I believe that will be it for tonight."

Kee watched as he went and gathered their equipment with a frown. She gingerly touched the cut on her lip and peered at the blood that coated her finger. She rubbed the blood off on her pants and then ran her tongue along the cut to try to get the rest of it.

"Stop," he rasped. "*Please.*"

She looked up and flushed to see Lucas staring at her with hungry eyes, his grip tight on the bucket of their supplies. She quickly covered her mouth with her hand and gave him an apologetic look when he stormed past her. She grabbed the earmuffs and goggles she had thrown before silently following after him.

Lucas set the bucket down on the counter with more force than needed but didn't bother to explain himself to the two vampires. They merely bowed their heads in respect and started putting the equipment away. He didn't wait for his employee, or her pet, before he walked outside. He just needed some cool air. How could he have let himself slip up like that? Why did he cross that boundary in the first place? She was his employee; that should have been it.

*Should have.* He repeated to himself despondently.

"Lucas?"

He tensed slightly at her soft voice and turned to look at her. He felt the wolf's glare on him, but didn't bother addressing him. Clearly Conrad wasn't an idiot, but he would offer him no explanation. Even if he had one to give. "I have a job for you tomorrow night. I will be in contact with more details later."

Kee let out a heavy sigh as he left. She felt Conrad's hand on her shoulder and looked at him to see his brow furrowed with worry. "What's wrong?" She asked.

"You're hurt." He growled low. If the vampire had struck her, he wouldn't be idle about it. While Lucas unnerved him, he wouldn't let him hurt his alpha and get away with it. This was someone she was supposed to trust.

She blushed. "It's not what you think," she explained in a small voice. Oh gods, she had kissed Lucas. She covered her mouth again when she realized what that meant. She cheated on Cain.

*How could I? How did I let myself get so caught up? Although, with how we left things, I'm not so sure we're even together anymore. How can we be?*

Her bottom lip trembled as the earlier emotions raged like a storm within her once again. The anger at the pack, the hurt from Cain, the pain of being a shapeshifter, and now the confusion of kissing Lucas.

"Damn it!" She cursed as her eyes stung with unwanted tears once again.

"What's wrong?" Conrad repeated softly as he followed her to the car.

"Everything." She hissed as she dug through her back pocket and handed him the keys. "Can you drive? Please? I just can't focus on anything right now."

"Sure." He said simply because what else could he say? He unlocked the car and flinched when she got in and slammed the door shut. With a heavy sigh, he slipped into the driver's side and started the car.

She didn't say a word on the way home, or when they got back to the apartment. He waited as she got ready for bed and slipped under the covers before he went to the bathroom. He stripped down, shifted into his wolf form, and then walked back into the bedroom. Leaping up on the bed, he hesitantly nestled down next to her, not sure if she wanted the company. He released a soft huff of relief when she threw an arm over him, cuddling him and pressing her face to his back.

"I'm sorry," she breathed tiredly into his fur. "We'll talk tomorrow, but for now I just need this."

Conrad rumbled contently, glad he could help his alpha.

# *Twelve*

"Are you sure this was what you saw?" Warren asked coldly, glaring at his younger brother. He had to be one hundred percent certain that what he was insinuating was true.

Wyatt matched the glare, ice blue clashing. "I know what I saw, Warren. I was going to go let off some steam at the gun range, but when I got there they told me they were closed for a private party. I was pissed, so I went back to my car to have a smoke. Lucas showed up and a few minutes later, so did Cain's woman and another guy. They met each other there."

The alpha growled low in his throat as he hunched forward, resting his elbows on his knees. "Did you see them do anything suspicious?"

"Suspicious like what? Isn't them meeting enough of a red flag? Especially outside of the city?" Wyatt shoved his hands through his short black hair. "Come on, Warren! You can't leave this alone! If he finds out, he'll flip out!"

"I know I can't, Wyatt, but this is a delicate matter. Our beta has chosen her as his mate. Her initiation task has already been stated. I can't simply revoke it, it would raise too many questions." Warren pinched the bridge of his nose in frustration.

*What was Kee's relationship with the vampire? And who was the other man with her? Has she been conspiring against us from the start? Or, is it all some strange coincidence?*

"If she's cheating on Cain then we should just kill her anyways! It would be better for him because if he finds out it will *crush* him! We protect our own, even from their bitch!" He snarled, slamming his hands down on his brother's coffee table, the wood creaking in protest.

Warren flared his aura and growled low in warning, not letting up until his brother backed down. He waited until he removed his hands from the table and took two steps back, head tilted off to the side in submission. "We don't know for sure if that is what you saw, Wyatt. You said they chatted for a second before they went into the building. No hugging, no kissing, no physical contact, right?"

"She punched him in the arm." He grumbled angrily.

He resisted the urge to roll his eyes at his brother. "Yes, they *must* be fucking," he commented sarcastically. "What about when they left?"

The younger werewolf gave a stubborn shrug. "I don't know, they barely looked at each other. They walked out, had a short talk, and then left separately." He exhaled loudly. "But why else would she go all the way out to Inglewood to meet him? And with another man?"

"I'm not saying there isn't the possibility. But, as I stated, we need to handle this with care. We are stuck in the middle and our actions have to be well thought out."

"Are you going to tell him?" He asked quietly after a few moments of silence.

He didn't need his brother to elaborate on whom he was referring to. "I have to. From there we will see what he wants to do."

"In the meantime?" He pressed as he crossed his arms over his chest.

"I want you to keep occasional tabs on her. Inform me if you discover anything else, or find any proof of their relationship." He lowered his tone. "Do not tell anyone about this, Wyatt. Not Katie, and not Nat. Understand?"

He nodded begrudgingly. "Yeah, I got it. I just think that the quicker we deal with this, the better."

"I know, but it isn't up to me." Warren said and then dismissed his brother with a wave of his hand. "I will keep you informed with what happens." He waited for him to leave the room before sighing heavily and leaning back against his couch cushions again.

How could this new werewolf be causing him so many problems already? He originally just wanted to dominate her by sheathing himself inside her tight little body after her display of dominance, but now he didn't know what to do. She was Cain's chosen woman, but was also fraternizing with their enemy. However, he wasn't really sure what the status was of her and Lucas' relationship yet. Perhaps it was just a coincidence. Or, maybe they were just friends. But, Wyatt was right, why would they go all the way to Inglewood?

He realized he was trying to make excuses for her. Mostly because he still wanted to fulfill his needs with her, but also keep his beta happy. However, excuses or not, he knew that this would end badly. Anyone who was close to Lucas would suffer, it just depended on when the order was given.

He rubbed the bridge of his nose once again. Why couldn't Cain just like one of the females in their pack? Why did he have to pick a stray? This was why he always demanded to meet new wolves when they moved to the city; so he could get to know them before accepting them into his pack. That way he knew what he was getting into.

Admittedly, he sensed something was off with Kee when he met her, but had disregarded it when he learned of her past. A late blooming gene was always tricky to accommodate to. But, now that Wyatt had come to him with this information, could there have been a different reason behind it? Was she their enemy from the beginning? Was she using Cain?

He tensed. Wait, did Cain know of her relationship with Lucas? Was he collaborating against him for the title of alpha?

Warren shook his head. No, there was no way. Cain was his loyal beta. He was like a second little brother to him and Natalie. Cain had shed blood for him before and wouldn't hesitate to do it again. Warren knew this with absolute certainty.

Releasing a heavy sigh, he knew he had to stop dwelling on the issue. For now, there was nothing more he could do. He could only hope Wyatt would fail to find any proof, but he knew in his gut that it wouldn't matter what proof he did or did not find. Her fate was already sealed.

Taking a deep breath, he reached for his phone and pulled up one of the first numbers on his contact list. He glanced at the time. It was just before midnight and he knew that Alexander would be up.

"*Yes, Warren?*" Came the impassive greeting.

"I've got some news for you." The alpha replied as he tried to relax against the cushions of the stiff couch.

"*Regarding?*"

"What else? Your enemy, of course."

"Our *enemy*," he stressed. "*He stands in the way of accomplishing our goals so he is both our enemy. Don't forget that.*"

"Right, well, *our* enemy has a friend."

"*Oh? And who is this friend?*"

He paused ever so slightly, his instincts flaring in warning. It was too late though, he had made his choice. "A wolf, but not one from my pack." He started and then proceeded to tell him what Wyatt had seen.

"*Then kill her.*" He said it bluntly, as if it were the most obvious thing to do.

"There is a complication with that, Alexander." He growled, not liking that he had been right. He knew he would have to give this order.

"*Which is?*" The vampire asked with a bored tone.

He sighed heavily. "My beta has chosen her to be his mate."

He was quiet for a few moments. "*And this is a problem, how, exactly? I understand your second-in-command is important to you, but if this girl is working with Lucas, then she must be eliminated.*"

Warren clenched his jaw. "We don't know if they are working together. We have no proof."

"*Who cares? Even if she isn't a colleague of his, they still know each other well enough to meet outside the city. Anyone who is important to him will be killed. Hell, even if they aren't important to him, I want them eradicated. I want him to be standing alone with no one to support him the next time we fight.*"

"What am I supposed to tell Cain?" He asked angrily.

"*Quite frankly, my dear wolf, I don't give a shit what you tell him. Make her disappear, make it look like a homicide, I don't care. Just get rid of her.*" He snapped and then took a deep breath as if to regain his composure. "*Look, Warren, each ally we kill brings us closer to our goal. Remember, the two of us are the superior races.*"

"Humans are beneath us," he added quietly. He agreed that were-animals and vampires could take over the humans of the city. Technically, even if all vampires and wereanimals banded together, the humans outnumbered them, but they were weak and would never stand a chance. "They belong on their knees."

"*Exactly. Your beta's unknown sacrifice will be for a greater cause.*" Alexander cooed before his tone turned serious. "*Just make sure he does not find out. I can't have your pack divided, or have your position compromised, Warren. I need you on my side."*

"He won't find out," he growled. "I'm not going anywhere."

*"Good."* He practically purred. *"I have to go pick off other members of Lucas' coven. Call me after she has been taken care of."*

Warren pulled the phone away from his ear when the call ended and sighed heavily. He ran his hand through his long hair and then down his face. It was too bad he would never get to fuck the dominance out of Kee, but the end game was more important that his desire.

He clicked on his brother's name on his phone and only had to wait one ring for him to pick up. "Wyatt, don't bother keeping tabs on her. Plans have changed."

# *Thirteen*

Kee let out a tired sigh as she walked down the hall towards her apartment. Lucas was consistently pushing her limits with her shifting, but these last few nights had been draining. She couldn't handle it. Shifting took a burst of energy and the longer she held the skin, the more it siphoned. Holding a skin for hours on end the last five nights was taking a toll on her, but she was determined to trudge through it. She even quit her job at Shifters to try so she could recharge during the day.

Lucas had told her he suspected Alexander was killing off his coven members. Every night since the fight, a member from Lucas' coven has been found down. Each time, no one was around to witness it. Lucas suspected that one of the murderers was a newer vampire made by Alexander.

Unfortunately, due to the lack of proof, he couldn't act.

That was where she came in.

It was her job to follow Alexander's vampire. The first couple nights she followed him around the streets of Ventura, trying to confirm if he was assisting Alexander in the murders. Newer vampires were clumsy, not quite used to their new senses, and therefore were easier to trail. She scurried around in a variety of animal skins as she followed the baby vampire, making sure to stay out of sight. She saw him feed from a few willing humans, but nothing stood out to her as suspicious.

Until tonight.

He was on a date with a slender, Asian woman with beautiful pale skin. Honestly, Kee had almost given up on following them until he finally made his move. In her black cat skin, she watched as he snapped the woman's neck when he went in for a kiss. The break didn't kill the fellow vampire, but it did disorient her enough that she couldn't defend herself when he pulled a switchblade from his pocket and thrust it into her chest.

"Alexander sends his regards to your lord." He had spat before slicing down her torso.

Kee almost gagged as she remembered how he ripped open her ribcage with his bare hands before fishing out her heart. With his grip on the plastic handle, he stabbed the silver blade into her heart and watched as it sizzled before disintegrating into ash. Kee had ran back to her car, shifted into her human form, and immediately texted Lucas. He told her he had a meeting at 9:30, but would meet her afterwards for details.

*Which I'm nervous as fuck for.* She thought as she bit down on her bottom lip.

Every conversation between them since the gun range had been through text messages and strictly work related. Neither one brought up what happened. She didn't know what to make of it, honestly. Then there was the fact that she hadn't spoken to Cain either. He hadn't reached out to her and she was scared to do it first. She had hurt him, and then betrayed him.

She was just as drained mentally as she was physically.

Thank whatever gods were above that she had Conrad. He had

been nothing but supportive. He silently put up with her mood swings, cuddled her when she was upset, and made her coffee when she couldn't get out of bed. She was so glad that he had chosen to stay by her side. She really didn't know what she would have done without him around to keep her grounded. She owed him. Big time. Maybe she should order them takeout when he got home.

Nodding in agreement to herself, she unlocked the door, put her hand on the handle, and froze. Every hair on the back of her neck stood up in warning. It was similar to when she found Lucas in her apartment, but this time she could sense an aura behind the door. It wasn't pleasant.

She clenched her jaw as she racked her brain for who could be in her apartment. She was supposed to meet Lucas after his meeting, and Conrad said he would be back in about half an hour. So who, or what, was in her apartment? Was it Cain? She knew he was probably still upset, but for his aura to be this vicious?

Swallowing thickly, she twisted the knob and pushed the door open. She stepped in and closed the door behind her, pressing her back to it as she scanned her apartment. She instantly saw a man standing in front of her fridge, his back to her as he inspected the pictures. Her brow furrowed when the man turned towards her, holding the glossy image of her and Cain in his hand.

"Wyatt?" She asked cautiously.

"Yo," he stated casually as he held up the picture of the couple. "Cute picture."

"Thanks." She replied slowly, her hands flexing at her sides nervously. "Why are you here? Did you need something?"

"Do you love Cain?" He questioned as if she hadn't spoken. His artic blue eyes finally looking at her, his expression was anything but friendly. "He's crazy about you, you know," he continued on as he waved the picture at her. "He wants you to be his mate."

*Cain? Is that why he's here? Because of our disagreement? Because I don't want to fuck their alpha?* Her stomach twisted in dread. *Did he tell his pack the truth about me? About why I don't want to join their pack? No, he wouldn't do that to me. Right?*

"No answer? What a shame." He said lightly as he crumpled the picture in his hand and dropped it to the floor before he stepped towards her.

She instantly darted to the right towards the living room so that her back wasn't against the door. Her eyes widened when she saw two other werewolves emerging from the hall that led to her bedroom. They were in their hybrid form, a mix between human and wolf. They were covered in fur and stood on their hind legs, their faces that of a wolf. The wolf in front was a rich brown, eyes a golden yellow. The other was a tawny color with dark chocolate eyes.

She knew the color of their fur didn't always correlate with their human form, especially if they were turned into a werewolf and not born as one. She didn't know many werewolves, but she had seen this one before. The slight offset of their snout only confirmed her suspicion.

*It can't be.* "N-Noah?"

His eyes widened slightly in what she assumed was surprise before scowling at her. Her pulse kicked into gear, her heart pounding hard against her rib cage, as if it was trying to break free of its prison. Her breath came out in short spurts as she watched the three wolves start to close in on her.

"What do you want?" She asked shakily as adrenaline began to spread through her veins.

Wyatt smiled cruelly at her. "Did you think we wouldn't find out?"

She clenched her hands into fists as sweat slicked her palms. *So Cain did tell them.* She felt her rapidly beating heart stop for a second before it twisted in pain with betrayal. *How could he?*

"And you intend to kill me because of it?"

"We have our orders. Shame, Katie really liked you." He comment-ed unapologetically before his eyes shifted to something more primal and hungry.

She could do nothing but watch as he shifted into his hybrid wolf form, black fur covering him from head to claw. Fear grabbed her in a vice grip as unwanted memories attacked her, but she quickly shook her head clear of them. She wasn't a little girl anymore. She would be damned if she didn't at least put up a fight.

Filtering through her collection of skins, she tried to find one that would save her. Or at least give her a fighting chance. She selected one and focused on the image, but her temple thrummed in warning, reminding her of her exhausted state.

But she didn't have a choice. She had to fight.

Accepting the image, she began to shift. Her clothes ripped apart as her body expanded and thickened. Coarse, chocolate brown fur sprouted from her skin as she took on the form of a grizzly bear. She stood on her hind legs, now the same size as the wolves.

Wyatt suddenly launched himself at her so she forced strength into her right arm and smacked him to the side, sending him crashing into her entertainment center. She began to turn towards the other two, but roared in pain when the wolf she didn't know leapt onto her back, claws digging into her skin. She went down on all fours and ran the short distance to the wall by the front door. She flung herself at it, curling in so her back would hit. The wolf yelped as he was crushed between the wall and her massive weight. She felt something pop and the wolf whimpered as she stood. She cried out when his claws ripped down her shoulder, but slammed her back against the wall again to dislodge him.

Kee was panting, her temples pounding. The base of her skull tingled and she knew she was pushing herself too far. Her limbs trembled as they tried to hold the skin, the pain in her shoulder not helping her concentration. She could feel something wet gather and drip from her nose and knew it was blood from the straining herself. Her ears would be next.

Growling low, she forced herself to focus. She looked up to see Noah coming at her. She met his paws with hers, stopping his claws from ripping out her throat. She pushed back against him, but he was stronger. He used his grip on her paws to turn and throw her. She tumbled into her dining room table, knocking it over before her head smacked hard against the wood floor.

The skin left her as her breath did, her body shifting back into her naked human form. Pain shot through her skull and neck when the shock from the initial impact wore off. She felt blood trickle from her ears, but didn't have time to worry about it before Noah's form was on top of hers. He had shifted back into a person, his naked body kneeling over hers. She couldn't bring her hands up in time to block his next attack and was rewarded with a backhanded slap. Her head snapped to the right, her neck straining from the force.

"You dare embarrass me in front of my pack?! In front of my alpha?!" He screamed at her, drawing his fist back to punch her already bruising face. "I can't believe you're a *shapeshifter*," he spat the word like it was a curse. "Of all the disgusting things for Cain to bring home!"

Noah couldn't believe that his best friend's girl was the monster of all monsters. Had his friend even known? Had she tricked him, too?

He originally had doubts about killing her when Wyatt came to him with Warren's order. Cain had told him what her initiation was supposed to be and that she refused. He was there when Cain told Warren, and stopped his friend from attacking their alpha out of rage. Cain had blamed Warren for their fight, blamed him for possibly losing the only woman he ever loved. Noah knew Warren was angry with Kee's decision, and was livid that she had driven a wedge between him and his beta, but he never would have thought Warren would have ordered her death.

Had he been pissed that she embarrassed him in front of everyone? Fuck yeah, but he wasn't convinced she deserved death until he saw her morph into a bear in front of him. He had seen her wolf form before, watched her shift into it when Cain invited her to go camping with them.

A pup being carried by *any* wereanimal barely made it full term due to the need to shift on the full moon. But, if the child survived to birth, and their parents were two different wereanimals, the more dominant beast gene would be passed on to the pup. Never both.

So that only left one thing for Kee to be. *A fucking shapeshifter.*

All his anger had exploded within him, fueling his beast with the need to kill her. "I'll enjoy killing you." He sneered down at her.

Kee slowly turned her head back so she was looking up at him. Her lip stung from him splitting it open, and she had to close her right eye as blood dripped into it from the laceration on her brow. Her heart pounded in fear, but she refused to show it. "How's your nose?" She asked quietly, her one good grey eye staring defiantly up at him.

His rage doubled at the reminder of his embarrassment, a nasty snarl marring his face. He wrapped both his hands around her frail neck and squeezed. Using his hold on her neck, he lifted her upper body from the floor and shook her. "You were lucky, *shapeshifter*, nothing more! Do you really think you could win against me?"

She gagged as her throat was all but crushed in his grip. Her hands flew to his, her nails clawing and digging into the skin of his fingers to try and alleviate the pressure. She tried to gasp in air, but he had firmly sealed off her airway. She felt her lips go cold, her fingertips tingling.

"Look at you. You're just as pathetic as the mutt you tried to save."
He brought her face close to his, their noses almost touching. "I will
kill him, too, just to spite you."

Fire flared in her at the mention of her wolf. *Yes, my wolf.* She was
protective of Conrad, especially after all he had been through and
done for her.

She tightened her hold on his hands and used the leverage to
quickly bring up her knee between his legs. He wailed in pain and
abruptly released her. She sucked in a painful gasp and immediately
started coughing.

*Move, Kee!*

She jabbed her foot straight at Noah's face when he growled at her,
crushing the healing bones of his nose once again. When he howled
in pain and covered his nose, she leapt to her feet and cursed as she
wobbled. Darkness hazed the edges of her vision, but she forced
herself to keep going. She stumbled towards her sliding glass door,
but wheezed when something latched onto her hair and yanked her
back. She was swung and then slammed down on her glass coffee
table. She let out a scream as the glass shattered beneath her, shards
of it cutting into and embedding themselves deep into her back as she
landed hard on the ground.

Her breath left her a second time from the impact and she tried
to focus as Wyatt's black furry form hovered over her. Pain jarred her
body as her senses started to come back. She squeezed her eyes tight
as the pain consumed her, tears stinging her eyes.

Wyatt slammed one hand down below her left collar bone and
sunk each of his four claws into her flesh, smirking when she cried
out. He then proceeded to drag his hand down through her skin to
her right hip, his smirk widening as she screamed and writhed in
agony.

He turned and snarled at Noah when he approached them. "No,

you had your chance." He rumbled threateningly.

Noah snarled. "After what she did to me, I deserve this!" His voice came out nasally, blood still pouring from his nose.

"You had your chance!" He repeated. He removed his claws from her torn flesh and admired his handy work as her eyes glazed over and became distant. "I'll finish this. Brandon is having trouble breathing. Take him and leave."

He went to protest, but Wyatt snarled at him again, his aura pressing on him. "Fine," Noah grumbled as he walked over to Brandon's human form and helped him stand. After looping his arm across his shoulders to keep him upright, he glared at Kee's bleeding form. "Just make it hurt, Wyatt." With that, he grabbed the duffle bag of their spare clothes and walked out the door.

"Intend to." He purred as the two wolves left. He then bent over his victim's form, tilting his head innocently at her. "Passing out already? We can't have that."

Kee's eyes snapped open and another scream ripped itself from her abused throat when she felt his claws sink into her left side. A spasm shook her body at the painful feeling of his claws knocking and sliding against her ribs. She felt something wet work its way up her throat and knew it was blood once it hit her tongue. She choked before coughing it out. Her body was wracked with pain, her torso so cold it made her body tremble. Or, was she hot? She couldn't tell anymore. She could almost feel her brain shutting down, trying to protect itself from the overload of pain.

She wasn't aware Wyatt had been talking to her until he tapped her bruised cheek.

"*Tsk*, you're dying too soon," he frowned down at her. "I wanted to draw this out."

Her head lolled to the side, suddenly too heavy. Unfocused eyes landed on a familiar small, black box under her couch. It took a few seconds for her to realize and remember what it was. Her heart skipped a slow beat when she recalled the gun Lucas got her. Determination jolted her mind awake. If she was going to die, she was going to take Wyatt with her.

"The scent of your blood is intoxicating, I have to admit," he hummed as he bent down close to her and inhaled deeply, his snout centimeters from the bleeding wounds across her torso. "Do all shape-shifters smell like this?" He licked his lips before flicking his tongue at a puddle of blood on her stomach. His eyes widened and a shudder ran through his body.

The taste! He ran his tongue along part of the wound again and again, filling his mouth with her blood. Oh, gods! It was delicious! *More, I need more!*

While he was distracted with her blood, Kee begged her body to move. She didn't want to die in vain. She needed to take at least one of her assailants with her. Her arm sluggishly reached out for the box. She missed a couple times, her vision swimming, until she finally got it. She froze when she heard Wyatt release a needy, ravenous growl. She waited for him to stop her or yell at her, but it never came, his tongue still lapping up her blood like a starved man. She slipped her hand into the box and wrapped her fingers around the cool metal grip of the gun. She clicked off the safety as Lucas taught her and glanced at Wyatt.

Why? Why did she taste so good? Her blood was exotic and rich. It was warm and inviting, like a lover's embrace. His wolf ears twitched when he heard a click and he lazily looked up from his meal, his head heavy as if intoxicated. It took him a few seconds to realize the barrel of a gun was pointed at him. By the time he understood what was happening, she pulled the trigger.

It took everything in her to muster up the strength to pull the trigger, but she was satisfied. The bullet had gone straight into his forehead and splattered out the back of his head. Her arm dropped lifelessly at her side, the gun skittering along the broken glass. His deadweight fell on top of her and her lungs burned at the extra pressure on them, but she didn't have the strength to push him off. She couldn't feel her limbs anymore and darkness was creeping along her vision again.

*Well, at least I took Wyatt with me.*

# *Fourteen*

It was a little after ten when Conrad thanked the Uber driver and got out of the car, taking grocery bags with him. He made his way up the apartment stairs and tensed when he reached Kee's floor. There was a heavy scent of blood in the air and he briefly wondered which of the neighbors had hurt themselves. He approached Kee's door and stuck his key in the lock, but frowned when he realized it was already unlocked.

*That's weird. I wasn't expecting Kee home until later. Isn't she working for Lucas tonight?*

He twisted the knob and a cold wave of dread washed over him as the scent of blood grew stronger when he parted the door. He practically kicked it open and dropped the grocery bags as he took in the chaos of the apartment. The kitchen table was toppled over, blood splattered on the floor. Turning to the living room, he saw the entertainment center ruined, the television shattered and useless. The wall next to him was dented and cracked, smear of blood running along it. His heart pounded in his chest as he saw a pair of large feet peeking out from in front of the couch.

Silently and cautiously, he made his way to the living room. He peeked over the couch and saw a naked man lying on his stomach where the coffee table should have been. His eyes traveled up the man's bloodied back and then blinked when he realized part of his head had been blown apart, clumps of skull matted with bloodied hair.

He felt his blood freeze in his veins when he realized there was a small body lying under him. "Kee!"

He leapt over the couch, his shoes crunching on the broken glass, and ripped the lifeless man off of her. His breath caught in his throat and time seemed to slow as he looked down at her battered, naked, motionless body. Why did this happen to her? What did she do to deserve this? He glanced at the dead body he had thrown off of her and felt a growl vibrate in his chest when he realized it was Wyatt.

*Why is he there? Why did he do this to Kee? Did Cain have something to do with it?*

Conrad fell to his knees by her head, not feeling the bits of glass that sunk through his jeans and into his flesh as he took in her beaten, bloodied body. He carefully lifted her head and cradled it in his lap. Shakily, he reached out and pushed a blood matted strand of hair from her cool forehead. He bent over her still form and lowered his head to hers. He pressed his cheek against hers and put his fingers to her neck. A grief-stricken whine escaped him when he felt nothing.

Alphas could draw power from their pack, but he wasn't sure it would work with just him. Or with shapeshifters. His initial cold numbness was quickly replaced by an overwhelming ache as he mourned the only alpha he ever respected.

He jerked his head up when he heard her cell phone ring. Finding the phone nestled in torn denim an arm's length away, he reached for it and felt desperation consume him when he saw the name. He slid a bloodied thumb along the green bar, having to swipe it a couple times before the phone registered it, and then pressed the phone to the side of his face.

"Help!" He pleaded.

"*What?*" Came the stunned reply.

"Kee! You have to help! I don't know what to do!" He felt his inner wolf thrash in him, howling for their loss.

"*Slow down, Mr Novak. What happened?*" The vampire asked slowly.

"I don't know!" Conrad shouted in frustration as tears filled his amber eyes. "I came home and the apartment was wrecked! There's blood everywhere! Wyatt was dead on top of her, and when I pulled him off of her—*fuck!* It's bad!"

"*I will be there shortly. Do not move her.*"

He closed his eyes tightly as he whispered, "Please, hurry."

—

When Lucas had approached the apartment, he knew from the heavy scent of blood in the air that it would be bad. However, as he stepped through the door and made his way over to Conrad, he didn't anticipate it to be *this* bad.

Emerald green orbs slowly traveled across the expanse of her torso and chest, taking in each of the four slashes that ripped diagonally across her naked flesh. Her skin had been punctured and torn apart carelessly, the attacker clearly meaning to do detrimental physical damage. In one of her gaping side wounds, he could see a sliver of a milky white rib coated with the tempting nectar that was her blood.

Lucas' eyes traveled up to her once beautiful, slender neck. Now it was discolored, obvious finger-shaped bruises darkening her pale skin. Although Conrad's hands still cradled her face, he could see that her bottom lip was split at the left side, leaving it puffy with a smear of blood next to it. Her left cheek was swollen, the flesh a dark purple hue. Her right eye was swollen shut, a deep gash sliced into her brow. The other eye was closed as well, but it remained unharmed. Streams of blood went from each nostril to the corner of her lips, similar streaks trailing from her ears to her neck.

He glanced over at the dead body that Conrad had mentioned on the phone and snarled, fangs bared with the sudden wave of anger that hit him. He didn't know who Wyatt was, but he was sure he was a werewolf.

*Was this Cain's doing? Because she refused to be part of his pack?* He asked himself, but then shook his head. He had seen the way the wolf was with her, there was no way he would have wished this upon her. Or, had he somehow found out about the kiss? She had finally shown interest in him and look at where it had gotten her.

Lucas squatted down next to her body. "Keira." He sighed, his chest tightening with loss as he cupped her cold cheek.

He had wanted to keep her a secret. Wanted to keep her safe. Not only was her talent a rare gift that he used for his own purposes, but *she* as a person was something he wanted just for himself. He had hated it when she started dating Cain and had to keep himself from ripping the wolf to shreds. That restraint nearly snapped when she told him that Cain had put his hands on her.

Lucas slid his hand down to her abused neck, gently stroking the discolored skin. He had always desired to sink his fangs into the creamy flesh, to taste the source of her being again. After tasting it once, the need only grew. Now he would never have the chance.

His hand twitched and his body went rigid. He instantly pressed his pointer and middle finger to her pulse point and inhaled sharply. Had he imagined that? Was his need and regret toying with his mind? He bent down and pressed his ear to her chest, not caring that he was coating the side of his face in her blood.

"What are you doing?" Conrad croaked, his voice rough with emotion.

"Hush." He commanded as he listened. The silence seemed to stretch on forever. His eyes fluttered shut in aggravation. Damn his mind for—

...*thump*...

His eyes flew open, his pupils dilating. "Keira!" He called, resisting the urge to shake her battered body. He grabbed her hand in his, giving it a firm squeeze. "Keira, can you hear me?" She didn't reply to him, but her pinky finger twitched just the slightest bit. "She's alive."

"What? Kee!" Conrad exclaimed.

Lucas leapt to his feet as Conrad started calling her name over and over again, telling her to hold on. He snatched the blanket from the couch and lightly draped the soft fabric over her naked form. "Let go, Conrad." He calmly ordered him.

"What are you going to do?" The wolf asked as he removed his hands from her face.

"I am going to take her to my home." Lucas hesitated slightly before sliding his arms under her shoulders and knees. She was so terribly wounded, he didn't want to cause more damage. As carefully as he could, as if she was a precious porcelain doll, he lifted her into his arms, cradling her to his chest.

Conrad almost mirrored her whine, wanting to take his alpha's pain. "What can I do?"

Lucas paused briefly as he thought about it. If Cain did set this up, and if she did survive, then maybe it was best if he thought she was dead. His eyes met the wolf's amber gaze. "Grab some clothes for her, valuables you think she deems important, and any money she has stashed away. Hurry." He watched as the wolf obediently ran to her bedroom and was gone for a few minutes before returning with a backpack.

"What about Wyatt?" Conrad bit out as he glared at the dead body.

"I will have someone take care of it. Come."

When they pulled in the backlot of Byte minutes later, they hurried to the building and through the back entrance. "Giovanni!" Lucas called as he rushed in and made an immediate right in the kitchen. He nodded to the werewolf to open the plain, black metal door that led to the basement of the building.

Conrad followed the lord down the staircase and down a hallway lined with doors. He growled low in warning when a few vampires opened the doors and watched with curiosity. He saw their nostrils flare at the scent of Kee's blood and clenched his jaw. "Do you trust them?" He asked quietly.

"I am their lord, Mr Novak. They will not disobey me." He answered as he came to a stop at a door at the end of the hall.

"You called, Lord Lucas?" Giovanni asked as he stepped in front of him and opened the door without hesitation. He looked at the blood on the side of his lord's face, glanced briefly at the man standing next to him, and then at the very pale woman in his arms. "Should I get my supplies?"

"Yes, hurry." Lucas carried the shapeshifter to his bed and gently set her down. He carefully peeled the blood soaked blanket from her, careful not to cause further harm. He looked up when Giovanni reappeared with his bag of medical supplies and moved to the other side of the bed so he wasn't in the doctor's way.

Gio set the bag down next to the naked woman and looked at Lucas as he slid on a pair of latex gloves. "What happened?"

"She was attacked." Conrad replied as he looked down at his alpha's pale face.

"Who is she?" Gio inquired, not looking away from his maker.

Lucas met his subordinate's hazel eyes. "Someone of great value to me." He was glad that Giovanni merely lifted an eyebrow at him in response before turning back to his patient.

Gio grabbed his stethoscope and put in the ear pieces. Seeing her wrist had the least amount of damage, he chose that to check her pulse. As he listened, he carefully inspected her wounds, checking the amount of damage she sustained. He quickly pulled away when a tremor shook her body, blood splattering from her mouth. Ignoring the tantalizing scent of her blood, he looked up at his maker seriously. "She isn't going to make it on her own."

Conrad's brows knitted together in anguish. "No, you *have* to save her."

He glanced at the wolf and then back to Lucas. "I can't heal the internal damage she's suffered. I can stop the external bleeding and stitch her up, but I can't do it quickly enough. Her blood loss is stunting her natural wereanimal healing. She will die before her body can heal enough to last through my stitching."

"So we need to accelerate her healing more," Lucas concluded and then met Giovanni's knowing gaze. "If I give her my blood it will form a bond between us."

"Only if you have taken her blood as well." When Lucas just stared at him, he bowed his head. "The decision is yours, Lucas."

Conrad glared at Lucas. "You drank Kee's blood?" He growled when the vampire ignored him to climb on the bed so he was kneeling next to Kee. "Don't ignore me, Lucas. What kind of bond will this form with my alpha?"

"It is a connection, Mr Novak. We will just be more aware of each other," he replied and then looked at Giovanni. "Start stitching her up, I will give her my blood." When his second-in-command began cleaning Keira's wounds, he bit into the soft flesh of his wrist until blood welled up from it like a spring. With his other hand, he cupped Keira's jaw and applied enough pressure until her lips parted. He then pressed his wrist to her mouth, letting the blood drip inside.

Conrad kneeled by the side of the bed, making sure to stay out of

Gio's way as he began stitching up her torso. He watched carefully as Lucas rubbed Keira's bruised throat with his other hand, encouraging her to swallow. After a few weak, forced gulps, his brow furrowed when her swollen face flinched. His hackles raised when her uninjured eye suddenly shot open.

"Kee?" He called hesitantly.

Lucas felt the connection with Keira click into place and felt the pain that was starting to gather like a tidal wave inside her as consciousness came back to her. He blocked out the pain right before she let out a blood curdling scream. He heard Giovanni curse as she thrashed and saw Conrad leap to his feet so he could pin her shoulders down.

Being restrained made her grey eye frantically dart around in its socket like a frightened, caged animal. When her gaze landed on him, his chest tightened at the desperation there. Her bottom lip trembled and she weakly tried to move her hand towards him. With their new connection, he knew what she wanted. He grabbed her hand in his and squeezed it.

"Keep fighting, Keira." He ordered in a soft tone. She managed to hold his stare for a little bit longer before her eye rolled back into her head, her body going limp once again.

"Kee!" The werewolf called worriedly.

"She's just unconscious, Mr Novak." Lucas assured him as he looked down at her abused face. "It's better this way. She cannot feel the pain."

Conrad nodded reluctantly, noticing that the vampire still held her hand. The trio remained silent as Gio finished stitching up her torso and then moved to her side. When he was done, Conrad helped gently turn her on her side so that the doctor could start picking the glass shards out of her back and clean the slashes on her shoulder. After another long stretch of silence, he and Lucas helped prop her up so Giovanni could wrap bandages around her torso and shoulder.

After carefully lying her back down, he glanced up uncertainly at Lucas. "What happens now?"

"We wait." Lucas answered simply, his hand not once releasing Keira's.

"I mean after she wakes up." He clarified as he sat down on the edge of the bed after Gio pulled the blankets over her.

He sighed and met the wolf's inquiring gaze. "It will be up to her. We do not know how long it will take for her to recover, if she does. For now though, I believe it is best that we let others think she is dead."

"Cain, you mean." He growled, his hands clenching into tight fists. He was there when the couple got into their fight, had seen how hurt and angry the beta had been. Had he been the one who orchestrated this? "I can't believe he would do this to her."

"Would he, though?" Lucas questioned seriously. "Is he such a coward as to not do it himself?"

Conrad clenched his teeth and looked down at her battered face. "I didn't think so, but I've learned to never put anything past my species."

Giovanni interrupted them as he cleared his throat. "My apologies, Lucas, but it is nearly dawn."

The vampire frowned at the reminder. He still had to feed for the evening, especially after giving Keira blood he didn't have to spare. He reluctantly released her small hand before looking at her pet once again. "You are permitted to stay here with her, Mr Novak. I am entrusting you with her safety while I am asleep."

"I'll keep her safe." He told him confidently as he stood to take the place Lucas had been.

"Good. I will see you in the evening." With that, he turned and left the room with Giovanni.

Conrad waited until they were gone to strip down to the nude. He shifted into his wolf form and cautiously settled down next to her. He rested his head on her hand and stared sadly up at her, a whine in his throat.

She had to make it through this. He needed her. He knew she would keep them *both* safe. If she died, he didn't know what he would do.

# *Fifteen*

Natalie sat on her cream couch, legs pulled under her as she read a Cosmo magazine on her tablet. Her light blonde hair was pulled up into a fashionable, yet effortless bun, her face free of any makeup. She sipped a cup of tea and then set it down on her coffee table when she heard muffled shouting from Warren's office. She glanced at the closed doors, tilting her head slightly so her ear faced that direction.

"…do you not know?" She could make out her mate asking.

"I just don't…left early…told to." She could barely make out Noah's reply, only picking up little pieces.

She set her tablet down next to her mug and stood with the intention of heading towards the office. However, she stopped when the front door banged open, their beta's wild energy rapidly filling the downstairs. "Cain?"

He all but stumbled into the living room, dark blue eyes falling on the wolf queen. "*Nat.*" His voice was strangled with emotion.

She quickly went to him, reaching him as he crumbled to his knees. She kneeled down in front of him and let him fall into her lap. "Cain, what is it? What happened?" She cooed, cradling his head when he wrapped his arms around her waist.

"Kee," he began, his throat tight. "I took your advice and finally went to see her."

She nodded, gently stroking his hair to try and calm him down. She knew the past couple days had been hard on him. When he came to them after Kee declined Warren's initiation, she saw how heartbroken he was. Distraught, he tried to fight Warren in retaliation. Noah and Wyatt had stopped him, preventing him from making a mistake that would permanently disrupt their pack. Still, she couldn't blame him. It had been nearly a week since then, the scruff on his face had grown out, his hair disheveled.

She glanced up when Noah and Warren appeared from the office, their faces carefully blank. Her instincts went off like a warning bell. "What happened?" She asked Cain, but her eyes remained on the two.

"I shouldn't have waited six days, Nat," he cried, closing his eyes tightly. "I could have protected her."

"Protected her?" She echoed softly, running her fingers through his thick, dark brown hair. "What do you mean?"

"She was attacked, Nat! Gods, her apartment, you should have seen it!" He tightened his hold around her as anguish seared through him.

When he went to Kee's apartment, he was prepared to tell her that he was determined to keep her. He was going to tell her that she didn't have to join his pack, that they would make it work either way. He had bought her peach colored roses, which were her favorite, and a bottle of sweet moscato. As he waited for her to answer the door, the scent of old blood wafted from within. Alarmed, he grabbed the handle and pushed the door open. The wine bottle hit the floor and shattered, rose petals scattering around a discarded bag of groceries at the sight.

"There was so much blood. *Her* blood."

"Oh, Cain," she breathed when he buried his face in her stomach, his shoulders quivering. She tightened her hold on him, trying to comfort the wolf that was like a brother to her.

"Was there anyone in the apartment?" Warren asked. His eyes widened slightly when his mate shot him a withering glare.

"No," Cain croaked. "No one was there."

"Her body?" Noah questioned as he forced himself to move forward towards his best friend. He kneeled down next to him and tried to ignore the scrutinizing look Natalie gave him. There was no way she knew anything. He had no reason to look guilty. "Maybe she's still alive?"

"You didn't see all the blood, Noah," he whined. "It would be a miracle if she survived."

"Did you get any other scents? Maybe we can find the people who did this to her." The alpha suggested softly.

"The scent of day old blood was too strong. There were other scents, but I couldn't make them out." He answered as he sat up stiffly, wiping his hand across his eyes to dry them.

Warren walked over and set his hand on his beta's shoulder, squeezing it with comfort. "I know you are angry at me, Cain, but if I can help you find who did this, I will."

He put his hand on his alpha's and looked up at him. "Thank you, Warren. That means a lot."

"Cain, why don't you go shift and run? Go stretch and clear your head. You can stay here tonight and I'll make dinner, okay?" Natalie offered as she cupped his face in her hands.

He nodded and looked at his friend. "Run with me? I could use the company."

Noah forced a smile. "Of course, man. Let's go." He helped his friend to his feet and clamped him on the shoulder as he led him to the backyard.

She waited until they left and then glared at her mate. "Warren, what did you do?"

"What?" He asked as he helped her from the floor. His beast shrunk back at the heat in her glare. Nat was his mate, the love of his life, but damn could she scare him in a way no one else could. "Why are you looking at me like that?"

"I'll ask you one more time, *what did you do?*" She seethed when he turned his back on her and started walking towards his office. She grabbed the cup of tea from the coffee table and hurled it at him. It exploded when it hit the wall by his head, denting the drywall and chipping the paint. "Don't fucking turn your back on me, Warren."

His beast went from cautious to angry in a split second. He slowly turned towards her, his ice blue eyes practically glowing with the presence of his beast. "Say you're sorry, Natalie."

"No," she growled, baring her white teeth. "You promised not to keep things from me, Warren. You did something, I know you did. And so help me, if you killed Cain's girl, I won't forgive you."

He had to check his emotions to make sure he gave nothing away. Instead of pouncing on her and forcing her to submit to him by biting her throat, he looked away from her. "Do you really think I would do that? Cain is like our brother."

"Maybe." She commented and then crossed her arms over her chest. "Tell me, Warren, where's Wyatt? Where is our *real* little brother? It's been nearly a week since he's been around and Katie has been texting me asking if I know where he is."

He tensed, but tried to keep himself calm. "I'm sure he's fine, Nat."

"*Are* you sure?" She scowled when he simply shook his head and disappeared back into his office, the lock clicking into place. She let out a frustrated growl and sunk down on the couch, burying her face in her hands.

*Please, please, don't let my mate have anything to do with either of their disappearances.*

# *Sixteen*

Kee awoke with a start when a jolt of pain shot through her stomach as she tried to roll over. Her eyes flew open, but one protested the motion and only opened halfway. A wave of panic washed through her when she realized that she wasn't staring up at her bland white ceiling. Instead it was a dark grey, almost charcoal color. Where was she?

She let out a short yelp when she tried to sit up, another spasm of pain running through half her body. She glanced down at the dark maroon duvet covering her and pulled it back. Her eyes widened when she saw her torso wrapped in bandages. Her brow furrowed as she gently ran her fingers over the gauze.

*What happened? And who did this?*

Kee forced herself into a sitting position and immediately had to lean against the headboard as a surge of nausea made her stomach churn. She took a few deep breaths and then ran her hand down her face.

"Fuck!" She cursed as she was immediately met with pain from the action. She gingerly ran her fingertips along her face, checking the damage. She felt the scabbed cut on her brow, then her swollen cheek, and finally the almost healed cut on her lip. Had she been in an accident?

She let her hand drop from her face and scanned the unfamiliar room. It was decorated in sleek black furniture with dark red accents. On the other side of the rather spacious room was a black leather couch with crimson pillows. The coffee table was black, a dark red bowl with golden glass balls arranged within it. There was black bookshelf with gold etchings against one of the walls, the shelves overflowing with books both worn and new. The large bed she was lying on had a black frame with matching nightstands.

She swung her legs over the bed and shakily got to her feet. Damn, her body ached. Using the bed as support, she walked over to the two doors on the right side of the room. The first one she opened was a large walk-in closet, the second was what she had been hoping for. She stepped into the black and white bathroom, bracing herself along the walls as she walked further in. She stumbled towards the black countertop and gasped at her reflection.

*What the fuck...?*

Her face and neck were covered in fading bruises, the deep purple mixed with the pale green that came with healing. The cut on her eyebrow was stitched, but a scab had formed around it. Her bottom lip had a gash on it as well, but it was small and mostly healed. Dried blood was coming off in flakes around her ears and nose, but she knew that was from pushing her shifting limits.

Kee lifted her hands and reached for the knot on her gauze. She undid it and slowly uncoiled it from around her, hissing in a breath from the movement. The more of her body that was revealed, the more the color drained from her face. She let the gauze drop to the floor and her mouth fell open in horror.

Four pink, angry, jagged cuts went from her left shoulder to her right hip. The two outer ones had snagged on her breasts, the left one just barely missing her nipple. The slashes had been cleaned and stitched together carefully, but little crusts of blood were still splattered around them. Horrified, her gaze dropped down to the four puncture holes on the side of her ribs, little lines of stitches holding them together as well.

She lifted a shaking hand and followed the marks with her fingers. Her eyes widened when she realized they were done by claws. *Wyatt's claws.*

She sucked in breath as the memories came rushing back to her, pulling her under and drowning her in a wave of anguish. She shrieked and stumbled away from the mirror, landing on her ass on the cool tile. Her breaths came out in short, rapid pants as she was forced to vividly relive her assault. All of it. Brandon on her back, Noah punching and choking her, and Wyatt painfully dragging his claws through her flesh.

*No, no, no.* She had to get clean. She had to wash off the blood and the touch of them on her body. She crawled to the shower, put her hand on the door's handle, and used it as leverage to stand on shaking legs. She stepped into the black tiled shower and turned on the water. She didn't care that it was freezing when the water first beat down on her, she just needed to get clean.

She turned the water to warm and leaned against the tile as the flashes of her attack hit her once again. She sunk to her knees as her chest heaved, her breath coming out in quick, little bursts. They became shaky as tears filled her eyes. She didn't try to hold them back and there was no slowing them once they came. She wrapped her arms around herself as she sobbed, unable to stop as she came to the only conclusion as to why this happened to her.

"*Cain!*" His name came out as a heartbroken, strangled cry.

Kee wasn't sure if minutes or hours had passed when she heard the door open, but she wasn't expecting it. She quickly scampered to the corner of the shower, sliding along the tile as she tried to get away from the hands reaching for her. "No!" She screeched, holding up her hands to try and fend off the person coming near her. "*NO!*"

———

Lucas had been violently pulled from his slumber when he shot Wyatt in the head. Well, not him, but Keira. He was reliving what happened to her as if he had experienced it himself. He quickly jumped out of Giovanni's bed and ran to his room when he realized she was conscious. He looked around his bedroom and cursed when he didn't see her or Conrad anywhere.

Hearing the water going, he opened the door, and instantly went to his shower. He yanked open the door and felt his stomach drop when he saw her huddled on the floor, arms wrapped around herself as she sobbed. Seeing her breaking apart in his shower made him feel an odd, uncomfortable pang. He stepped in the shower with his lounge pants still on and reached for her. His body tensed when she screamed in terror, trying desperately to scramble from him.

"Stop," he said softly as he kneeled in front of her and pulled her into his arms. When she immediately started struggling, he tightened one arm around her waist and used the other to grab the back of her neck. "*Keira*, look at me." He demanded.

She opened her eyes at the familiar voice. She stared at Lucas, her heart beating painfully in her chest. His black hair was wet and clung to his forehead as the water sprayed over him. "L-Lucas," she stammered, her bottom lip trembling. Her eyes filled with tears again as she wrapped her arms tightly around him, pressing her face to his neck. "Lucas!"

He arranged her in his lap and just held her as she got it all out of her system. He pushed her wet mane from her back and examined the skin. His eyes raked over her back, his fingers lightly gliding over the soft flesh. He was pleased when all he felt was wet, smooth skin, the cuts on her back and the scratches on her shoulder gone. He rubbed her back until her sobs died down to sniffles, her breathing slowly evening out.

"How bad is it?" She finally whispered as she rested her cheek on his bare shoulder. She took a deep, shaky breath and released it, trying to rein her emotions back in.

"Not at all," he replied, his hand doing another sweep of her skin before resting on her lower back. "It healed perfectly."

"That's good," she mumbled and slowly pulled away from him. She looked at his naked, pale chest and at the soaked, dark blue pajama pants he wore. "I'm sorry you're all wet."

Lucas lifted a black brow at her, his green eyes gleaming with amusement. "After everything that happened, *that* is what you say?"

She flushed and crossed her arms across her chest, suddenly very aware that she was naked. "What am I supposed to say?"

He simply shook his head and pushed a few persistent wet strands from her face. He then cupped her abused cheek, his face growing serious. "I thought you were dead."

She met his eyes, her bottom lip threatening to quiver again. "Me too, but you saved me."

His brow furrowed. "Conrad told you about the blood?"

"What blood?"

At that moment, the bathroom door flung open again and they heard feet slapping against the tile as someone ran to the shower without opening it. A rushed, but weary, "Kee?" echoed in the room.

Conrad had been upstairs in the club's kitchen. He had made a phone call and fixed himself some lunch when he finally couldn't ignore the pang in his stomach anymore. After finishing off his sandwich he made his way back down to Lucas' bedroom and froze in the doorway when he noticed the large bed was empty. Fear gripped him before his sensitive hearing heard the shower running in the bathroom.

"Conrad." She greeted as she looked away from Lucas.

He put his hand over his heart as relief flooded him. "You're awake," he stated, but it was more for himself. He looked at her blurred form on the floor through the textured glass. "Do you need help?"

"No, I had a freak out, but it's over. I just want to get clean now." She replied honestly.

He tilted his head when he realized the vampire was in the shower with her. "Okay, I'll let you shower and go make you something to eat."

"Sounds good." She told him although she had zero appetite. She waited until the door closed and then dropped the forced smile. She let Lucas help her to her feet, but clutched his hand when he moved to leave. "Please, don't leave yet." She whispered.

*I'm not ready to be alone.*

Lucas looked down at her pleading eyes as the water beat over them. As much as he wanted to keep her naked in his shower, he wouldn't let himself baby her any further. He didn't want her to confuse comfort with feelings and mix them up later down the road. Especially with their new connection.

He turned so his back was to her. "Now that you have calmed down, you need to think of how you want to move forward, Miss Quinn."

She wrapped her arms around his waist, making sure to be careful of her stitches when she pressed her body to his. "Don't go back to calling me that." She breathed miserably.

She didn't want distance between them again. The five days of tense texting had been hard and she refused to go back to that. She lifted her head to tell him as such, but halted when she noticed a patch of raised flesh on his left shoulder blade. The white scar tissue, she realized as she looked closer, was a deep, intricate design of a sun. There was an almost perfect circle for the center of the sun, but the rays that jumped off of it varied in length, depth, and thickness. To her, it was beautiful.

Lucas froze when he felt her touch his brand. His undead heart did a strange flutter when he realized she had lightly pressed her lips against it. He stepped out of her arms and turned back to her. He framed her face with his hands again and put a thumb on her lips to prevent himself from kissing her. "Get the rest of your emotions out. We have much to talk about when you are done."

Kee watched him leave the shower and saw his silhouette grab one of the towels from the wall before walking out the door. Releasing a heavy sigh, she braced her hands against the cool tile and closed her eyes tightly. *Gods, what am I doing?*

She didn't cling to people, didn't rely on them for support, and yet she had basically begged Lucas not to leave her. Still, he had made her feel safe. She wanted to curl into his arms and never leave. It was true that he had been the one who saved her, even if it was indirectly. If he hadn't bought her that gun, she knew Wyatt would have finished her off.

After another ten minutes of scrubbing every speck of her attackers off, she stepped out of the shower and began drying herself off with the other black towel hanging on the rack. She used it to wipe the fog from the mirror and forced herself to look at her reflection again. She grit her teeth and took in the damage to her body once again.

Three werewolves had ambushed her in the comfort of her own home all because of what she was. Noah had been so disgusted, so repulsed by the truth of her person. Brandon she didn't know personally, but he had been there and attacked her and that was enough for her to surmise he felt the same way. And Wyatt, well, he didn't matter anymore. She blew his brains out and would do it again if she got the chance.

Her hands tightened on the towel. She had *killed* someone, stole their life away. And yet, she only felt a small amount of guilt for killing Wyatt. Even then, she realized it was because she felt bad for Katie. She glanced down at her white knuckles when they began to ache and slowly eased her hold on the towel.

*When my anger cools, will I regret it? Will I feel ashamed?* She glimpsed at her reflection in the mirror and scowled at it. Even if she did, she knew it was a life for a life. His or hers, and she had made a decision.

She jumped when the door opened, Conrad handing her a pile of clothes. "Here, I gave you one of my shirts so it wouldn't hurt your stitches."

"Thanks, Con," she said earnestly as she took the small pile. "I really appreciate it." She added with a forced smile.

"Of course." He replied before leaving the bathroom once again, lips turned down into a frown. He knew his alpha was forcing herself, but didn't comment on it. He tied the top section of his hair back into a bun and flopped down on the leather couch with a sigh. If pretending was better for her at the moment, then he would let her. When she stepped back out of the bathroom in leggings and his white shirt, he gestured her over. "Here, you need to eat."

Kee sat down on the plush leather sofa and looked down at the peanut butter and honey sandwich waiting for her. Next to it was a cup of raspberries, her favorite fruit, and a bottle of water. She reached for the water first and looked at Conrad when he stared at her. "What?" She winced when it came out as a snap. "I'm sorry."

He looked at her red rimmed eyes. "It's fine, I understand. I'm just glad you're alive, Kee."

"Mm," she hummed. "Barely."

"You scared me," he admitted, his amber eyes hardening as he clenched his hands into fists on his knees. He wasn't sure what would have happened if she had died. "When I found you, I thought you were dead. Wyatt was on top of you and there was so much blood. You were so pale and—"

"Shh," she set the bottle down and scooted closer to him. She put her hand on the back of his neck and pulled him down so their foreheads touched. "I'm okay now." Honestly, she wasn't sure she was, but she had to at least act like it for Conrad. He nodded against and they stayed like that for a few more seconds before she pulled away. "Where are we?"

"Lucas' club. The basement is like a one story apartment complex." He explained, watching as she took a sip of water. "They have a big common room too."

"Byte?" She questioned as her eyes swept along the studio-style room once again. "Is this Lucas' room?" She wasn't sure why she asked when she knew it was. It seemed like his style.

"It is. You have been staying here while you are recovering." Lucas answered as he stepped back into the room, dried and dressed in black jeans and a plain grey t-shirt.

Kee's eyes swept over him. She had never seen him dressed in anything casual before. "Thank you." She ended up saying formally, feeling a lingering awkwardness from the shower incident. "I hope I didn't kick you out of your own room."

He walked over to the couch and sat down on the arm. "You are welcome." He replied nonchalantly, running his hand through his damp hair. "And I stayed with Giovanni, so do not trouble yourself."

The werewolf glanced between them, feeling the sudden tension. "He stayed by you when he was awake," he informed her, gaining both of their attention. "He's also the reason you're alive." He added as he looked at Lucas expectantly.

She flushed as she had brief memories of emerald green eyes staring down at her in concern while his hand held hers. She took another sip of water to distract her thoughts. "He saved me with the gun," she began. "I blew out Wyatt's brains before he could finish me off."

Conrad shook his head. "No, Kee, not just that way. You don't understand," he hesitated and licked his lips. "You weren't going to make it. The doctor said your body wasn't healing itself fast enough because you lost too much blood."

The color drained from her face when she was told just how close to death she had come. "How did I survive then?" She asked quietly.

"I gave you my blood," Lucas responded as he looked at her. "Blood from a lord vampire can accelerate a body's natural healing process."

"And the side effect?" Conrad pushed.

The vampire restrained himself from punching the wolf. "It is not quite a side effect, Mr Novak. It only occurs when blood has been swapped on both sides."

Kee looked from Conrad to Lucas with a furrowed brow. "What are you guys talking about?"

Lucas sighed softly. "Since I drank your blood a while ago, when I gave you mine it created a bond between us. I relived your attack as you did and could feel the fear in you. That is how I knew you were awake. That is also why I am conscious instead of sleeping." At her questioning look, he gestured to the antique clock on the wall. "It is three in the afternoon, not in the morning."

"So you wake up when I do? What else does this bond entail?" She inquired quietly, looking warily at him.

"No, I woke up because of the memory. You had so much emotion, so much fear and anxiety, that it pulled me from my sleep," he explained calmly. "Feeling each other's strong emotions will be one side effect. It will also make us drawn to each other, like two magnets, if you will. If we need to find each other, we will be able to so."

"Explain the drawn to each other." She demanded.

He should have known she would have picked up on that. "Physically and mentally."

Kee felt anger simmer in her chest. "So just now, in the shower—"

"I am going to stop you there," he said as he held up his hand. "I would have comforted you without the bond."

She would have asked about her need for him to stay, but felt Conrad staring at her in worry. She cleared her throat and took another gulp of her water. She gave Lucas a look that clearly told him she wasn't done with this topic before looking at her wolf. "How long have we been here?"

He pushed the plate closer to her. "You've been unconscious for almost three full days, Kee. That's why you need to eat."

"Three days?" She echoed in shock. "Did anyone try to get a hold of me?"

"Ah, *some* people," he nervously met her eyes. "Lucas thinks it's a good idea if everyone thinks you're dead."

*He means Cain.* They both came to the same conclusion she had. She tightened her hand on the bottle, the plastic crinkling in protest. *How could he? How could he?!* She scowled even as her chest tightened. *If he had been on top of me instead of Wyatt, would I have been able to pull the trigger?* Her lips curled up into a snarl when she realized she might not have. *No! Cain deserves to be punished for doing this to me! Brandon and Noah, too!*

"Cool your anger." Lucas told her lightly as he stood from the couch.

"Don't tell me what to do," she scowled at him and looked at Conrad when he picked up the bowl of raspberries and tried to hand it to her. "I don't want any!"

"Eat," Conrad pressed as he picked up a raspberry and held it in front of her lips. When she cringed away, he glared at her. "Damn it, Kee, your body needs the nutrition! It's been fighting for days on empty. Help it!"

*We've only been together for a little while, but when has he ever raised his voice to me?* Her fury subsided when she saw the worry behind the irritation in his eyes.

She sighed in defeat and took the raspberry from him with her fingers. She ate it without tasting it and continued with the rest. When she finished the last one, she set the bowl down on the coffee table and then pursed her lips at him stubbornly. "Happy?"

"I'd be happier if you ate the sandwich." He glowered.

She shrugged and winced as it pulled at her top stitches. "I'm not hungry, Con; I'm still trying to get a grasp on everything."

"I guess I'll take what I can get," he grumbled unhappily. He then turned fully to look at her, his expression grave. He reached out and gently grabbed one of her hands in his, his frown deepening when she stiffened. "Who did this to you?"

She tensed and looked away from his prying stare. "Wyatt, Brandon and Noah."

Conrad's mouth fell open in shock. "Noah? Cain's best friend?"

"The one and only," she muttered. She glanced at him when he squeezed her hand. His face was angry, but his eyes were horrified. She softened and put her hand on top of the one holding hers. "He threatened to kill you after me," she began. "I thought he would be the one to kill me, honestly. But, when he said that, I got a second wind. I was enraged at the thought of him coming after you. I got fuel to fight back and broke his nose again. So, you too saved me, Con. I couldn't let him go after you."

"He might still come after me." He let out a soft, humorless laugh, but the emotion in his eyes shifted to something else. Once again, she had fought for him, even when he wasn't there. She was truly worthy of being his alpha.

"No, he won't." She stated vehemently.

"How do you know?"

She took a deep breath to steady herself. "Conrad, listen to me very closely, okay?" When he leaned in closer, his brow furrowed in confusion, she continued. "I don't think you should follow me anymore."

His chest tightened in rejection, his eyes widening. "What? Why? How could you say that?"

"*Listen*," she was pleased when he immediately complied and looked at her like a lost puppy. "I'm going to get revenge. I'm going to hunt down Brandon and Noah and kill them. Then, I'm going to kill Cain. And if any wolf gets in my way, I'll kill them too. Do you understand? I'm going to assassinate members of your wolf pack."

He stared at her, eyes never leaving hers. He saw the anger and determination there, the seriousness of her words. "They're not my pack." He finally told her, his teeth clenched. "How many times do I have to tell you that? That you are my alpha? You're going to get revenge? Good. I'll help you."

She shook her head. "I can't ask you to do that."

"You're not asking me to do shit," he growled as he leapt to his feet. "I want revenge for you. I want you to kill the people that did this to you! I can help you! I can go back in my wolf form and get information you need. We're a team, Kee, you're not getting rid of me."

She just stared at him, the sincerity in his voice calming the surge of rage that swelled in her. She finally rose to her feet and wrapped her arms around him. "You're too good to me, Conrad."

He hugged her to him with a relieved sigh. "We'll do this together."

"The three of us will," Lucas added as he walked over to them. "And, we will start with training."

Kee pulled away from Conrad and looked at the vampire. "What kind of training?"

"Shifting training." He smirked at her, green eyes blazing mischievously. "You are going to start shifting into people."

# *Seventeen*

*Kee's breath left her as she was slammed down onto the coffee table, shards of glass flying around her.* No, not again! *She cried as she realized she was back in her living room, her body tense from pain. Her throat burned, her neck stiff from the earlier abuse. She heard growling above her and suddenly Wyatt was there, snarling down at her.*

*His paw swung down, claws sinking into the flesh below her left collar bone. She screamed as he dragged his claws through her skin down towards the opposite hip. His wolf face was sneering down at her as he spoke, but she couldn't make out his words. Instead, she felt him stab his claws into her side and scrape against her ribs. She remembered fading in and out of consciousness at the time, but now she was painfully aware of what was going on.*

*"No, stop!" She pleaded.*

*"You should have just joined us, Kee." Cain's voice came. She jerked her head to the side and saw him standing by her head, arms crossed with a blank expression.*

*"Cain, please! Help!" She cried. "Help me!"*

*He shook his head. "You gave me up, remember? Didn't want to fuck my alpha, didn't want to join my pack. Now look at you."*

*A sob tore its way from her throat. "I'm sorry! I love you. Save me and I'll do whatever you want me to!"*

*He scoffed. "Pathetic."*

*Cain's image shifted until a painfully familiar face was above her. She hadn't seen him since she was twelve and that was thirteen years ago. His dark blonde hair was cut short to his head, his blue eyes staring down at her with rage and resentment.*

*"You're pathetic, Kee!" Liam drew back his hand and struck her.*

*"I'm sorry, daddy!" She sobbed as she had all those years ago.*

*"This is your fault!" He growled, smacking her once again.*

*Pain coursed through her face. "Please, no! I can't control it! I'm trying, I'm trying! I don't know how!"*

*"Learn!" He snarled.*

*The scene shifted again, her great-grandmother frowning disapprovingly as she struggled to shift. "You must learn, Kee."*

*"I don't get it, Nana. How do I shift into a wolf? I stare and study the image, but I can't change into it." She whined tiredly, sitting down on the floor cross-legged.*

*"You have to learn. People can't know what you are. If they did, I mean, look what happened. Your father, that pathetic alpha Christian, and even my own daughter," she scoffed, taking a long drag of her cigarette. "You know, she blames me for your mother's death and yet she refused to take in her own granddaughter."*

*Kee went rigid at the reminder of how grandma had looked at her the day grandpa brought her home from the boundary line. "No, it's my fault mommy died."*

*Nana was quiet for a moment. She then tapped the ash loose from her cigarette and gestured at her great-granddaughter. "Then learn, Keira."*

"Keira."

She startled awake when someone touched her, her body twitching almost painfully. She blinked when she saw Lucas squatting next to the edge of bed, staring at her intently. She closed her eyes, took a deep breath and reopened them after releasing it. Her eyebrows knitted together when he wasn't there. She almost convinced herself she imagined him until she felt the mattress dip. She rolled over onto her back and watched him crawl onto the bed next to her where her wolf had been sleeping.

"Where's Conrad?" She murmured.

"I am not sure. It is early in the morning so he could have left for the pack already." He explained tiredly.

"Oh." She forgot they had agreed that Conrad would start going back to the wolf pack to get information for her. She wanted to know if the pack had talked about her and Wyatt's disappearance. She was curious if anyone, mainly Cain and the left over wolves that attacked her, had spoken about it.

She blinked when she finally processed what he said about early in the morning. Guilt hit her in the stomach. "You're awake again because of me." She stated softly.

"It is fine." He replied as he laid down on his side of the bed.

"It's not okay that I forced you awake again, Lucas. I woke Conrad up last night, too." She sighed as she remembered how he had shaken her awake, trying to get her to stop screaming.

"You have gone through something traumatic and I will experience it with you until we get used to this new bond, Miss Quinn." He felt irritation surge through the bond and turned on his side to face her. "Why are you mad?" His voice was drained, tone almost exasperated.

"I don't want you to call me that. It's too formal." She grumbled and rubbed her eyes. "I don't need formality in my life anymore. I don't want that distance between us. I'm sorry I asked for you to stay and comfort me in the shower yesterday. I was weak and it won't happen again, okay?"

Lucas exhaled a breath he didn't need. Breathing was a habit he had difficulty shaking. "I chose to comfort you, but I did not stay because I did not want you to get confused with the bond."

"What do you mean by confused? Which reminds me, we never finished our conversation about the bond." She rolled onto her side so they were facing each other. She frowned when she saw how pale he was. He was naturally pale as a vampire, but he looked almost sickly as he looked at her with dark circles under his eyes. "Should we talk about this later? You don't look good."

He closed his eyes when she reached out and traced one of the circles with her thumb. "It's because this is the second time I have been awake while the sun is up. Even though we are underground, my body knows that the sun is up and that I should be slumbering."

"Are you in pain?" She questioned.

"Not particularly. My body just wants to shut down." He opened his eyes and saw her concerned frown. He gave her a small, humorous smirk. "Do not worry. It's not as if it will kill me; I'm already dead."

She gave him a deadpan expression. "You're so funny," she rolled her eyes when he let out a grunt of a laugh. "We can talk about the bond later."

Lucas closed his eyes again. "We can discuss it now. As I said, we will feel each other's strong emotions and be able to find each other should we need to."

"How will we be drawn together?" She pressed as she recalled their conversation yesterday.

"A need to be around each other, to have physical contact. Touching each other would be an accurate example. The bond will always seek to strengthen itself and that will only happen when it is fed more blood." He lifted his hand and gently cupped the side of her bruised neck. "So it will constantly yearn to bring us together. However, the stronger the bond, the more side effects."

"Like?" Kee pressed.

"Shared durability and a longer life, if you were human. Immunity to other vampires' compulsion is another benefit and you would gain some of my strength." He told her, his thumb absentmindedly stroking the soft skin of her neck.

"If I were human." She clarified.

He gave a single shrug. "Vampires often bond with wereanimals as well and they also have some of those effects. They are called our bonded animal. For example, if you were a wolf, you would be my bonded wolf. Though I am not sure how it will be with you."

"Because I'm a shapeshifter."

"Correct." He wasn't sure to what degree she would receive the benefits from their bond. Everything was different with her.

She sighed and put her hand on his. "What are the downsides?"

He frowned. "If I compared you to a wereanimal, I would say that your downside would be that I am technically your alpha."

Her grey eyes widened a little. "What does that mean?"

"I would not be able to compel you, but you would still feel the desire to fulfill my orders." He explained calmly.

She glowered. "I refuse to have an alpha. Alphas tear packs and families apart, Lucas. I've experienced it enough times to know I'm not wrong. I won't have one." First her father's pack, then Cain's.

"This is if we feed the bond with blood, Keira," he told her firmly when he heard her heated reply. "I will not feed from you again."

She calmed down at his explanation. She slid her hand down to his wrist and rubbed circles on the inside of it with her thumb. "Would you have comforted me without the bond?" She breathed tiredly as her eyes closed.

"I told you I would have. I relived what happened to you because of the bond," his eyes shut as well, his lids heavy with exhaustion. "But even if I hadn't, seeing you in a ball, crying on my shower floor made me uncomfortable. I did not like seeing you like that."

His voice was soft, a little louder than a whisper, but it warmed her chest. She shuffled closer to him so that their knees bumped. His hand slid up to her cheek and she parted her eyelids to see he had done the same. He leaned his head closer to hers and pressed a cool kiss to her forehead.

"I'm sorry I upset you." She mumbled as his eyes closed again. He hummed in response, too tired to form words. His hand slid down so it rested comfortably on her waist before his body visibly relaxed as the need to be asleep finally claimed him. "Good night." She murmured before letting sleep claim her again.

# *Eighteen*

Kee was exhausted, yet restless. Her bunched muscles longed to relax, to ease out of their prolonged tense state. Her mind buzzed with an underlying sense of anxiousness, panic threatening to take over at any moment. With her mind and body at odds, staying in bed for a third day was out of the question. Every time she closed her eyes she was back in her apartment, her limbs twitching in anticipation for the agony to come. She couldn't lay there any longer despite Conrad, Lucas, *and* Gio nagging her to do so.

On stiff legs, she slowly made her way up the stairs that were tucked in the back left corner of the club. Byte was closed for another hour and she was taking advantage of the emptiness to explore. The club's building, like many of the ones in downtown LA, had multiple stories and she was curious as to how many were connected to the club.

She hobbled down the hall of the second story, glancing at the empty VIP rooms and over the guardrail to take in the empty club. Some of the VIP rooms were completely private, but most were missing a fourth wall so that the patrons could enjoy the club beneath them without actually being in the crowd. Passing Lucas' office, she found a second set of stairs behind a door that had been painted the same matte black as the walls.

Ignoring the discomfort and protests of her body, she finished climbing the second set of stairs and stopped to survey her surroundings. There was a wide hallway with a single door on either side plus another one at the end. She approached the one on the right and cautiously twisted the handle and pushed it open. She poked her head in and was surprised to see a long table of polished oak in the middle of the room, plush leather chairs lined neatly around it. The walls were painted a rich brown with white crown molding. Two gold chandeliers with crystal embellishments dangled over the table from the vaulted ceilings, matching the sheer gold curtains that parted over the thoroughly painted windows.

*I wonder why Lucas has a boardroom.*

She shut the door and turned towards the other. She turned the handle and opened it just enough to peek in. She blinked at the mirrors that lined the back wall of the room and pushed the door open so she could step inside. Curious, she started to walk towards them, but halted when someone grabbed the back of her neck. She was quickly spun and pushed up against the wall next to the door. She yelped in pain as her torso slammed against the wall, her wounds protesting the rough treatment.

"Who are you?" Snapped a rough voice close to her ear.

She winced when he pushed her harder against the wall. "Kee!" She blurted out.

"I know no one of that name. How did you get in here?" He demanded, hand tightening around the back of her neck.

"I've been here for six days," she rasped. "I've been staying in Lucas' room."

His other hand pulled the neck of her shirt to one side and then the other. "And yet I see no bite mark."

"That's because he didn't drink from me." She retorted. When his hand flexed on her neck, she quickly added, "I'm bonded to him!"

"His bonded animal?" He asked, loosening his hold. "Turn around. Slowly."

She did as she was told and then leaned back against the wall as they studied each other. He was closer to her height, but had beautiful, smooth dark skin and light brown eyes. He kept his head bald, but a short, clean trimmed beard adorned his face. After a long, drawn out, awkward moment of him persistently staring, she clenched her jaw. "Satisfied?" She snipped as his eyes fell to her chest.

His face was impassive as he pointed to the stain of fresh blood on her shirt. "You're bleeding."

Kee pulled Lucas' shirt away from her chest, looked down the neck hole, and cursed. Two stitches under her collar bone had ripped free, making a small gape along the slash. She pressed the shirt to the wound to stop the bleeding and looked back up at the vampire. She quickly angled her body away when his eyes focused intensely on the hidden wound. "What is this room?"

"The training room," he answered as he took several steps back from her, distancing himself from the tempting scent of her blood. If she really was Lucas' bonded wereanimal, he wouldn't risk a taste. He feared his friend's wrath and preferred his skin in a solid state with his head where it was. "How long have you been bonded to Lord Lucas?"

"Not long." She glanced over at the other door in the room towards the back. "What's in there?"

"A small gun range." He told her as he walked over to the punching bag hanging from the ceiling.

Kee walked around the room and realized the windows had been blacked as well. She glanced back over at the vampire and watched as he began throwing punches at the bag. "What's the other room at the end of the hall? I know across the way is a boardroom."

"The door at the end of the hall is not a room, it's another staircase to the next floor. Up there are a few rooms for visiting officials." He explained as he jabbed at the bag.

*Lucas had spare rooms this whole time? Then why have I been staying in his room?* "Why does Lucas have a training room up here? And a boardroom?" She pressed.

"The boardroom is for when the other coven lords come to town for meetings, just like the bedrooms," he said between punches. "And the training room is for the purpose of its name. Training."

She rolled her eyes at the dry sarcasm in his tone. "Obviously," she drawled out. "Why would vampires need training? Don't you all already have inhuman strength?"

"*Obviously,*" he mocked. "But what good is it if you don't know how to fight? What if you're up against another vampire who is skilled?"

"Point taken." She looked at the punching bag then back to him again. "Do you train them?" She asked, an idea forming in her mind. Sure, Lucas had said he would help her with the shifting, but she needed strength, too.

"Some."

"Can you train me?"

He lowered his hand and looked at her quizzically. "Train *you?*"

She shrugged, hoping she wasn't overstepping. "I didn't realize until just recently how weak I am."

His eyes dropped down to the stain on her shirt again. "I take it that is why you're here." When she didn't respond, he stepped around the punching bag and approached her. "Are you sure you want me to train you? I'm not nice. I won't go easy on you just because you're a girl. Or because you're Lucas' bonded wolf."

The shapeshifter met his eyes defiantly. "I didn't ask you to."

He smirked and stuck his hand out towards her. "Dante."

She grabbed his hand. "Kee."

His smirk disappeared as he gripped her hand, pulled her forward, and spun her until he had her wrapped in a choke hold. "First lesson, never let your guard down."

She gasped and tapped his arm. "I get it!" She wheezed out. The door suddenly flung open and Dante's hold on her instantly vanished. She steadied herself on her feet as she saw Lucas storm in, his eyes flicking from her to Dante, before setting into a hard glare. "Lucas?"

Dante swallowed thickly and flinched when his lord made a straight line towards him. "Lucas—"

Lucas grabbed his subordinate by the front of his shirt and jerked him forward. He kicked Dante's feet out from under him, making him fall to his knees, Lucas's hold on his shirt the only thing keeping him up. Lucas lowered his face to Dante's, fangs bared. "You will not touch her again."

Kee's eyes widened and she quickly grabbed one of Lucas' arms in an effort to get him to let go of Dante. "Lucas, stop! It's not what you think! I asked him to train me!"

He glanced at her from the corner of his eye before glaring down at Dante. "Is this true?"

"Yes, my lord." He replied quietly.

He scowled, but released his shirt. He turned to Keira with poorly concealed irritation. "If you insist on training, you need to wait until your stitches are removed." He ran a finger over the growing stain on her shirt. "No more of this," he gestured to the blood on his fingertip. "You are not healed enough to do strenuous activity and my people do not need the temptation. Do you understand?"

"Sorry." She murmured like a scolded child. "It was an accident."

He turned to the other vampire. "Reserved strength, Dante. Understood?"

"Yes, sir." He replied dutifully, keeping his eyes cast down.

Satisfied, Lucas put his hand on the small of the shifter's back and led her towards the exit. After closing the door behind them, he guided her to the stairwell and stopped them on the landing halfway down the stairs. "You need to be cautious with your blood, Keira."

She turned and looked up at him with a cocked eyebrow. "Why? Do your vampires not have any self-control?"

"Of course they do. If they did not, I am sure your lifeless body would currently be lying in a heap on the training room floor." He stared down at her seriously. "Your blood is unique. The smell, the taste," a small shudder ran through his body as his fangs pulsed hungrily. "It's something I have never experienced before. It is like a succubus trying to seduce its next lover."

She remembered Lucas feasting on her wrist in her bedroom and how Wyatt had been distracted as he lapped at her wounds. She grabbed the stained part of her shirt in a tight fist and cautiously stepped down two more steps. "That explains a few things." She muttered, looking away from him.

He closed the distance between them and tilted her chin up so she met his eyes. "I will not drink from you again, Keira. I gave you my word and I will keep it." His cool hand moved to cup her cheek, noting approvingly how much the swelling had gone down.

Her eyes fluttered shut when his thumb brushed over her cheekbone. The tender caress made her eager for more. Cuddling with Conrad's furry form at night helped soothe her, but the soft touches from Lucas momentarily erased the mental scars left by her attackers.

"I trust you." Kee whispered.

Lucas nodded once, but kept sweeping his thumb over her cheek. "I also trust my people to not hurt what is mine, but do not give them a reason to break my trust."

Kee's eyes snapped open and she knocked his hand away angrily, albeit a small part of her protested the lost contact. "I don't belong to anyone." She bit out defiantly as she glared at him.

If he was angry about her refusal, he didn't show it. "We are bonded to one another," he reminded her. "That makes you mine as much as it makes me yours. It is better for my vampires to be informed of this so that they know to stay away from you." He watched as some of the heat cooled from her scowl.

"Well when you put it like that." She muttered.

He gave her a knowing smirk. "Now, I understand you wish to get stronger to carry out your revenge and I will assist you where I can, but you need to give your body time to heal. Not just physically," he tapped his temple. "But mentally as well. I live your night terrors with you, Keira. I know they still plague you."

*Damn, I was hoping he wasn't on the receiving end of those still.* Grey met green as she met his serious gaze. "I will get better."

"I know you will," he agreed as he held his hand out to her. When she slid her hand into his, he led her the rest of the way down the stairs. "And you will be stronger than ever."

*At least one of us thinks so.* She whispered in her head.

# *Nineteen*

Kee sat at the bar, brown eyes staring down at a pint of orange wheat beer. It was nearly three in morning and she, once again, couldn't sleep. Lucky for her, vampire clubs and bars got a pass from the city to stay open later as long as they remained strict with their serving policy. The bar, by California's law, had to stop serving alcohol by 1:30am. Technically, the drinks had to be consumed and out of sight by 2:00am, but she wasn't giving up her beer. The bartender had tried to take her drink away three times, but gave up when Kee practically bit her head off.

She combed her fingers through her short, black hair, pushing the foreign bangs from her forehead. She jumped in her seat and tensed when she heard a loud crash behind her. She slowly turned her head and, from the corner of her eye, saw a drunk human laughing as he picked himself off the floor. She relaxed marginally but kept her focus on the vampire who helped them up. She narrowed her eyes, knowing the woman was anticipating the blood rush. From what Lucas had told her, vamps got a buzz when they drank from an intoxicated person. The more drunk the person, the bigger the effect.

*How long has this vamp been watching her prey? Was she the reason he was so drunk?*

She turned back to her lukewarm beer and took a sip, listening to the melody of the crowded bar. There were current hits playing from the DJ, people talking and laughing over the loud music, glasses chinking, and moans of people getting bit. She could smell the spilled alcohol on the ground, the lingering smoke from a cigarette, and the scent of arousal growing the later the time did.

*How many people are banging in the VIP rooms upstairs? How many are blood whores?* She wondered, her eyes glancing up at the railing that lined the second story ledge.

She then thought about the people who frequented the club. *Did any change their mind about being bit once they were here?* Lucas told her that it wasn't mandatory for patrons of the bar to feed vampires. He said that the ones who did feed did so willingly, but she was curious about when they had second thoughts.

*What about the ones who get drunk and change their mind? Even the ones who signed the waiver?* She was assured that there was security lurking around in the club to intervene if such an occasion occurred, but she had doubts.

She looked up at the bartender when she cleared her throat before stepping away. That was all she needed to know who was behind her. Her mind warmed a second before he braced one of his hands on the bar top and bent close to her. That was the only way she could explain the odd feeling of Lucas being near her. It was similar to noticing something in her peripheral vision, but she saw it in her mind and not with her eyes.

"You should not be up so late, Miss Quinn." He purred in her ear.

Kee resisted the urge to shudder and calmly lifted the glass to her lips to take a drink. "Did you use the bond to find me?"

He smirked and swiveled her barstool around so she faced him. "I did not have to. You may have been able to change your hair, but I know you too well."

*And here I thought I did a good job.*

She huffed and looked away as she took another sip. "I changed my eye color, too. I made myself look different enough that no one would notice me." She murmured so only he would hear.

"I am fairly certain that Mr Donovan would have noticed you if he looked hard enough." He said as he held out his hand to her.

Her eyes narrowed at the mention of Cain. "I dare him to come looking for me," she grumbled as she downed the rest of her beer and set the empty glass on the bar top. She put her hand in his and let him pull her to her feet. She pulled out money from her back pocket to pay for her tab, but the bartender shook her head and nodded at the owner of the bar. She turned and puffed her cheeks out at Lucas. "I can pay for my drinks."

"There is no need, it is my bar and you are my guest," he replied as he led her to the back kitchen and down the stairs to the living area of his coven. "Giovanni has returned."

She brightened at the mention of the doctor as they walked into Lucas' bedroom. "I'm excited to get these fuckers out of my skin. They itch like crazy."

"And you will be able to try full body shifts," he pointed out as he closed the door behind them. He watched as her hair grew back down to her waist, fading to her natural dark blonde as her eyes switched back to grey. "You will also be able to work with Dante more. He has been holding back with you."

She had only been training with Dante for five days, but she liked him. He had zero tolerance for weakness and was a hard ass, but still had a sarcastic, humorous side to him.

"Yeah, because he's scared of popping anymore of my stitches." She replied with a small smirk when she remembered how Lucas had nearly bit Dante's head off the second time a couple stitches ripped free.

He gave an impossibly elegant shrug. "I warned him to be careful."

She rolled her eyes and smiled at Giovanni when he came into the room with his medical bag in his hand. "Welcome back, Gio." She greeted and then sat down on her side of the bed.

Kee looked over at the other occupied side of the bed and couldn't stop the warm smile that curved her lips. She reached out and stroked Conrad's fur, giving him another smile when one of his eyes cracked open. It stared at her for a second before sliding shut when sleep claimed him once again.

Conrad had been training with her and Dante, but also hung out around the pack to gather information. He had said the only ones at the house had been Natalie and Warren, but that there was a pack meeting in three nights. Between training, spying on the pack, and her nightmares, she knew he was exhausted. She had consistently woken him up with whimpers and groans, but he just curled his furry body close to her in comfort.

"Thank you, Kee," Giovanni replied as he approached the bed, medical scissors in hand. "If you will remove your shirt and lie back against the bed."

She put her hands on the hem of her shirt and went to pull it up, but looked at Lucas. She flushed and looked away from him. "Don't look," she murmured. Honestly, she was embarrassed of the marks that marred her body. She didn't know how bad they would be until the stitches were removed, but she was nervous to find out.

Lucas narrowed his eyes at the feel of her mortification, but turned his head away from her. "There."

She eyed him for a moment before tugging off her shirt. Unclasping her bra and covering her breasts with her hands, she reclined back against the bed. She stared up at the ceiling, avoiding Gio's gaze as he stood over her and began snipping. When Gio tapped her hands, she moved them so he could cut the threads that lined part of her breasts.

She knew there were a ton of stitches, a little over a hundred and forty, but it felt like he had been removing them for hours.

"It's curious that you didn't heal as quickly as other werewolves," Gio commented offhandedly as he cut the last few stitches. He set his scissors down before grabbing alcohol and gauze pads. He peered at her expectantly as he wet the gauze and slid it over the pink marks on her torso. "Normal werewolves would not have had to have stitches for more than three days, yet you had yours for eleven."

"Giovanni." Lucas warned, but kept his gaze away from them.

"Nor would they have had any scarring." Gio added. He watched her jerk her head towards him and sit up before raking her eyes down her body. The pink from her scars would fade, as most scars did, but he had no doubt that pale white lines would mar her body for the rest of her life. From the way her eyes watered, he knew she had come to the same understanding. "They will not be too bad."

"The fact that they're there is enough." She growled and lightly ran her fingertips down the scars. She clenched her jaw angrily and tugged her clothes back on with jerky movements.

"Think of them as battle scars." Lucas said as he finally turned to look at her once she was clothed.

"Maybe after I kill them," she glanced at Gio when he continued to stare at her expectantly. "I don't know what you want me to say, Gio, but my parents were werewolves."

His eyes hardened when he didn't sense any deceit from her. Still, he knew something was off. He turned fierce eyes on his maker. "I am not only your second-in-command, Lucas, but also your blood son. I deserve to know the truth!"

"Giovanni, you overstep yourself. Stop." Lucas demanded as his eyes narrowed.

"You have willingly bonded yourself with this female when you have done so only once before." Gio continued as he gestured to the silent girl on the bed. "Why is she special?"

"Do not make me repeat myself." Lucas seethed as he took a step towards his second.

He was not ready to back down. "You said there would be no secrets between us, but omitting the truth is no different! *What* is she?"

Kee cowered back on the bed as Lucas' power filled the room to a suffocating level. She watched as red bled into the green of his irises, his pupils minute as he locked eyes with Giovanni. She covered her mouth as she watched Gio's knees instantly hit the ground, his eyes wide and clouded over. "Lucas..." She bit her lip when he merely held up a hand to silence her.

Lucas' eyes never left Giovanni's. "I am your maker, Giovanni. I am your lord and above you in power. When I give you a command, you listen. Do you understand?"

"Y-yes," he stammered almost painfully, unable to break away from his lord's gaze.

"I do not like to compel you like a simple human, Giovanni, but you give me no choice when you disobey me." He blinked, releasing him from the spell.

Gio crawled forward and held up a wrist. Lucas gently grabbed his wrist and bent to press a soft kiss to it, accepting his submission. Gio rose to his feet, keeping his gaze on the ground. "I apologize, Lord Lucas."

Lucas always felt some sliver of remorse when Giovanni and Dante addressed him as lord. When they were in private, he appreciated that they dropped the honorifics since they were his most trusted people.

He put his hand on his shoulder, silently apologizing. "If you want honesty, Giovanni, I will tell you that it is not my secret to tell."

Kee frowned when Gio turned to look at her. "Maybe in time, Gio, but I'm not really ready to trust anyone right now."

He nodded once in acceptance and then glanced at the clock on the wall. "If it is acceptable, I will make sure the club is clearing out. It is closing time and you know we get stragglers."

Lucas waved his hand at the door. "Please, do." He waited until he left before looking at Keira and the awakened Conrad. "My apologies for waking you, Mr Novak."

"Is everything okay?" He mumbled tiredly after shifting into his human form.

"Quite," he answered as his eyes drifted back to his bonded female. "Since he is awake, we should discuss what is going to happen in three days."

"Kee's going to shift into my wolf form and join the pack meeting," he said as he rubbed the sleep from his eyes. "Most of the pack will be there. I think only Alyssa, Mason, and a handful of others are excused for work."

Lucas glanced at Keira. "That means Cain will be there."

She stiffened and looked away from his knowing look. "And?"

"I do not think you are ready to see him," he explained bluntly. "Your emotions are still too raw right now."

She clenched her hands into fists. "I'm allowed to be angry."

"You need to control your anger better, or it will be your downfall."

"I *am* controlling it!"

"Yes, such control, I see."

"Fuck you!" His eyes narrowed angrily at her outburst and her heart fluttered. *Fuck, that was a mistake.*

Lucas' lip lifted in a snarl, a white fang showing. He was on her before she could defend herself, pinning her to the bed by her shoulders. Conrad moved towards him, but Lucas met his gaze and held it. "Stay back, Conrad." He commanded, pulling on his compulsion.

Kee watched as her wolf simply stared at the vampire with vacant eyes, the tension leaving his body. He sat there like a life-sized doll, amber orbs blank and unseeing. The apology died on her tongue as a new wave of rage crashed through her. "Let him go! Release him from your spell, Lucas!" She shouted as she struggled against his hold.

"I will once we have a little talk, Miss Quinn," he promised as he glared down at her. "You need to calm down and get your emotions in check. Before your attack, you never lashed out like this. And when you did, you would immediately apologize."

*I'm not the same person.*

She matched his glare. "What, you going to compel me to say sorry? Trap me like Conrad? He's my wolf, Lucas. His wellbeing is in my hands, so let him go!"

"If I could compel you, I would have already," he snapped. "You are immune to me now because of our bond and so I must use measures like this. Your wolf is fine, I will not harm him, but you need to listen to me." He relaxed his hold on her. "You can trust me, Keira."

Kee blinked up at him, surprised by the vehemence of his statement. "Fine," her eyes softened marginally and she took a deep breath. "And I'm sorry for snapping at you."

He nodded in acceptance and released his hold on her shoulders. He snapped his fingers and looked at the wolf. "I apologize for using force, Mr Novak, but I had to get through to our shapeshifter."

Conrad blinked back to reality as soon as the fog in his mind cleared. He growled at Lucas, but then quickly shifted his attention to his alpha. "Are you okay?"

"He didn't hurt me, Con," she replied with a forced smile. "But, he made a point."

"Which was?" He asked.

"I'm being too emotional. I won't be able to face Cain like this. I'll either attack him the moment I see him, or burst into tears. I can't do either, especially if I'm in your form." She explained with a heavy, defeated sigh. She rubbed her temples and then gingerly touched the permanent bald spot on her eyebrow. She had a small scar that went right through the arch of her brow.

"What do you want to do then?" Conrad asked seriously. "I should still go. Warren told me it was important, but wouldn't explain what it was about."

"No, you have to go. If anything, I want to know what it's about. My bet is that he's going to discuss the disappearance of me and Wyatt." She pursed her lips together. "You said Mason was going to be at work?"

Conrad nodded. "Something about working late on a project."

"What are you thinking, Keira?" Lucas asked, practically seeing the wheels in her mind turn.

She couldn't help but smile at him. She loved when he used her real name. "Brandon is mated to Mason." She explained.

Lucas saw her smile, a real one for once, but why did he feel the surge of happiness from her as well? "Brandon is one of your attackers, if I remember correctly."

"Yeah. So, what if I ambush him at home? He'll be my first target." She started, a plan already forming in her mind. "I can pose as Mason, coming home early as a surprise, and then kill him."

"What if Mason comes home?" Conrad questioned.

"If he's working late, then I should have a small window to work with. Cain never came home too late after a pack meeting," She tried to ignore the way heart clenched. *Stop it, Kee, he's dead to you.* "Warren always makes them early in the evening."

"You are going to try to do a full body shift in three days? And hold it until the job is done? You have not practiced it yet." Lucas pointed out with a frown.

She grinned. "We better start now then, huh?"

# *Twenty*

Conrad glanced at the rows of werewolves sitting in Warren's backyard. They made a wide half-circle on the grass, leaving a standing space for their alpha. He wanted to stay near the back, away from certain werewolves. Noah especially. His eyes fell on Katie. She sat at the back of the pack, her aqua eyes red and puffy from crying. He padded over her on all fours and sat down next to her.

She jerked her head up as if she had been pulled from a daze and looked down at him. "Conrad," she breathed, the sadness in her voice almost palpable. "Where have you been?"

*Poor Katie, she has no idea.* He thought to himself as he tilted his head. He felt bad for her. She had never been mean to him and had always given him apologetic smiles when Wyatt harassed him. He gently nudged her shoulder with his snout before rubbing his cheek on it.

Her eyes welled with tears and she wrapped her arms around his furry neck "I miss him so much, Conrad." She wailed, burying her face in his fur. "I know he was rough around the edges and a little mean, but he wasn't that way with me! He always told me I was his exception! I want him back!"

His heart hurt for her, it really did, but she had no idea just what kind of demon she had fallen in love with. He rumbled in his chest, trying to soothe her as she sobbed into his fur. His hackles suddenly rose when a familiar scent flooded his snout. He looked up just in time to see Cain come and sit down close behind them.

Katie removed herself from Conrad and allowed Cain to pull her back into a hug, her back to the beta's chest. "Cain, I miss him so much." She sobbed, holding Cain's arms tightly to her.

Cain held his hurting pack mate, resting his cheek on her head as his own eyes watered. "I know how you feel, Katie. I miss Kee so much it hurts." He mumbled sadly before closing his eyes tightly.

Conrad watched the two, his heart hammering in his chest. There was nothing romantic about the embrace, it was simply two devastated people clinging to each other for comfort. He frowned inwardly. How could such raw emotion be flowing between the two of them when one of them is at fault? He glanced away from them when Cain opened his eyes and looked at him. He tensed when Cain's hand came and gently rested on his head between his ears, stroking his fur softly.

"You must also be hurting," he murmured. "I know you liked Kee."

Conrad closed his eyes, his ears flattening back against his head. *How can Cain be so sincere in his pain? How can he act so distraught? Was it that he regrets his actions? Yes, it had to be guilt. That's the only explanation.*

"Were...were you there when it happened?" Cain asked quietly. The one arm he kept around Katie tightened. "Did you see what happened to her?"

Conrad opened his eyes at the anguish in Cain's voice. He looked him in the eye and felt a whimper work his way up his throat. He shook his head once and closed his eyes again. How can Cain look at him like that?

"Pack!" Warren's voice suddenly boomed over them.

The trio, along with the rest of the pack, looked at their alpha as he stood in front of them. Natalie stood to his left and two steps behind him, her hands clasped in front of her. Her eyes were guarded, but a glimmer of sorrow shined in them.

Warren took a deep breath and slowly released it. "My wolves, by now I am sure that you have noticed we are missing not one, but two of our own. Wyatt, my brother and Katie's intended mate, and Kee, Cain's chosen mate, have been missing for a week and half now."

Katie sucked in a shaky, mournful breath as the pack turned towards her and Cain. She closed her eyes tightly and tried to disappear into the beta's hold. She didn't want to see their sympathetic stares. She couldn't handle it.

"We will find who did this to them, Katie," Cain spoke low to her. "I promise."

Conrad's head whipped back towards him. *How can he make that kind of promise when he's the one who did it?* Suddenly his instincts were screaming at him that something was wrong.

"Our pack mates are hurting," Warren declared solemnly. "Someone, or some people, have decided to make us their enemies. They have struck us the lowest of blows and we will not stand by idly."

Natalie felt her heart skip a painful beat as her instincts went off like a warning bell in her head once again. She stepped forward so she was next to her mate. To put on a show, she slid her arm around his waist and looked over at their wolves. They were pack. They all hurt for the loss, all shared the pain. They shared a bond unlike any other creature. When one mourned so deeply, they all did.

"We don't know if this was premeditated, or two random acts of violence," Natalie started, ignoring the flare of irritation her mate sent her. "But their bodies have not been found, so there is hope. We want everyone to stay on alert, to be cautious." She looked up at Warren and couldn't keep the coldness from her eyes when he looked down at her. "We may not know for sure what's happening, but we *will* find out."

He put his arm around her shoulders and squeezed her shoulder with a little more force than necessary. "Love your family, friends, and especially your mate, because they will be your greatest comfort in this time." He tore his eyes from her and looked at their pack. "As your wolf queen has said, be cautious and alert until we find the people who did this."

Conrad stared at the mated pair before looking back over at Katie as she started sobbing again. He watched as Cain tried to calm the hysterical woman, letting out low, rumbling growls to try and soothe her even as his own face still twisted with pain. Conrad tore his eyes from them to stare down at the grass. Either Cain was a brilliant actor, riddled with guilt, or innocent.

*How am I supposed to tell Kee?*

—

Kee was lying down in the backseat of the borrowed black Jeep Grand Cherokee. They were parked about two miles away from the Erickson's house and the wait was killing her. She saw movement outside the window and froze until she heard four taps on the glass. She reached and hit the unlock button. She watched the door open, revealing a very naked Conrad, his skin slick with sweat from running.

"Everything go okay?" She asked.

"Yeah, I waited until most of them left before hurrying here," he replied as he crawled into the backseat and tossed a small, black leather book at her. "I got the pack's address book." He said as he started tugging on the clothes he had brought.

She caught it and flipped through it. "Perfect," she cooed and then climbed into the passenger's seat, her veins already beginning to fill with icy adrenaline. She smoothed her hands down the loose shirt she wore. She had practiced shifting into Mason countless times over the last three days. With the help of Lucas and Conrad, they found clothes that fit the smaller man. "How was the meeting?"

Conrad tensed slightly. Did he tell her his suspicions about Cain? No, he would tell her later. He didn't want to distract her from what she was going to do. He swallowed thickly as he crawled into the driver seat and buckled himself in.

"You were right, it was about you guys missing." He pushed his hair from his face and then took the address book. He found Brandon and Mason's address and put it in the GPS.

She nodded once, her hands nervously rubbing together. She wanted to ask about Cain, to ask if he said anything about her. If he even asked about her. The questions were on her tongue, but she swallowed. It wouldn't matter. She had made up her mind.

"I see." She said instead.

His hands tightened on the steering wheel as he began to drive. "You alright?" He questioned quietly.

She nodded. "Nervous, I guess." A humorless laugh escaped her. "Is that wrong? That I'm nervous to shift into someone's lover to kill them?"

His amber eyes hardened. "No, it's to be expected. Just don't let yourself feel guilty, Kee. You earned this right."

"Did I?" She asked quietly. She killed Wyatt because she wanted to take him with her. Noah she wanted to kill because of everything he had said and done to her. "Brandon had barely scathed me compared to the other two."

He widened his eyes in disbelief. "He came into your apartment with the intent to kill you, Kee! They all did! Just because he didn't do as much damage as the other two doesn't mean he wouldn't have if he had the chance!"

*That's true.* If he had the chance, he probably would have hurt her too, or even killed her.

She took a deep breath and nodded, but didn't speak again until he came to a stop. She looked at the GPS and saw he had parked a few blocks away from their destination. She looked at her wolf and saw he was looking at her expectantly. "I guess it's time."

"When we drove by there was only one car in the driveway, so Mason hasn't come home yet." He put his hand on her shoulder and squeezed. "You can do this, Kee. I'll be here waiting for you."

She nodded and closed her eyes, letting her new skin knit around her. Shifting into a person was still foreign to her. It was nothing like changing into an animal. Mason was only marginally taller than her, but she felt her body expand and swell until the skin fit like a glove around her body. She opened her now light green eyes and looked at herself in the mirror, still surprised to see Mason's face looking back at her. She ran her fingers through the short blonde hair and studied her reflection. She had only met him once, but studied his social media pictures like a textbook. Admittedly, as soon as she shifted into him, she knew she had done it right. She wasn't sure how she knew, it was just a feeling. She took a deep breath and gave Conrad one last nod before getting out of the car and walking towards Brandon's house.

When she reached the front door, she frowned when she realized she didn't have a key. She reached for it anyways and almost sighed in relief when it opened. Her heart hammered hard in her chest when she pushed open the door and took a few hesitant steps inside. Palms slick with sweat, she silently walked down the entryway and made her first left into a large living room.

*Where is Brandon?*

She looked around the spacious, well decorated room, but didn't see him. She turned to the right and headed through an archway that led to the kitchen. As she started to walk towards the island, she suddenly felt someone grab her and panic surged through her. Arms wrapped around her and she almost screamed, but bit it back when lips found the side of her neck.

"Your pulse is racing, Mase," Brandon hummed against his mate's skin. He playfully nipped at the smooth flesh, his arms pulling Mason tighter against him. "Did I scare you?"

It took Kee a couple times to find her voice, her nerves flaring as her adrenaline spiked. "Y-yeah, I didn't expect you to sneak up on me."

He smirked against his skin, his hands sliding down to Mason's hips and pulling them back against his. "I wanted to show you how excited I am to see you."

Kee felt her stomach drop when she felt his erection pressing against her ass. She tore away from him and then cursed at her own stupidity when Brandon's face faltered in confusion. "I'm sorry. I just, I mean—"

Brandon sighed and closed the distance between them, cupping Mason's face in his hands. "Mase, is this because of that accident I had with Noah? It's been almost two weeks since then. I told you my ribs healed after they were reset. I can breathe again just fine."

She blinked. *Was that the excuse the two of them made up to explain the wounds I gave them? A fucking accident?*

"I just don't want you to strain yourself." She told him cautiously as she walked over to the fridge, feeling his eyes follow her. She opened the polished metal door, but her eyes kept flicking towards the knife block next to it. She grabbed a random soda from the shelf, closed the door, and casually set the can down on the counter next to the block.

Brandon furrowed his brow as he walked over to his mate, standing behind him. "What are you doing? You never drink Coke."

She grit her teeth at her second slip up. *Fuck, I don't know anything about Mason. Think, Kee. You can do this. Use his arousal to your advantage.*

She popped open the tab and turned so her back was against the counter. She took a tiny sip and then offered him the can. "I had a long day," she began with a small pout. "And maybe I just wanted to share something sweet with you." She added a little heat to her tone, trying to sound sultry.

He grinned and took the can from him so he could set it down on the counter. He stroked his mate's soft cheek and then grabbed his chin, angling his pretty face up towards him. He flicked his tongue along Mason's bottom lip, tasting the faint trace of the soda. "You're sweet enough for me."

Every fiber in her body threatened to tense, but she forced it away. She silently cursed when she felt that familiar tingle in the base of her skull. The warning that she was already pushing herself too much. That was another problem with the new shifts; she still had to build her endurance to them. She cursed the timing and tried to reinforce her hold on the skin.

*I can do this. Just hold on.*

She pressed her lips hard against his, earning her a needy growl from Brandon. She felt his hips push against hers and turned up the passion. She parted her lips against his, her tongue playfully coming out to tease his. When his growl turned possessive, his mouth now devouring hers, she parted one eye and slowly reached for the knife block. Her hand encircled the top handle and she had to tighten her grip when sweat made her hold slippery.

Brandon's ears picked up the *shink* of metal and opened his eyes. Right as he pulled back, he felt something cold stab and thrust itself into his neck. His eyes widened when his mate's normally loving eyes were cold and spiteful. "M-Mas—" Blood spewed from his mouth before he could finish, choking him as it gurgled in his throat.

Kee twisted the thick blade in his neck and violently pulled it out, making sure she completely severed his jugular to prevent his lycanthrope healing from saving him. She pushed him away from her as he fell to his knees, his face full of confusion and betrayal. His eyes shined with heartbreak and she briefly wondered which pain hurt worse. Her own heart twisted a little when she realized she had used the love for his mate against him.

*Don't pity him.*

She watched impassively as the light began to fade from his tearful eyes. She felt blood trickle from both her nostrils and released the skin. Her body immediately shrunk back to her form, her bones and muscles crying with fatigue as they adjusted back into place. Normally it would have been painful, but her adrenaline was so high she was practically numb.

She saw his eyes widen when he saw her for *her* and not as his mate. His mouth opened, but only wet, strangled sounds came from it. She squatted down next to him, the blood pooling around her shoes. "Wyatt failed to finish the job. Sucks for you, doesn't it?" She taunted. She straightened up and watched as the rest of his life faded away. His eyes remained open as his body lay motionless.

Kee carefully stepped around the large pool of blood and pulled out the small bottle in her pants pocket. Lucas had given it to her, telling her to spray it heavily in the house to hide her scent if she couldn't hold the image. She did as he said, damn near emptying the bottle as she sprayed the strong smelling liquid continuously on her way back to the front door. She slipped out of the shoes that were too big for her, sprayed them down with the rest of the bottle and left them by the front door. She quickly adjusted the color of her eyes and hair before casually strolling out of the house towards the Jeep.

She didn't realize she had been holding her breath until she nearly doubled over once she reached the car. She exhaled loudly and greedily sucked in air. After a few heavy breaths, her adrenaline ebbed and nausea started to set in. Her knees buckled and she sank to the ground.

*I murdered someone. I watched the life leave them. The blood*— Her back hunched as she dry heaved and she knew what was coming. She felt hands grab her hair and pull it away from her face right as she threw up in the gutter.

"It's okay, it's okay." Conrad said calmly, but quickly as he held her fake platinum hair with one hand, his other hand rubbing her back. "I'm sorry to rush you, but we need to go, Kee. Before Mason comes home."

She retched one more time, emptying whatever was left in her stomach. She wiped her mouth with the back of her hand and let Conrad help her to feet. She flopped into the passenger seat and shakily buckled herself in. She let her hair and eyes shift back to normal as she pressed her back to the seat. She pulled her knees up to her chest and reached a trembling hand over to her wolf.

Conrad immediately grabbed her hand and laced their fingers together, his eyes never leaving the road. "It's okay." He told her again as her hand squeezed his tightly.

# _Twenty-One_

When they arrived back at Byte, the werebear security duo let them in through the back. Kee had changed into a hoodie and leggings in the car, leaving the bloodied clothes in a pile in the back seat. She was exhausted, but she wanted to see Lucas.

She knew that he could usually be found in his office on the second level during business hours so she told Conrad she'd be back and went in search for the vampire. Not having the energy to change her appearance, she pulled up the hood of her grey sweatshirt and pushed her way through the crowd. She approached the roped off stairs and glared at the tall, bulky vampire who blocked her way.

"Wristband?" He asked roughly, arms crossed over his chest as he eyed the drying blood around her nose.

"I don't have one. I just need to speak with Lucas." She replied as she took a step towards the stairs.

He instantly stepped in front of her, fangs bared. "No wristband, no admission."

"Look, he knows who I am. He's expecting me." Which wasn't exactly the truth, but he would know she was back with their bond. "I'm his bonded wolf."

"That's what they all say," he rolled his eyes and then quickly grabbed her shoulder when she tried to push past him. "Hey!"

Her body froze and her muscles coiled as his cold hand grabbed her left shoulder. She could only stand two people touching her right now and he was not one of them. "Don't fucking touch me!" She screeched at him.

Ignoring the few patrons that turned at the commotion, she grabbed the hand on her shoulder with her right one and raised her elbow on the arm he was holding. She spun towards him, forcing him down as his wrist and elbow strained from being bent at an odd angle. With his body bent towards the ground, she quickly drew up her knee and hit him straight in the nose.

He gave a wail of pain and covered his face with his hands when she dropped him. Recovering from his pain, he leapt to his feet and started towards her, but stopped when his boss stepped in front of him. "Dante! This wench—"

"Is Lord Lucas' bonded wolf," he finished, eyes warning him from saying anything else. "She is the one I have been training." He ignored his employee when he grumbled and looked at Kee. "I'm sorry for Brent, but he's very serious about his job."

She shrugged. "Sorry about his nose."

Dante gave her a proud smile. "Very good wrist and elbow lock, by the way."

She gave him a small, tired grin. "Thanks, I have a good teacher," she gestured at the stairs. "I'm going to go see Lucas. See you later, Dante."

"Have a pleasant night." He replied with a fang-tipped smile.

She trudged up the stairs and started walking along the hallway, her hand lightly running along the metal railing. She glanced down at the dance floor below her, watching as the bodies swayed together to the tempo. She turned the corner and walked towards the first door.

She lifted her hand to knock, but the door opened before she had a chance to.

"You are back early Miss Quinn," Lucas began with a small smirk. His lips quickly pressed into a hard line when he saw the blood smeared around her nose. He stepped aside and ushered her into the room. When he closed the door, he lifted her chin so he could inspect her nose. "Are you hurt?"

"Hurt?" She echoed. When he gestured at the front of her sweatshirt, she saw drops of blood had soaked into the fabric. She lifted her hand and touched her face, finding a damp trail running from nose to lip. "It's from holding the skin." She wiped at the remaining blood with her sleeve. He watched the tempting substance smear along her skin, leaving it stained a soft red. He quickly stepped back from her and crossed his arms across his chest. "How did it go?"

Kee sighed heavily and plopped onto his couch with her face in her hands. "I killed him," she told him quietly. "And it made me sick to my stomach. Literally."

"Your first kill will always be the hardest." Lucas commented.

"Wyatt was my first kill." She pointed out as she looked up at him.

"Ah, but that was in the heat of the moment, my sweet." He explained as he uncrossed his arms. "It was self-defense, technically. Tonight was the first time you planned to kill someone and carried it out."

*My sweet?* Her eyebrows knitted together at the nickname, but it also made her heart skip a beat.

"I guess," she sighed again and moved so she was lying along the couch. "It just didn't feel the way I thought it would."

Lucas approached her prone form. "Not satisfying, you mean?"

She bent her legs to give him room to sit on the couch. "Yeah, I thought I would feel better, but I don't. Really, I kind of feel bad." She admitted. "I could feel his love for Mason, even without him sticking his tongue down my throat. The betrayal in his eyes was heartbreaking."

He blinked at her. "Wait a moment, you kissed him?"

She shrugged. "I didn't know what to do. First he shoved his dick in my back and I damn near ran away from him. It raised a red flag so I kissed him. That's how I got my opening." She shuddered as she remembered stabbing the sharp knife into his neck. How easy the sharp knife sunk into his skin. Her gut clenched uncomfortably.

Lucas kneeled in front of her bent up legs and put his hands on her knees. "I hope that will not be your method for the other two."

She looked up at him, taking in the strands of black hair that fell across his forehead when he leaned over her. Her hand twitched with the need to push them back into place. "I plan on being Cain when I take out Noah. If I kissed him, it would be really weird." She told with a small laugh.

"And for Cain?" He shot back, ignoring her joke.

*What the hell?* She frowned up at him. "Why do you seem irritated?"

"I'm not."

"You are," she pressed. "I can feel it, Lucas. What's wrong?"

He stared down at her for a moment before glancing away. "Perhaps I do not like the idea of someone else touching you."

He had said it so quietly, she wasn't sure if she had imagined it or not. Her pulse sped up when he looked down at her again, eyes uncertain. "Is that because of the bond?" She asked softly.

His expression hardened. "I believe you already know that I was attracted to you before that."

She instantly recalled their kiss at the gun range and blushed. "Why didn't you ever tell me?" She whispered. "That you were attracted to me?"

The vampire relaxed again. "You seemed quite content with Mr

Donovan. Plus, I did not want to mix business and pleasure." She parted her knees so that they rested on either side of him and he took the invitation to crawl further up her body.

Kee felt his body brush against hers, their hips nearly touching as he hovered over her. She reached up and cupped his face in her hands, smoothing her thumbs along his high cheekbones. "Why the change of heart?" She could feel her heart thrumming in her throat as she waited for his answer.

She had always been attracted to her boss, but he had never acted interested so she never pursued him. Then she met Cain and was swept off her feet. She had loved Cain, she really did, but maybe a small part of her had longed for Lucas at the same time.

She thought about the shit storm her life had become in the last two weeks. The only two constants she had were Conrad and Lucas. They kept her grounded, kept her sane when her mind turned against her with nightmares of the attack. Not only had Lucas saved her life, but he had also been supportive and accommodating. He let her stay in his club, let her practically move into his room, supplied her with anything she needed, helped her plan her attacks, and even helped take her shifting to a level she had never even considered. What would have happened if he hadn't been there for her?

Lucas frowned when her eyes misted over. "Why are you crying?"

She started at his comment and gingerly touched her cheek. "I'm not crying," she mumbled as she blinked away the moisture. "I don't cry."

He couldn't stop the knowing smile that spread across his lips. "Now you sound like the Keira I knew before this," he pressed his forehead against hers. "But with a new strength that suits you much better."

Kee's eyes watered again. *It's like he knows exactly what to say and how to say it.*

It didn't matter if she was angry, upset, or even happy; he knew what to tell her. Butterflies small in her stomach. She couldn't find words to reply to his thoughtful comments. Instead, she tilted her head and slanted her lips against his. She felt the relief that echoed through their bond when he kissed her back. The kiss was delicate and sweet, nothing like the heated one at the range, but just as amazing. She slid her hands into his hair, running her fingers through the black silk.

Lucas could taste the dried blood around her upper lip and felt his fangs throb again. He had fed earlier and yet her blood called to him as if he hadn't fed in days. He broke the kiss, planted another quick peck on her lips, and then pulled back. He gave her a reassuring smirk when she pouted at him in confusion. "Your blood does odd things to me, Keira. I do not want a repeat of our time in your bathroom."

She sighed softly at the reminder. "I'm sorry, I forgot."

He shook his head. "You have nothing to apologize for. I just do not want to scare you away by doing something foolish."

"I understand," she replied quietly. She waited until he removed himself from her to rise from the couch after him. She stretched her arms above her head and watched as he leaned against his desk. She took in his black slacks, black button up, and black dress shoes. To anyone else, she was sure he looked imposing with the black clothes and hair. To her, it made him look all the more alluring, especially with his green eyes shining like polished emeralds.

Gods, he was handsome.

Lucas smirked at her. "You are looking at me like I am your next meal, Keira."

She blushed when she was caught staring. "Sorry." She turned towards the door, took a few steps, but then stilled at the pang of longing she felt both in chest and between her thighs.

*I don't want to leave. I don't want to leave* him. *I want more.* Nerves fluttered in her stomach, but she fought through them. She was a new person and she refused to be as timid as her old self. She knew what she wanted and she was going to have it.

He raised a single eyebrow when she suddenly whirled around to face him. "Yes?" He watched as she stormed towards him with determination. He was surprised when she grabbed the front of his shirt and pulled him down so she could kiss him hard. He gently cradled her face in his hands and drew back so he could look down at her. "Fangs, Keira. I do not want to cut you again."

"Shut up and kiss me, Lucas." She growled, staring up at him with need.

"I do not want to draw blood," he warned, but his grip tightened ever so slightly with anticipation. He wanted this just as much, had for nearly a year. "I do not want to drink from you."

"Then don't bite me." Kee replied hotly. She unwaveringly met his stare, daring him to move.

He slid his hand down and cupped her jaw, holding it firmly while his tongue skimmed along her bottom lip. He was pleased when she gave a soft sigh of approval. "Part your lips, but keep your tongue still." He demanded with a breath against her lips. "If you prick yourself on my fangs, I will stop." When she did as told, he slipped his tongue past her lips. She let out a breath of a moan when his tongue slid along hers and explored her mouth. She tried to reciprocate the action, but he tightened his hold on her lower jaw to keep her in place. Eager to settle the need to touch him, she ran her hands down the expanse of his torso and then back up until her fingers found the buttons of his shirt. Once she had them all undone, she parted the fabric and let her hands run over the smooth, firm skin.

Lucas bit back a groan as her small, warm hands roamed over his chest and abs. He broke away from her mouth and shrugged out of the shirt when she pushed it down his shoulders. He ran his hand into her hair and fisted it when she leaned forward to place wet kisses on his skin. His eyes closed in pleasure when her teeth gently nipped the flesh between kisses, her tongue soothing any sting she caused.

She drew back and watched with satisfaction as his eyes flew open when she suddenly palmed his erection through his slacks. Her pussy clenched when those green eyes blazed with hunger. A surprised squeak escaped her when he suddenly lifted her and sat her on the edge of his desk. She wriggled against him when he stood between her thighs, trying to push her core against him as he grabbed the hem of her sweatshirt.

Kee froze when she realized she was naked beneath it. The pink had faded from the scars, but white lines still disfigured and marred her skin. She put her hands on his wrists to stop him. "Don't." She whispered.

He felt her humiliation though their bond and frowned. He tipped her chin up so she looked at him. "What are you embarrassed about?"

She pursed her lips together. "My scars," she bit out.

He shook his head and began tugging at her sweatshirt again. When she tried to stop him, he gave her a warning look that stilled her hands. "I can rip it off, if you prefer."

She looked up at him with a horrified expression. "But it's my favorite hoodie," she pouted. When his face didn't so much as flinch, she sighed, "Fine." As soon as he pulled it over her head, she crossed her arms over her bare chest.

Lucas scoffed and grabbed her wrists, pressing her back against his desk with her hands above her head. She squirmed against his hold, but he held her down firmly. "These scars," he breathed against her skin as he dipped down to place a kiss on the scar on her eyebrow. "Are just another thing that makes you, *you*." He brushed his tongue over the beginning of each scar under her left collar bone.

She writhed under him when he kissed and trailed his tongue

diagonally across her body, following the marks. She let out a soft moan when he licked the outside two that ran across the outer edges of her breasts, stopping to give each nipple a quick, teasing bite. He released her wrists and put his hands on her waist as he finished adoring the scars that stopped at her right hip. She was trembling when he finally looked up at her from the length of her torso.

"They are a testament to how far you have come after what you have been through." He told her softly as he slid his hands to her hips, his fingers sliding under the waistband of her leggings.

Kee let him tug off her pants and thong, leaving her bare on his cold desk. "Is that how you feel about your scar?"

He stiffened slightly, his hands pausing on his zipper. He looked down at her and saw only curiosity in her eyes. "My brand is just a constant reminder of something I can never have again, Keira."

"The sun," she murmured, her heart aching for him. "For what it's worth, I think it's beautiful."

He blinked at her before giving her a rare, gentle smile. "From you, it is worth a lot." He told her as he removed the rest of his clothing. He put his hands on her hips and pulled her closer to the edge of the desk before dropping to his knees. "Allow me to show you how much."

She sucked in a breath when the pad of his thumb slid between her nether lips, tracing up and down her seam. Up and down. He rubbed firm circles along her clit each time he reached it, making her toes curl in pleasure. He then varied the amount of pressure he used as stroked. One swipe light, the next hard.

"Lucas," she cried when he pulled back.

Lucas parted her lips, opening her pussy to him. "So wet." He praised before flicking his tongue along her slick heat. He swirled it around her clit before sucking. Mindful of his fangs, he had to pull away when she gasped and bucked against his mouth. He placed a hand on her groin to hold her down before going back to his feast.

"Lucas!" She cried when he nibbled at her clit before sliding down to her entrance to fuck her with his tongue. Her hands went to the top of his head as heat gathered in the pit of her stomach and flared towards her chest. The tension in her mounted as his mouth returned to the sensitive ball of nerves at the top of her sex before his finger plunged inside of her. "Fuck!"

He turned his head and gently bit the tender flesh of her inner thigh as he slid in a second finger. "Come for me, my sweet, so I can fuck you properly."

His words, combined with the overwhelming sensation of his fingers fucking her and the stroke of his tongue over her clit, tightened her stomach until the waves of ecstasy crashed over her. Her back arched off the desk as she came with a cry.

Lucas ran his tongue along her seam a final time and stood. He admired the flush on her chest and face before leaning down to kiss her. He slipped his tongue into her mouth, making her taste herself as he readied himself between her bent legs. He grabbed his cock and rubbed the head of it along her folds, coating him in her slick release.

Feeling him nudge the tip of his erection into her, she inhaled sharply. Meeting his questioning gaze, she explained, "It's been a while."

He bent over her, his lips brushing the shell of her ear. "You can tell me if it is too much, my sweet," he slowly eased into her, male pride swelling when she let out a soft gasp once he sheathed himself completely within her. "But I know you can take it."

She clenched around his girth, trying to get used to the stretch she felt within her. He was thicker than Cain and her body was attempting to get used to the difference. When he shifted his hips and slid out to push back in, she moaned.

"Good girl," Lucas praised, withdrawing until just the head

remained before thrusting back in. He did it again, quicker this time.

"*Fuck.*" The curse came out breathless as he found a steady pace. She reached above her, grabbing the edge of the desk to anchor herself as he began to thrust harder.

He pounded into her, only noticing how much his desk was moving when a cup on pens fell over. Not trusting his shaking monitor to not topple over, he reluctantly pulled out of her. Sliding his hands under her ass, he lifted her and was pleased when she immediately wrapped her legs around his waist. He carried her over to the couch and sat down so she was straddling him.

He fisted her hair in his hand and kissed her deeply before nipping at her chin and then her throat, making sure not to break the skin. "What do you need, Keira?"

She leaned forward, pressing her pebbled nipples against his hard chest. She took his bottom lip between her teeth and gently tugged. "You." She responded once she let it go. She lifted her hips and reached down between them to grasp his hard cock. She gave it a firm squeeze, stroking him with her juices still coating him. She smirked when he grunted, his hand tightening its hold on her hair.

He thrust into her hand. "Be careful of what you ask for."

"I don't want to." She aligned his head with her pussy and sunk down, impaling herself on his girth. They both released a moan when she bottomed out. She gripped his shoulders, using them as leverage to lift her hips and drop back down.

He groaned at the feel of her wet heat gripping his cock snugly. He untangled his hand from her hair and gripped the back of her neck firmly while his other hand snaked around her waist. Holding her firmly in place, he bucked his hips, driving himself deep within her.

Kee mewled her pleasure as he took control. Her nails dug into his skin as he thrust into her, tugging her down as he went up. She tossed her head back as he moved faster, breathy moans escaping her with each powerful thrust. He attacked her throat with kisses and scrapes of his teeth, his grunts and groans music to her ears.

"More." She pleaded in a breathless whisper.

Lucas was more than happy to oblige. Without leaving the warmth of her body, he spun them so that she was laid out beneath him along the cushions. "Touch yourself, Keira. I want to feel you come on my cock."

His words made another wave of heat course through her. She never thought she was one for dirty talk, but Lucas and his deep baritone were proving her otherwise. Especially since his normally light accent became more pronounced with his arousal. So, she did as told, reaching between them to rub her clit as he began to piston his hips at a relentless pace. Her abs clenched as her body began to build up towards another release.

He watched her face intently as she pleasured herself while he fucked her. She squeezed her eyes shut, her cheeks flushing as her pleasure mounted. The moan on her lips turned into a cry as she came. And Gods, was it beautiful. A growl rumbled in his chest as her pussy gripped and fluttered around him, making his orgasm come too soon. After a few more jerky thrusts, his back stiffened and he grunted his release.

They stayed locked together, both panting and trying to recuperate. Kee stroked his back when he dropped his forehead to her shoulder, relishing in the pure masculine groan of contentment he gave. After a few minutes, a soft whimper escaped her when he eased out. Effortlessly, he rolled them over so she was sprawled on his chest.

"Wow," she mumbled, curling up to him and smiling tiredly as he wrapped an arm around her.

"Indeed," he stroked her hair tenderly. "Safe to say we thoroughly mixed business and pleasure. I do not believe we can ever go back.

Although, I will admit I am not fond of the idea of doing so." When she didn't respond, an odd pang hit his chest. "Keira?" He lifted his head to look at her and the pang instantly dissolved into warmth when he saw she had fallen asleep with a small smile on her lips.

# Twenty-Two

Conrad sat on Lucas' bed, biting the skin at the corner of his thumb as he ran through the pack meeting over and over again. He wanted to tell Kee, he knew he should, but he was nervous to. What if he was wrong in his thinking? What if Cain had just been acting?

*But what if he hadn't?*

He looked up when the door opened and watched as Lucas and Kee walked in. He tilted his head slightly at the sleepy, content smile on his alpha's face. His eyes shifted to Lucas who seemed relaxed as he looked down at Kee. His amber eyes widened slightly when the lingering traces of arousal hit his nose. Is that were they had been the last hour?

"I need a shower before I go back to sleep." Kee stated as she gave a suggestive smile to Lucas. "Join me?"

"You are a minx, my sweet." He replied with a smirk.

"Actually, Lucas, can I talk to you?" Conrad suddenly asked as he rose from the bed. He noticed his alpha flush as if she just noticed him and gave her a small, reassuring smile before looking at Lucas. Seeing him about to protest, he rushed out, "Please, it's important."

Lucas took in the wolf's serious expression and nodded. He

planted a quick kiss on Keira's lips before urging her on. "I will be here when you are done."

She looked at Conrad's solemn face. "Are you okay, Con?" She asked softly.

He forced a smile. "Everything's fine, Kee. I just need to talk to him about something."

She glanced between the two uncertainly. "If you're sure." When he nodded, she shrugged and headed to the bathroom for her shower.

Conrad waited until he heard the water running before turning and focusing on Lucas. "We might have a problem."

Lucas listened carefully as the werewolf told him what happened at the pack meeting. He silently sat down on the edge of his bed as he digested what he was told. "We still do not know for sure that he did *not* have something to do with Keira's attack."

Conrad combed his hair back with his fingers. "That's the problem, Lucas. I'm pretty sure he didn't. You weren't there. The sincerity in his voice, the anguish, it was real."

"The problem is that if Cain did not plan it, who did?" Lucas questioned. "He is the only one who had a motive."

He growled in frustration. "I know! I was there when they broke up, but seeing him today makes me question if it was him."

"What are you thinking, Mr Novak?"

He hesitated. "Should we tell her?"

Lucas looked up at the ceiling as he thought about it. *What if it wasn't Cain? What would Keira do? Would she leave?*

His hands fisted in the duvet. He didn't want her to leave. Not after he finally had her in his hands. Not after she became what he knew she could be. "I do not know if that is best as of yet."

"Why?"

"Because it does not change the fact that she was attacked. Until they are all dead, she will not be satisfied." He told him. "She still has one more."

Conrad nodded. "That makes sense. Whether it was Cain or someone else who ordered it, she'll still wipe out the ones who attacked her."

"Yes, and she does not need doubts to distract her." He added. "After she kills him, we can tell her."

Conrad nodded again and looked at the door when a light knock tapped against the door. He ventured over and opened it to reveal a pretty human with dyed, platinum blonde hair. The hair stopped at her shoulders with bangs that hovered right above her blue eyes. He lifted an eyebrow at her, keeping his body in the doorway to prevent her from coming in. "Can I help you?"

She scowled up at him. "I'm here to talk to Lucas. Is he here?"

"Let her in, Mr Novak." Lucas instructed. When the wolf stepped aside, he held out a hand towards the woman as she approached him. "Aubrey is my bleeder."

Conrad was familiar with the term. Vampires, especially the ones higher up the command chain, usually had one or more humans they fed from on a regular basis. Contracts with rules and expectations were drawn up and signed between both parties. It usually had the basics of no substance abuse, unprotected sex, or anything that could disrupt the quality of the bloodstream.

Along with bleeders being compensated with money, goods, and sometimes sex, they were often given a status higher than vampires that served under the lord. The humans were also guaranteed to be turned should the vampire fail to protect them. Some bleeders turned the option down, but many yearned for the chance at eternal life.

"Lucas, I'm going home for the night. It's almost one and I'm exhausted," Aubrey pouted as she sat sideways in his lap. "And I haven't seen you since I got here."

"I had a small snack when I woke up so I have not been hungry." He told her as she wound her arms around his neck, her fingers running into his hair.

"Do you want to feed before I leave?" She murmured seductively in his ear.

He grabbed her wrists and removed her hands from him. Finally being with Keira made him loath Aubrey's affection more than he already did. He had told her before that he didn't like her, or other people, touching him so intimately. Keira had been an exception even before their bond. Aubrey, however, believed it was her right to touch him after he made the mistake of once bedding her.

"Just a feeding, Aubrey." He warned.

She pouted at him as she pulled the neckline of her low cut shirt to the side, exposing the junction of her right shoulder. "You're no fun anymore."

"I told you that I would release you from your contract if you wished for it." He reminded her as she readjusted herself so she was straddling him.

"No way. Your bite is too good." She gathered her hair away from her shoulder for him. "Plus, I love when you take me with you when you travel."

Lucas chose not to reply to her. He flicked his tongue along her flesh, coating it with the endorphins from the backs of his fangs before sinking them into her skin. Her moan echoed in his ears and it reminded him of Keira mewling in pleasure under him not even an hour ago. He could feel her nails digging into his shoulders as they did when he thrust into her body. He could picture her body flushed, her heartbeat thrumming visibly in her neck as she came.

He felt Aubrey grind against him and opened his eyes as he was brought out of his drinking haze. His eyes locked with stunned grey ones and he quickly pulled his fangs out of Aubrey's neck. "Keira," He licked his lips, cleaning any traces of lingering blood. "This is Aubrey, my *bleeder*." He quickly explained.

"Oh, hello." Kee greeted awkwardly as she held a towel around her wet hair. She wasn't sure how she felt about seeing Lucas drink from the beauty in his lap. Especially when it was clear she was enjoying herself. What she didn't like was how Aubrey sent her a dirty look as she crawled off Lucas' lap.

Aubrey stood on shaky legs and gave the other woman a once over. She sneered at the pajama shorts and tank top. "And who are you to him?"

"That's none of your concern." Kee replied nonchalantly as she dried her hair.

The human scrunched up her face in distaste. "*I* am his bleeder."

Kee scoffed at her. "Good for you for being a personal blood bank."

"Lucas' *only* blood bank," Aubrey hissed. She turned and cupped Lucas' cheek in her hand, pouting when he jerked away. "I knew you still wanted me. Call me when you don't have company." She told him with a sultry smirk as she pulled away. She walked towards the door and glared at the taller girl. "It would be in your best interest to stay away from him. He only needs one human and it's not you."

The old Kee would have ignored her and walked away. The new one, not so much. As the girl tried to walk past her, Kee latched her hand around Aubrey's throat and slammed her into the wall. Aubrey wheezed as the breath left her, but Kee kept the human pinned there, eyes hardened into glare.

"Then it's a good thing I'm not a human, isn't it?" She watched Aubrey's eyes widen in fear, her pulse racing against Kee's hold.

"Keira, let her go." Lucas warned as he rose from the bed.

"Your bleeder challenged her," Conrad pointed out as he crossed his arms. "It's her right as an alpha to eliminate any threats."

The vampire scowled at him. "Perhaps if they were *both* werewolves." He stepped up to Keira and put his hand on her shoulder. "Release her, Keira, she will not be so foolish as to threaten you again," he glanced at Aubrey. "Will you?"

Aubrey rapidly shook her head and greedily gasped in air when she was released. She muttered a quick apology and then swiftly ran out the door, not once turning to look behind her.

Kee tried to seem unaffected by the situation as she picked up the towel she had dropped. She didn't have any claim to Lucas, and they certainly weren't dating, so why was she bothered? She met Lucas' guarded eyes and gave a sarcastic smile. "Well, at least she seemed to enjoy herself."

He frowned. "I had to feed, Keira."

"Did she have to dry hump you while you did?" She countered as she sat down on the side of the bed she claimed during her stay there.

"She thinks she is the one who aroused me, but she was not the one I was thinking of." Lucas explained as he sat down next to her.

Her cheeks warmed, but she didn't comment on it. "It hurt when you bit me. Why did she enjoy it so much?"

He sighed softly. "You triggered my blood lust so I did not have the foresight to release my endorphins. It is a much different experience with them."

"Why didn't you feed from her that night instead of coming to my apartment?"

"I did not want to show up here covered in blood. I also do not always choose to feed from her. She is my bleeder, but that does not mean I am limited to her."

"Do you care for her?" Kee suddenly asked.

He held her stare. "I have to."

She broke eye contact with Lucas and glanced at Conrad when she felt his uncomfortable aura brush against hers like a whisper. She cleared her throat and patted the spot on the bed next to her.

"Come to bed, Con. We've had a long day."

Conrad released a relieved sigh. "Sleep sounds amazing." He shifted into his wolf form and obediently leapt onto the bed next to her. He rumbled contently when she pet him, her hand sweeping down the fur on his back in soft, even strokes.

She smiled down at her wolf and then looked at the vampire. "Conrad and I will go back to my apartment next week."

Lucas' face darkened with frustration. "You are going to punish me because I fed and answered your questions truthfully?"

She shook her head. "Relax, that's not what I meant. I need to pay rent before they evict me. Plus, I have some of Cain's clothes there. I want to train more with Dante before I try to hammer out the plans to kill Noah, but I know I'll need those clothes." She glanced down at the comforter. "But, I'll admit that I'm nervous to go back. I'm scared to relive it like I do in my nightmares, but I think I just need to face it and get it over with." She heard Conrad whine and put a hand on his head when he set it on her lap.

"I assure you it has been cleaned," Lucas reminded her softly. "When you are there, I recommend you officially get rid of your apartment instead of paying your rent."

"Yeah, I don't think I can live there again, but I'll have to pay extra to break the lease. Plus, what am I going to do with all my stuff? My furniture? My clothes?"

"You may bring the rest of your things here, if you wish." He offered.

It was her turn to frown. "You want us to move here permanently? We can't do that, Lucas."

"And why is that?"

She gestured at the room. "We have taken up your room for almost two weeks. You have to keep sharing a bed with Gio and I feel bad."

"Then I will share the bed with you." He smirked. "We will be quite the threesome."

She rolled her eyes despite the blush spreading across her cheek. "We can't all live in the same room and the rooms you have here are all for your vampires. We don't really belong here."

"Stay in one of the rooms upstairs then. They are all vacant."

"I don't want to take advantage of you and your hospitality, Lucas."

His smirk slipped away. "Where will you go? Surely not your apartment."

"No, we will find a different place. A two bedroom apartment somewhere."

"Will you stay in the city?"

"If not, then close by. I have this needy boss who makes me work odd hours of the night." Kee teased.

His smirk returned. "He sounds unreasonable."

"He's an asshole, but the job has its perks." She finally smiled when he gave her one of his rare laughs.

"Go to bed, Keira. When I close the club in a few hours, I will be joining you and Conrad." He informed her as he got up from the bed.

She blinked and glanced at Conrad when he tilted his head in question. "You were serious?" She asked as she looked at Lucas once again.

"But of course. The bed is more than big enough. Also, I believe Giovanni has some lady company tonight." He tilted his head in thought. "Or was it a gentleman this time?"

"He's bisexual?" Kee asked curiously. She hadn't seen the doctor with any partner in her time there.

"Indeed. He was nearly dead because of it when I found him." At her horrified look, he explained. "Homosexuality wasn't legal in Italy until 1889 and we met in 1860. If you want the full story, you will have to ask him."

She nodded in understanding. "Well, this is your room so if you want to join us I won't tell you no."

"Do you wish to tell me no?" He inquired softly.

She gave him a small, seductive smile. "No."

"Then I will return later." He bent down and pressed a kiss to her lips before leaving the room to attend to his club.

She flopped back against the bed and curled on her side so she was facing Conrad. At his knowing look, she blushed. "Don't look at me like that." She murmured. He huffed, but closed his eyes and snuggled closer to her. She smiled and scratched the fur between his ears until she nodded off to sleep.

# Twenty-Three

Kee stood in front of her apartment door almost two weeks later, disguised as one of the leasing agents to avoid being recognized by her neighbors. After planning her attack on Noah, she had decided to come back alone. She didn't want to keep relying on Conrad and Lucas for support. It had been a few days short of a month since her attack and she was stronger than ever.

After she killed Brandon, she spent every day with Conrad lifting weights, running on the treadmill, and working on endurance. At night, she would spar with Dante before the club opened, take basic anatomy lessons from Giovanni, and then spend the remainder of the night with Lucas once Byte closed.

She wasn't sure if she would be ready to face off against Noah, but she had already put it off a week longer than she had originally planned. She glanced down at her phone and pursed her lips. It was nearly five in the evening and she knew her time was running out. During Conrad's last trip to the pack, he had found out that tonight was Brandon's wake.

She had until seven to strike.

She had been finalizing her day since she woke up, trying to get all the details set out for the night. She would pick up Cain's clothes from her apartment, park a few blocks away from Noah's apartment complex, and shift into Cain to kill him. It was pretty similar to what she had done for Brandon, but this time she was bringing a gun with silver bullets, courtesy of Dante. Silver was every monster's weakness. It scalded them like boiling water and slowed down their healing process. A fatal shot with a silver bullet would kill them before their body could even think to repair itself.

"Oh, are you evicting that nice girl? I haven't seen her in a month!"

Kee started and looked at the elderly neighbor across the hallway. She forced a smile and told the lie she had practiced in case this happened. "Good evening, Mrs Brown. Miss Quinn actually submitted her 30-day notice almost a month ago. I'm just making sure nothing is damaged in the unit."

"Oh, I had no idea! I would have baked her some cookies. Well, I hope the new tenants are just as pleasant! Have a good night!" She commented merrily.

"Night." Kee waved at her and waited until she disappeared behind her door before turning back towards her own. She unlocked the door and hesitantly stepped into the entryway, shutting the door behind her. She let her skin drop away and was relieved when she didn't ache from the change.

As part of her training, she pushed her shifting limit, trying to maximize the time she could stay in a skin. Skins that were closer to her stature were easier to hold. That was why she had chosen the agent who was most similar to her in height and weight. She wanted something easy since she was going to hold Cain's skin for a longer period of time later.

Hesitantly, she scanned the dining room and then her living room. Lucas wasn't kidding when he said he had the place cleaned. If she hadn't been the victim, she never would have known there had been a fight. Her TV and coffee table had been replaced, her entertainment center repaired as well. The dents in the walls had been filled and painted, leaving them almost as perfect as before. There wasn't a speck of blood that she could see and the scent of it was nonexistent.

She went to head down towards her bedroom, but her feet refused to move. She didn't realize her knees were trembling until they threatened to buckle. She braced herself against the door and locked her knees back in place. *I will not crumble because of this.*

Clenching her teeth, she looked at the kitchen again. The table was upright and perfectly centered, but she could only see herself being thrown at it, toppling to the ground and smacking her head against the floor. She could almost feel Noah sitting on top of her, his hands around her neck. She winced and lifted her hand to her throat as if it still ached from being strangled.

Her eyes darted to the living room again and she sucked in a breath at the memory of her slamming down onto the coffee table, shards of glass impaling themselves in her skin as if it were rice paper. Her hand fell from her neck to run across the scars through her shirt. Closing her eyes, she tilted her head back against the door and took deep breaths to calm her racing heart. With her eyes closed, she vividly recalled how the back of Wyatt's head exploded from the gunshot. She opened her eyes and looked at where bits of his brains and blood had shot across the room to splatter on her wall. It had been the same wall she slammed Brandon against. She remembered watching the life fade from his eyes two weeks ago.

*They both deserved it. Noah will get what's coming to him, and then Cain will as well. They all deserve it.* She told herself as a mantra.

Kee pushed away from the door with determination and was pleased when her feet obeyed and took her down the hall. She entered her room and went to the last drawer on the right side of the dresser. She pulled it open and grabbed Cain's spare pair of jeans. She closed it and yanked opened the one that held her pajamas. A pang hit her when Cain's red shirt sat neatly folded on top. She stared at it for a long time before lifting it from the drawer.

She turned and gazed at her bed, remembering all the moments she and Cain had spent on it. The cuddling, her reading while he played on his phone, watching movies on his laptop, and of course their intimate times as well. Her breath hitched and she clutched the shirt to her chest.

*How could he have forgotten about all of our time together? How could he have thrown it all away just because I didn't want to fuck Warren?*

She found it somewhat bittersweet that she still ended up screwing another man anyways. Multiple times. She sighed and ran a hand down her face. She wasn't sure what was going on with her and Lucas, but her heart still clenched with Cain's betrayal. Being around the memories they shared only made it worse. Would she be able to kill him? To end his life for trying to do the same thing to hers?

*I have to.*

Swallowing her emotions and steeling herself with resolve, she twisted away from the bed. She walked over to her closet, grabbed Cain's worn pair of converse, and then took the small pile of clothes with her back down the hall. She changed back into the image of the leasing agent and walked out the door, not once looking back on her old life.

—

Kee knocked on Noah's door, or what she hoped was his door. Cain had taken her there only a handful of times and she hoped her memory had served her right. She looked down at the red shirt and snug jeans, appreciating how well they fit Cain's body. The shift had come so differently than the other body skins she created. It had expanded and filled her with a wave of ice so cold, it left her almost numb. Once it set into place, warmth washed over her with a rumbling growl that echoed within her. She didn't know why the skin for Cain was so different, but she would think about it later.

She scratched her chin and hoped she had made the right decision by foregoing the beard. Conrad had said Cain had facial hair the last time he saw him, but she couldn't take any chances. A bare face was easier to explain than the sudden appearance of a beard.

She dropped her hand and tried to keep her gaze neutral when the door opened, revealing the shorter, bulkier man. Her heart began to pound with hate, anger threatening to spill its way onto her face in the form of a snarl. Instead, she gave him one of Cain's easy going smiles. "Hey."

"Hey man, I wasn't expecting to see you until seven." Noah replied with confusion. "Weren't we going to meet at Mason's for Brandon's wake?"

*Be cool and play along with it, Kee.*

She shrugged and shoved her hands into her pockets. "I guess I just wanted to kill time," she answered smoothly. "I'm not really looking forward to it."

Noah relaxed as he nodded with understanding. "Should we down a few beers before we head out?" When Cain nodded, he stepped aside to let him in. He closed the door behind them before heading to the kitchen off to the left of the small apartment. "I only have IPAs, that okay?"

"I'll take anything, honestly." Kee answered as she leaned against the counter next to the sink. She made sure to keep her back from Noah, especially with the gun tucked in the jean's waistband.

"I feel you." Noah twisted off the caps and handed his best friend one. He sighed heavily and lifted his bottle. "To Brandon."

"To Brandon," she held her beer back slightly when Noah tried to clink his bottle against hers. At his confused look, she added quietly,

"To Wyatt and Kee, too." Her eyes narrowed ever so slightly when he frowned.

*Is he mad that Cain ordered him to do that? Or is that guilt for carrying it through?*

Noah tried to keep his breathing even as he nodded and knocked his beer against Cain's. "Cheers," he mumbled. He swallowed a swig of beer in a large gulp and wiped his mouth with the back of his hand. He kept his gaze away from Cain, but could feel the beta staring at him. He cleared his throat twice before speaking. "Who do you think did it?" He suddenly asked, inwardly cursing when his nervousness made his voice rise an octave.

"You mean who do I think killed Brandon?" Kee questioned him, keeping her tone neutral as her dark blue eyes stayed on his form. Why was he fidgeting so much? What was he thinking?

*Am I acting out of Cain's character?*

His brow furrowed as he tightened his grip on the bottle. "You think it was a different person who killed him? Than the person who attacked the others?"

"Wasn't it?" She countered almost too quickly. He knew damn well that it wasn't him or Wyatt who killed Brandon. Or, did Cain want her attackers dead as well? To hide the evidence?

Noah set his beer down on the counter, his pulse racing with dread. Had Cain figured out what Warren had sent them to do? Did he know he tried to strangle the life out of his mate? How? How did Cain know he had betrayed him? There was no way unless someone leaked the truth.

"Who told you?" He breathed, his teeth clenched tightly together.

It was her turn to knit her eyebrows together in confusion. "Told me what?"

"You know exactly what I'm talking about!" Noah suddenly snarled as he turned on his best friend. "Asking me all these questions when you already know! Who told you? Was it Brandon? Is that why he's dead? Did you kill him in revenge? Did you come for me next?!"

Kee almost took a step back in fear of Noah's sudden rage. It was just like when he had snapped in her apartment and attacked her. When he was trying to choke her to death. She stared into Noah's tormented brown eyes and made herself stay still as something foreign and primal growled low in warning inside her. Cain wouldn't step back. He was above Noah in the pack. Noah was supposed to cower to *him*, not the other way. He was beneath them. *They* were alpha to *him*.

**He has to submit.**

Her eyes widened when she realized the string of thoughts were not her own, but belonged to that snarling darkness that housed itself within her when she initially shifted.

*This...this is Cain's wolf,* she realized with a shock. But, how? She had created an image of Cain, a skin. So, how did she get his beast?

Cain had been quiet for too long, making the other wolf anxious. "Answer me!" Noah screamed, pulling Kee away from her growing confusion. "What do you want from me?"

"I think you know." She growled with Cain's beast as she took a step towards him.

"I don't!" He screeched as his guilt consumed him. He took two steps back when his friend started advancing towards him, Cain's aura pulsing with anger. He threw up his hands in desperation. "What did you come here to do, Cain? Am I right? Are you here to kill me, too?"

"And why would I want to kill you, Noah?" Kee mocked him in Cain's dry, humorless tone. She grabbed Noah's shirt in both hands and shoved the smaller wolf against the wall, glaring down at him with hatred.

Noah's eyes widened, but he wouldn't go down without a fight. Cain was the beta, but he wasn't weak. He pushed off against the wall with one leg, launching himself at Cain. He took advantage when Cain stumbled back and threw all his weight at him to tackle him to the tiled floor. Noah drew back his arm and punched Cain hard in the face.

Kee was stunned, her mind momentarily sending her back to when he was on top of her in her apartment. He hit her hard in the face, just like he had a month ago. Her eyes widened in fear when he saw his arm pull back for another blow. Suddenly the wolf within her snarled so loud, it shook her whole body like a miniature earthquake. She quickly snapped out of her shock and caught Noah's fist as it came sailing down at her again. Using Dante's training and Cain's strength, she pulled his fist towards her and quickly jabbed her other fist up at Noah's throat.

Noah instantly starting hacking, but didn't remove himself from her. Instead, he tried to punch her again, but this time Kee was ready for him. She grabbed Noah's right wrist before the punch could connect with her face and pushed it towards his stomach. She then grabbed the back of his shirt with her other hand while trapping his right foot with her left one. When he tried to hit her again, he lost balance and she used it to her advantage. She pulled his shirt and thrust her weight up, she rolled them until he was pinned under her. She punched him in the face, hoping she broke his nose for the third time.

He groaned as pain wracked his face, blood pouring from both nostrils. He heard the hostile growl come from his beta and tilted his head back in submission. "What do you want, Cain?!" He shouted in defeat, but kept his throat bared to Cain. "Do you want a confession? Is that what you want? Fine! I was sent to kill your girlfriend! I was sent to kill that *disgusting shapeshifter* you wanted to mate with! Did you know what she was? *Did you*? I saved you from her, Cain! I'm glad I helped kill Kee! There's your confession!"

"What?"

"What?"

Kee blinked when her question was echoed a split second after she asked it. She froze when she saw Noah's eyes widen in horror as he looked at her and then at something over her shoulder. Her heart stammered to a stop as she slowly turned so she could glance at the person behind her from the corner of her eye. She sucked in a breath as she saw Cain standing in shock at the edge of the kitchen.

Cain looked at *himself* on top of his friend and had to take a second to make sure he was not in some horrible nightmare. Noah had just screamed that he had been sent to kill Kee, that he was glad that he helped kill her. No, there was no way. This had to be a dream. Noah was his best friend, his right-hand man. Cain was going to make him the beta when Warren stepped down. He would never betray him like this. He couldn't have. Not when he helped keep him together after Kee's death.

Cain's head jerked up when his beast rumbled at Kee's name. He looked at his clone and stared at the red shirt it was wearing. It was technically *his* red shirt, but it had always been Kee's. He swallowed thickly, trying to force down the storm of emotions that was suddenly caught in his throat. "K-Kee?" He whispered with a small hint of hope. It had been over a month since he had seen her and had just started to cope with the probability of her death.

Kee's heart gave an excruciating twist when he breathed her name. She let her skin drop and shrunk back into her normal form. Her eyes misted over when Cain's did, but she quickly snapped back to attention when Noah growled under her. She quickly grabbed the gun from the loose waistband of Cain's jeans and pointed the gun at Noah's heart.

"Bitch!" Noah snarled, but stopped moving when the barrel of the gun pressed into him.

"Don't fucking move, Noah," she sneered. She felt Cain move behind her, but refused to look at him. "*Don't*, Cain!" She warned, but her voice cracked on his name.

Cain looked between his friend and Kee, panic swelling in him. "Kee, baby, put the gun down."

She took in a shaky, angry breath. "No! You heard what he said! I've earned this!"

"We had to have heard wrong," Cain said desperately, slowly inching closer to her. "Noah wouldn't do that to me, to us. Please, Kee, *please*. Put it down. I can't handle any more death."

Her bottom lip trembled as she looked at him, but she quickly shook her head to rid herself of the emotion. *No, I'm going to do this!* Her expression turned steely and merciless. "What's one more?" She questioned monotonously as she looked down at Noah and pulled the trigger without hesitation.

"No!" Cain cried as the gun went off. He moved towards them, but froze when she pointed the gun at him as she climbed off Noah's torso. His attention snapped to Noah as his body started to convulse, blood and steam spewing from the wound. "Jesus, Kee, *silver* bullets?"

"I had to make sure he died," she told him honestly. She silently made her way towards the front door, keeping Cain in her sight the entire way. She tried to ignore the anguish on his face as she backed away from him. She shifted back into his skin, ignoring the icy wave and the way the base of her skull tingled in exhaustion. She nodded towards Noah. "You might want to say your goodbye." She murmured before hurrying out the door.

Cain was torn. Did he run after her? Or did he say his final words to Noah? Numbly, he squatted down next to his friend and put his hand over the wound on his chest. "Noah, please, tell me it isn't true."

His wolf whined when he realized his friend was already dead. He replayed Noah's confession over and over again in his mind. He closed his eyes and saw Kee killing him. *No, this has to be a nightmare. There was no way any of this just happened.* He gripped his best friend's lifeless hand tightly in his and released a confused, mournful howl.

# Twenty-Four

Cain sat in the driver's side of his truck feeling numb from head to toe. The trip to Mason's house was a blur, his mind reeling as he tried to process everything that had happened. He was stuck in a quicksand of emotions, each thought sinking him further into a pit of despair. He looked up in the rear view mirror and peered at the body lying motionless on his backseat.

After Kee left, he grieved over Noah before calling Warren. Things were still rough between the alpha and beta, but this was a pack death and he had to be notified. Warren had been stunned into silence, especially since he was at a wake for one of his other wolves. After recovering from his shock, he told Cain to bring him to Mason's.

He took a deep breath and forced his tense limbs to move. He climbed out of the truck and went to the backseat. He opened the door and felt his beast whine at Noah's still body. With a heavy heart, he lifted his friend into his arms and kicked the door shut. The pack left the driveway empty for Cain to park in so he wouldn't have to walk far.

As he approached the front door, it swung open to reveal his alpha. "Warren." Cain greeted emotionlessly.

"Come, we prepared the dining room table." Warren replied solemnly.

As Cain carried the body into the house, his fellow wolves stood in two parallel lines, making an aisle to walk down. When he got to the dining room, Natalie and Mason stood at the table with teary faces. He carefully set Noah down on the white sheet and stepped back so the pack could mourn.

"Cain," Nat cooed as she came up to him. She was dressed in a sleek, long sleeve black dress, her blonde hair pulled back in a low ponytail. When he dipped his head towards her, she cupped his cheek with one hand and stroked his hair with the other. "I'm so sorry, brother."

They weren't related by blood, but they might as well be. Before he met Kee, the wolf queen had provided any emotional comfort he may have needed. He had turned to Kee during their time together, but Nat had been there in her absence. "What do I do?" He asked helplessly as he put his hand on her wrist.

"Oh, Cain." She cried for him. First he lost Kee as a mate because of Warren's decision, then lost her in a different way when her life was taken. They all felt the weight of Wyatt and Brandon's death, but Noah's death had to have hit Cain the hardest. Noah had been Cain's best friend, his choice for beta. *How much loss can one person take before breaking?*

Mason came up to them and nuzzled his head into the side of his beta's shoulder. "I'm sorry." He mumbled softly.

"I am, too. Neither one of them deserved it." Once again, he replayed Noah's confession in his head. He wasn't sure about Brandon's death, but maybe Noah had his coming. Hearing him confess to what he did to Kee made his blood boil and his wolf howl in need for revenge.

His stomach suddenly churned when he remembered Noah

comforting him after he found out about Kee's supposed death. He had consoled him, helped look for her, and ran with him through the woods. Noah encouraged him to stay positive when he *knew* differently. Noah had been the one to attack Kee and he acted like he had no idea what had happened to her.

*How could he have betrayed me in the worst way possible? We were supposed to be best friends!*

"Cain!" Warren snarled and clamped his hand on his beta's shoulder. Cain was gripping Nat's wrist tightly, his aura flaring wildly.

Cain startled out of his angry thoughts and saw Natalie looking up at him with wide eyes. He quickly released her and stepped back. "I'm sorry."

Warren tightened his hold on Cain. "I know you are hurting, but don't ever touch my mate like that again. Do you understand me?"

He looked off to the side in submission, not having it in him to challenge him or defend himself. "I won't."

"Good," he said and released him. "Come on, Nat."

She hadn't been scared of Cain. She knew he was heartbroken. She gave his forearm a reassuring squeeze before following Warren to the head of the table. "He didn't mean to, Warren." She whispered to her mate.

"I know." He replied in an equally soft tone. He approached his second *officially* dead wolf and his beast howled at the loss. He leaned over Noah's body to stare at the bullet hole in his chest. He could smell the charred flesh deep inside the wound and saw the smooth, pale burns around the rim of the entry point. "This was done with a silver bullet." He announced.

Natalie heard some of their wolves gasp in horror, others growling in anger. "It burned him from the inside. His body couldn't heal itself." She explained with a sad frown.

"Even if it wasn't silver, it's too close to his heart to say if he would have survived or not." Warren growled. He lowered his head closer to the body and inhaled deeply. He tried to find a foreign scent, but found none. He sneered and pulled away. "I can't scent the person who did it."

"Then it's like Brandon?" Mason asked miserably, eyes filling with unshed tears. "Do you smell the jasmine?"

Warren shook his head. "Whoever sprayed your house in that shit knew it would hide their scent. With Noah, all I smell is blood and Cain. It's a bullet hole so it's possible they weren't touching him when they shot him."

"I know this may seem silly, but did you see anyone suspicious, Cain?" Natalie asked softly.

He lifted his head and looked at her. "No, or I would have gone after them." He said carefully. Technically he wasn't lying. Kee wasn't suspicious, he just was stunned to see that she was alive.

*Kee's alive.* Cain repeated to himself and his wolf rumbled in happiness.

She nodded sympathetically and then snapped her head up when she heard a mournful howl near the end of the table. Katie was there, aqua eyes wide and pupils dilated. She tensed when the other girl's aura flared out of control. The hair on the back Natalie's neck stood up in warning as Katie's body started quivering.

"Katie!" She cried in fear when the girl let out another anguished howl. She wasn't afraid of her own well-being, but for what would happen next. If Katie didn't calm down, her wolf would go into a primal, instinctual mode. When a wolf suffered too much emotional trauma their human side, in essence, breaks. A nervous breakdown for a wolf could permanently cost them their sanity.

Cain moved before he could think. His instincts told him to save his fellow wolf and so he would. He had comforted Katie with Wyatt's disappearance and let her lean on him for support when Brandon was found dead. She had thrown a fit, but managed to keep it together with his help. Noah's death had just pushed her over the edge.

He reached her as her body convulsed, and pulled her tightly to his chest. He pinned her arms to her sides to keep them from flailing. "Don't change, Katie! If you shift you'll be lost to us!"

Warren ordered his wolves to back away from the duo and give them space. He took a step towards them, but his mate grabbed his hand and pulled him back. "What are you doing? I am her alpha and she needs me."

Natalie glared up at him. "Cain has been keeping her grounded since Wyatt went missing. What have *you* done for her?"

"Don't take that tone with me, Nat." He bared his teeth at her, but froze when Katie gave a high pitched scream.

Cain took her to the floor when she started thrashing harder. He pinned her hands above her head, the rest of her body trapped under his as he kneeled over her. His chest vibrated with a deep growl, his blue eyes blazing with his wolf's presence. "Listen to me, Katie." He rumbled as he pushed his power down on her.

She squirmed under him, the claws from her wolf coming through her fingertips as her body tried to shift. "This isn't fair! I can't keep doing this!" She whined. "I can't keep losing people I care about!"

"So your answer is to quit?" He sneered. "You're not allowed to give up. You're not the only one hurting!"

Tears pooled in her eyes and spilled down her cheeks. "I'm not strong like you." She cried as her body trembled, her beast calming a bit as it listened to the male above her.

"My wolves aren't weak," his wolf scolded. "And Wyatt would never choose such a feeble female." He remarked harshly.

She suddenly bared her teeth at him in a snarl. "Don't you dare say anything negative about him!"

Cain returned the snarl, lowering his face towards hers menacingly. "Then obey me," he growled. "Fight this shift and pull yourself together." When her body hesitated under him, he tightened his hold on her hands. "Wyatt wouldn't want you to lose yourself, Katie. Now, *obey me*."

More tears fell from her eyes, but she tilted her head back and exposed her throat to him. Accepting her submission, he bit her throat without drawing blood. When she submitted to him, her beast obeyed her alpha's orders and retreated back to its dormant state.

Cain released her throat and gave it a soft nuzzle. He stood and helped her to her feet, letting her lean into him for support. He patted her head once, but then let his hands fall to his sides. He felt nothing but protectiveness for Katie. He acknowledged she was pretty, but she wasn't Kee.

"I'm sorry, Cain." She murmured almost embarrassingly and wiped at her cheeks. "Thank you for bringing me back."

"It's okay, Katie. I know it's a lot to take in." He assured her. Feeling the eyes of his pack on him, he looked up. He felt a cold dread seep into his chest as he met Warren's glare.

He had just taken a wolf from his alpha. It was the start to becoming alpha, but he wasn't as happy as he thought he would be. Wolves submitting to him instead of Warren was just the beginning. If Warren didn't step down, it would come down to a fight for the position. The timing couldn't have been worse.

"Cain, come with me." Warren ordered as he stormed towards the beta.

Cain untangled his arm from Katie's hold and obediently followed after his alpha, his beast pacing nervously within him. He was silent as he trailed Warren into the backyard. He closed the door behind them and turned towards Warren with an apology on the tip of his tongue. He didn't expect the fist that connected with his face and stumbled back against the sliding glass door.

Warren fisted Cain's shirt and held him against the door. "First you grab my mate and then you take a wolf from me? Have you lost your mind?!" He snarled.

"I didn't mean to grab Nat, Warren. I was lost in my thoughts." Cain said calmly, not wanting to rile his alpha further.

"And becoming Katie's alpha? What's that about? Why are you turning against me?" He spat out, slamming Cain back against the slider once again, the glass cracking from the force. "What is making you do this to me? Tell me!"

Cain stared into Warren's crazed eyes and then quickly looked away so he didn't think he was challenging him. "I just didn't want her to lose herself. The pack can't take another loss. Katie is proof of that. I didn't realize what my wolf was doing until it was too late. I'm not going against you, Warren. Why would I?"

Warren studied Cain carefully, his heart pounding in his chest. Did Cain know what he did? Did Noah tell him the truth? All he could smell on Noah was Cain. Did that mean that he killed the other wolf?

"You don't have reason to take over as alpha?" Warren asked with a cold, skeptical voice.

Cain's brow furrowed in confusion. "Should I?"

"No," he said a little too quickly. "Did you kill Noah?"

Cain whipped his head back to Warren. "*What?*" He questioned incredulously. "Of course not! How can you ask me if I killed my best friend? Why would you even think that?"

Warren released the breath he was holding and then let go of his beta. "I had to make sure. I could only smell your scent on him."

"I wouldn't do that to him." *Or, would I? If I had been there when he attacked Kee, would I have killed him?*

"I know, I'm sorry I accused you." He mumbled and ran his hand through his long hair. "I just don't know how to deal with three pack members dead."

"It's four for me, Warren. My best friend and my mate. I felt the loss more than you, but you don't see me accusing you of killing them." He pointed out harshly. Warren didn't know Kee was alive and Cain didn't have any intention of telling him. Not until he knew what was going on.

"Wyatt was my little brother." He growled, trying to ignore just how nervous Cain's words made him.

Cain rubbed his temples in exasperation. "I'm not going to argue about this. I'm going to pay my respects to Brandon and then call Noah's sister. His family disowned him when he was infected with the werewolf virus, but they should still know." He turned to the door and looked over his shoulder. "I ask that you don't treat Katie any differently. I don't think she really comprehends that she changed alphas."

"I won't take it out on her." Warren agreed with a nod.

He nodded back and then slipped back inside the house to find Brandon's urn. Werewolves didn't believe in burials. The thought of trapping a wolf's body in a box beneath the ground they loved to run on was just cruel. He found the urn in the living room and placed his palm on the lid. He prayed that Brandon's wolf spirit would be wild and free once his ashes were spread along the earth.

He hugged Mason and Natalie goodbye, patting Katie on the head in farewell as well before leaving. When he got to his truck, he slipped into the driver seat and stared at the wheel blankly. A sense of numbness crept over him again, his wolf whimpering in anxiety. Too much had happened that night. There were so many questions, but not enough answers.

*Why did my wolf take Katie? Why did Noah attack Kee? Why did she kill him? Why was Brandon dead? Was Wyatt dead, too? If so, where was his body?* He needed answers.

With determination chasing away the shock, he stuck his key in the ignition. When the engine roared to life, he pulled out of the driveway and veered off towards downtown. He was desperate for answers and knew one person who could answer at least some of them. Now that he knew she was alive, he knew exactly where to go to find her and he wouldn't accept another lie from her boss.

# Twenty-Five

Something bad had happened, Lucas was sure. He had been concentrating on the bond with Keira since she left, keeping tabs on her emotions. She had been fine for a majority of the time, but then there was suddenly a tirade of emotions. Confusion, disbelief, regret, and an overwhelming amount of panic. He feared what the combination of emotions meant, but he was certain in his assumption the longer they remained.

The bond told him she was close and had been for a while. "Conrad," Lucas called from his seat behind his desk. The wolf broke his conversation with Dante to look at him curiously. "Keira is here and upset."

He frowned with worry and looked at the head of security. "I'm sorry, I think I'll need to start on another night." He had accepted Dante's proposal for working part-time security at Byte. If he and Kee were going to get an apartment together, he wanted a job to help split the costs.

"We can do the paperwork another night. The position will be waiting for you, Conrad." Dante said with a pleased smile. "Take care of your alpha."

"I will, thank you." He told him earnestly and then turned towards Lucas as he rose from his seat. He waited until they started making their way across the upstairs hallway before speaking again. "Is it bad?"

"Yes," he replied honestly as they went down the stairs and towards the kitchen at the back. "I fear she encountered Cain."

Conrad sucked in a breath and glowered at the floor as they approached the back entrance. "Do you think he hurt her?"

"Not in the way you presume." He answered quietly as he opened the door.

Kee sat shaking in the Grand Cherokee she borrowed from Lucas. She was frozen in the driver's seat, her limbs quivering as her heart beat painfully against her ribs. She didn't remember driving back to Byte, didn't recall parking in the back lot. Her hands were trembling so badly, she had to try three different times to press the red ignition button to turn off the car. Once it was off, she drew her knees up to her chest and rested her bare feet on the black leather as she tried to control herself.

*Cain didn't do it.* She shook her head and buried her face in her hands. *No! It's not possible! It had to be Cain!* But, Noah had admitted what he did to her. *Why would he have said that if Cain already knew? If Cain had orchestrated it?*

Because he didn't.

And, according to what Noah had said before that, Cain was never supposed to know what happened to her. So, who had planned her death? Who else knew she was a shapeshifter? Who sent Brandon, Wyatt and Noah to kill her? Who else wanted her dead?

*Who do I blame?*

She inhaled sharply and exhaled a shaky breath. She did it again, and then again, and again, until her chest was heaving unbearably.

*Who do I accuse of almost sending me to an early grave? Who do I make take ownership of the attack?*

She felt her chest grow cold, her fingers growing numb as she struggled to gasp in air.

*Who do I kill next? Where is my end game?*

There had to be a final person to annihilate. There had to be one more life she had to take away before she could move the fuck on with her life. There was the possibility she would never find out. She could be forever stuck wondering who the person got away with trying to kill her was.

*And for what? How do I face Cain knowing that he did nothing wrong while I murdered his pack members? That I had blamed him for being the reason I was attacked? What does this change? Everything; and yet nothing.*

She had slept with Lucas, had enjoyed the comfort his body had to offer her. She welcomed him with open arms. *Did we officially break up that night? Have I been cheating on him this whole time? And gods, that look he gave me when I killed Noah.*

"Kee?"

She jerked her head up and heard a wheezing sound. She saw a blurred version of Conrad, but when she tried to call out to him, she realized the noise was coming from her. He framed her face in his hands and heard him tell her to calm down.

"You are hyperventilating, Keira." Lucas told her as Conrad tried to gather her from the car.

She instantly started struggling when her beta pulled her from the car. She didn't want to be touched, didn't want to be held. She didn't want to feel constricted. When he let her go, she tumbled to the cracked asphalt and tried to follow Lucas' breathing instructions. Deep inhale, hold it, slowly let it out. She did it over and over until her heart slowed down enough for her to breathe normally.

Conrad had kneeled down next to her. He didn't touch her, but let her know he was there and she appreciated that. When she finally stopped quivering, she looked at him with an ashen face. "I'm sorry." She croaked. "I felt smothered."

He shook his head. "It's okay." He told her and stood up with his hand outstretched. "Can I help you up?"

She nodded once, a small jerk of her head, and put her hand in his. When he pulled her to her feet, she leaned into him for support. He put his arm around her shoulders and she sighed. "I saw Cain." She murmured, suddenly feeling exhausted.

"I assumed so." Lucas commented carefully as he walked behind them back to the club. "Are you feeling better now?"

She shook her head, but didn't say anything else on their trip down to Lucas' room. Once they were in the room, she sat down on the bed and put her hands in her lap. "I killed Noah." She announced, voice devoid of any emotion.

Lucas sat down next to her while Conrad sat down on the ground by her feet, his hands on her knees. "Did Cain see?" The vampire prodded softly.

She nodded. "But, before that Noah confessed when I was Cain. He said that he was sent to kill me," she turned tormented eyes on Lucas. "Do you know what that means, Lucas? He admitted to Cain that he tried to kill me! Why would he do that if Cain is the one who planned it?"

Lucas bit back a sigh. He had not wanted her to learn of the truth in such a way. "Keira, we had an inkling that perhaps Cain was not behind your attack." He said softly.

"What do you mean?" She asked and then looked down at Conrad whose eyes were wide like a frightened puppy. "What does he mean, Con?"

"At the pack meeting I had a suspicion that Cain might not have had anything to do with your attack," he mumbled. "He was so upset by your death. It's hard to fake such raw emotion, Kee."

She leapt to her feet and backed away from them. How could they keep such a thing from her? "You two knew?" She breathed, her heart slamming into gear again.

"No, Keira, we did not know for certain," Lucas calmly explained as he slowly stood up from the bed as well. "We had no way of knowing for sure, but we were going to tell you our suspicion after you killed Noah."

"Why wait?" Kee demanded, pushing away from him when he tried to pull her into his arms.

"Whether it was Cain or someone else, would you not have still gone after Noah?" He asked seriously. "Would you not have still killed him for trying to do the same to you?"

She clenched her jaw. "Of course I would have."

"Then telling you beforehand would have done nothing but distract you," he pointed out. At her angry, betrayed look, he sighed. "We were going to tell you, Keira, I promise."

"Well it doesn't matter now!" She huffed and pushed her hair back from her face angrily. "I now know for sure that it wasn't him!"

"And how does that information make you feel?" Lucas questioned with a carefully placed blank face. A part of him was nervous for her answer. They had grown close the past month and the idea of her and Cain getting back together infuriated him.

"It makes me feel relieved, Lucas," she admitted breathlessly. "My heart feels lighter knowing the man I love didn't betray me."

Conrad frowned and glanced at Lucas. He liked Lucas. The vampire was hard to read most of the time, but he was reasonable and supportive. But, more than anything, he cared for Kee more than he let on. It must have stung for him to hear her say those words about Cain.

"Lord Lucas, there's a problem at the front." Giovanni interrupted from the other side of the door.

Glad for the distraction, Lucas tore his eyes away from the fuming Keira and pulled open his door. He looked at his second-in-command with a neutral expression. "What is it?"

"A werewolf has pushed his way past security throwing a fit about seeing Kee. He's scaring some of the patrons in his hybrid form." Gio replied and then flinched when he heard crashing in the kitchen upstairs. "It seems he's coming."

"Cain," Lucas surmised and then looked at Keira. Her eyes were wide and he could practically taste her anxiety again. He sighed and glanced down the hall behind Gio when he heard cursing and stomping coming down the stairs. "What do you want to do, Keira?"

She cringed when an animalistic growl echoed down the hall, a hot power thrumming in the air around them. "I don't know." She answered honestly.

"Stop there, wolf!" Dante shouted as he finally caught up to the werewolf after being thrown aside earlier.

Cain snarled at him as he stood tall in his hybrid wolf form. Dark brown, almost black fur covered him from head to toe, his dark blue eyes practically glowing as he glared at the dark skinned vampire that stood in front of him. He lurched at him, grabbing his arm when Dante tried to shove him back.

Kee moved towards the door when she heard the bangs and scuffles of a fight. She gasped when she saw Dante and Cain fighting, each one landing blows and trying to subdue the other. They wrestled on the floor, fists and feet flying and connecting with the other person. She didn't like this. She didn't want them hurting each other.

"Lucas, stop them! I don't want them hurt." She pleaded as she turned towards him. All anger momentarily forgotten, she put her hand on his forearm in a pleading gesture.

"If you stop Dante, the wolf will come." Gio warned her with a serious expression.

"It's fine," she mumbled softly, her fingers tightening on Lucas's arm. "I have to face him eventually."

"No, you don't, Kee," Conrad finally said from behind them. "You killed Noah because he tried to kill you. You owe Cain nothing."

"But he has no idea what happened to me, Conrad. He heard Noah admit to being sent to kill me, but I murdered his best friend right in front of him before he could ask any questions." She defended. "He deserves to know why I'm killing his pack members."

"Noah's confession should be enough to explain it, Kee." Her wolf interjected. "You don't have to face him."

"Yes, I do." She shook her head and looked at Lucas. "He needs to hear it from me."

Lucas stared down at her. "This is what you wish to do? Think hard because if I call off Dante, I will not call him back to help should Cain get out of hand."

She straightened her spine. "That's fine, I'll handle him."

He stared at her a few seconds longer before turning back to the fight. "Dante, let him pass."

Dante hesitated for a moment before rolling away from the wolf's claws. He leapt to his feet, but pressed his back against the wall, leaving the hallway clear. He crossed his arms over his chest and sneered at the wolf when Cain rose to his feet and stormed past him. He watched as he ventured closer to Lucas' room and frowned. "Do you want me to stay?"

Lucas shook his head. "No, we will take care of it. Resume your position at the front."

"Yes, sir." He replied dutifully before heading back up the stairs to the club.

Lucas' eyes stayed on Cain as he closed the distance between them. He nodded at Giovanni to leave and then stepped aside to let the werewolf into the room. He closed the door and watched carefully as

Cain swung his head towards Keira, his claws flexing. "Kee." Conrad warned as he took a step towards Cain.

Lucas held up his hand to stop Conrad from advancing further. "Let's see what he does."

Kee stared up at Cain's wolf face, her heart thrashing against her chest. Her eyes met his and she took a single step back when he released a low growl. She lifted her hands into a defensive position when he started to move towards her. She was ready to fight him, ready to defend herself if she needed to. She opened her mouth to warn him, but snapped it shut when he shifted back into his human form and dropped to his knees in front of her.

"Kee." Cain breathed, his voice a strange mix of helplessness and relief. He wrapped his arms around her waist and pressed his face to her stomach, letting out a shaky breath.

He hadn't been dreaming earlier. She really was alive. He had barged into Byte with an agonized rage, wanting answers to fill some of the emptiness he felt. But seeing Kee again washed away his anger and filled his hollowness with relief. "You really are alive."

Her face softened as he held her almost desperately. She slowly lifted her hands and placed them on his head, petting his hair. He had trimmed his hair again, the sides shorter while the top was a bit more grown out. His facial hair was still longer than a stubble, but it was even and well groomed. Besides earlier that night, it had been over a month since she saw him.

"Yeah." She said softly as she stroked his hair. Her chest constricted when he looked up at her with glistening eyes.

"No fucking thanks to your wolf pack!" Conrad suddenly shouted, hands balled into fists.

"Conrad." Kee warned gently.

"Conrad?" Cain echoed as he looked at the fuming, blonde man next to Lucas. He inhaled deeply, catching the man's scent. His eyes widened in surprise. "You're in your human form?"

"Surprise." He replied sarcastically.

Cain climbed to his feet and stood at his full naked height, towering over Kee as he glared at Conrad. "You," he sneered and bared his teeth. "You knew she was alive and didn't tell me? You've been with her all along, haven't you? You saw me at the pack meeting and didn't think to tell me?"

"Why would I tell you when I thought you were the one who did it?" Conrad shot back with a growl.

"Did what?" He growled low, his aura expanding in warning.

"Leave him alone, Cain." Kee reprimanded.

He didn't ease his aura. "No, tell me, Conrad, what do you think I did?"

"Orchestrated the attack on Keira, of course." Lucas explained evenly when he sensed the wolves getting ready to attack each other. He respected Conrad, but he knew Cain would win in a fight. Cain was born to be an alpha, Conrad he wasn't so sure about.

Cain whirled to face the vampire with a snarl. "You're out of your fucking mind if you think I would hurt her!" A tremor went through his body when another wave of anger hit him. "And *you!* *You* lied to me! When she first disappeared, I came to you and asked if you've talked to her! When you said no, I asked if you knew what happened to her and you still replied no!" He gestured at Kee with claws protruding from his human hand. "Well, here she is with you. She's been here the whole time, hasn't she? You son of a bitch!"

"Yes, she has been here." Lucas answered with a smooth shrug. "And, I did not lie to you. She was unconscious when you came to me, still fighting for her life. So, I did not, in fact, speak to her, nor did I know at the time what happened to her. We wanted everyone to think she was dead, but I did not lie to you."

"Don't act like a damn fae, Lucas! The fae weave truths around lies, not vampires!"

"Wait, wait, Cain came looking for me?" She asked, looking at Lucas suspiciously. When he simply nodded, she glared at him. "When? And why didn't you tell me?"

"He came the day after you were attacked," he admitted, a knot forming in his stomach. "And I did not tell you because you were unconscious."

"That's a bullshit excuse!" She snapped. "You could have told me when I was awake! You've had a month, Lucas!"

"For what reason would I have told you? You were a ball of unstable, torrid emotions, Keira. You were setting up your plan to get your revenge and you did not need the interference." Lucas' eyes narrowed when she growled at him. "I did it with your best interest in mind."

"You mean like how you and Conrad chose not to tell me how you guys started to doubt that Cain had set the whole thing up? What if I had killed him tonight? What then, Lucas?" She accused angrily. "If I killed him when he was innocent, I never would have forgiven myself!"

She was suddenly mortified.

*Oh gods, I was going to kill him.*

"Why do you think I would have tried to have you killed, Kee? Why would any of you think that? I love her, I wouldn't hurt her!" Cain defended himself as his clawed hands fisted at his sides.

"But have you not already?" Lucas shot back with a knowing scoff. "I seem to remember a scuffle that ended in a broken phone."

She felt Cain's aura expand with a snap of energy that shocked her senses. Before she could put a hand on his arm to stop him, he shifted into his hybrid wolf form and launched himself at Lucas. "Cain!" She shouted incredulously.

Lucas was ready for him. The werewolf may be taller than him by over a foot in his hybrid form, but Lucas was faster. He caught Cain's furry wrist and spun around to kick him hard in the back. Cain faltered forward from the impact, but remained upright. Cain turned back to his opponent and lurched at him again. Lucas moved back, but Cain had a longer reach in his current form. He punched Lucas in the face with his right hand, and then in his stomach with his left.

"Stop it!" Kee shouted as she watched the two men fight. Her heart was constricted. She felt torn as she watched the two of them go at it. She didn't want either of them to get hurt. They both meant too much to her.

Lucas snarled and blocked the third hit. He ducked under Cain's arm and tackled him. They skidded towards the couch, knocking it over before they hit the floor. Lucas sat on Cain's chest and returned the punches without holding back. He felt Cain's cheek bone crack under the force from his first hit, his snout dislocating on the second.

Undeterred, Cain snapped his jaws at Lucas's neck, teeth sinking into his throat. He clenched down and tried to shake his head, but Lucas's hands gripped Cain's furry neck to hold him in place. Lucas tightened his grip, choking the wolf as Cain bit down harder. Lucas was strangling Cain to keep him from ripping his throat out, but he would break the wolf's neck if he had to.

"Stop!" Kee cried as she flung herself at Lucas's back. "Let go! Both of you!"

Neither one could talk, but the glares they gave each other spoke for them. They were at a standstill. Either Cain would rip Lucas' throat out, or Lucas would snap Cain's neck. Neither one wanted to give in first. Neither wanted to be the loser. Cain bit down harder making the vampire cough up blood. At the same time, Lucas tightened his hold, the werewolf's body shuddering from lack of air.

"I said stop!" Kee screamed. She fisted her hand in Lucas's hair while sliding her hand over his shoulder to grab a handful of fur on

Cain's face. She gave each grip a firm pull. "Let. Go."

"Kee, no one wants to be the first one to submit." Conrad explained, staying back from the power struggle. "They'll stay that way until the other hesitates."

She sneered down at them. "Are you kidding me? Stop this fucking pissing contest! When I count to three you both let go at the same time. If you kill each other, I will never forgive either of you. Do you understand me?" They both growled and she took it as affirmation. She released their hair, but remained molded to Lucas' back in case their egos got ahead of them.

She counted to one and the two men glared at each other, their eyes blazing with hate for the other. She got to two and their holds on each other flexed as if daring the other to do something. When she got to three, they simultaneously released each other.

Kee sighed in relief and pulled away when Lucas stood up from Cain's body. She frowned at the blood flowing from the gaping wound in his neck, flaps of his skin hanging from where Cain had torn his teeth away. She quickly covered the wound with her hand, trying to stop the bleeding.

She looked at Cain as he shifted back to his human form. Her brow furrowed when he started hacking and gasping for air. His cheek was swollen and blood gushed from his nose. "Cain, are you okay?" She asked as he sat up and put a hand to his neck.

"I'll live." He growled, his voice rough.

She gave him a relieved smile and then looked at Lucas when he put his hand on her wrist. "And what about you?" She questioned softly.

"I will survive," he answered as he pulled her bloodied hand away. "But I have to find Aubrey. I need to feed to fix this."

Something twisted in her stomach at the reminder of his feeder. *Was that jealousy?*

She stepped back from him. "I didn't know she was here."

"Even if she is not, I need to feed from someone." Lucas replied pointedly. He could feel her irritation through the bond and couldn't help but scowl. She had no right to be jealous when she clearly still had feelings for Cain. "Unless you are offering yourself up?"

"You mean so you can almost drain her like last time? Fuck no." Cain snarled as he got to his feet. "Or do you not remember attacking her in her home? Leaving her almost empty on her bed?"

Kee put her hands on Lucas' chest, keeping him in place when he tensed like a snake about to strike. "Don't," she pleaded and then shot Cain a glare. "Don't start up again, Cain. No more fighting."

Cain pursed his lips together and looked away, but his expression was still angry. "He made a jab at me for hurting you when he's guilty of the same thing."

Conrad growled at Cain. "But his people didn't try to kill her; yours did."

Kee sighed when Cain went rigid and looked at her with a confused stare. "It's true, Cain." She blushed when he moved closer to her, his nakedness making her eyes wander. "I'll tell you about it, but let me give you these clothes." She murmured as she gestured at the baggy clothes that were still on her. She looked back up at Lucas when he shifted away from her. "Will you be back?"

His eyes bore down into hers. "Do you want me to? Or do you want privacy with Mr Donovan?"

She frowned at his mocking tone. "He just needs to know what happened."

Lucas stared at her with a blank expression. He was foolish to think that she would forget her love for Cain so easily. He really thought she would be able to force herself to hate him. *I underestimated our situation. I was blind in my yearning.* "Then he will relive it the way I had."

"What?" She asked, but he pushed past her and approached Cain.

The hackles on Cain's neck rose as the vampire approached him with a cold glare. He lifted his fists when Lucas' eyes turned to him. "Stay back, or I'll rip your throat out for real this time."

"Let me compel you, Mr Donovan, and see what happened to our shapeshifter through her eyes." Lucas said as he caught Cain's gaze and called upon his compulsion, his eyes shifting to red. He tried to sink into the wolf's mind with his magic, but felt him resist. He scowled at Cain and flared his power. "Do you not wish to know what happened?"

Cain sneered, but couldn't break eye contact with him. He felt a mist of warmth blanket his head as he began to slip under Lucas's compulsion. He grit his teeth, hands fisted at his sides. "Don't make me." He bit out, trying not to sink under the wave of control.

"Then let me in and I will not have to force myself." Lucas growled back. He was weakening from the blood loss of his wound and spending the energy to compel the stubborn wolf wasn't improving his situation.

"It might be easier if you see it for yourself, Cain." Kee suggested gently, biting her lip. "That way you can understand it from my point of view and know why I did what I did."

Cain looked at her and grimaced when she nodded at him. "Fine." With a heavy, defeated exhale, he dropped his guard and let Lucas in.

Lucas didn't reply to him as he took advantage of the vanished mental block. He slipped into Cain's mind like a key in a lock. He stepped forward and cupped the sides of Cain's head, projecting the night of Keira's attack into his mind.

Conrad sauntered up to his alpha's side as Cain's eyes glazed over. He put a hand on her shoulder when she pursed her lips nervously. "It's better this way." He assured her.

She put her hand on his and squeezed it. "I hope so." She bit her lip when Cain twitched, his body flinching as he was forced to watch what happened to her.

Lucas waited until Keira fired the bullet into Wyatt's head before switching the scene to his point of view. He showed him her marred body and then the aftermath of the stitches before pulling away from Cain. He staggered back as a wave of dizziness washed over him.

He put a hand to his head and held up the other to stop Keira when she tried to steady him. "No," he told her as he backed up to the door and tried to ignore how hurt she looked. "I need to feed. If you touch me, I will bite you."

Kee slowly pulled her hand back and frowned as he quickly left the room. She turned towards Cain and saw him down on his knees. His face was scrunched up in hurt and confusion, his eyes lost. She hesitated before approaching him. She squatted down and gingerly touched his uninjured cheek. "Cain?"

He looked at her and then down at her torso. He gently grabbed the hem of the shirt. "I need to see it. I need to know this was real." He breathed with an undertone of panic echoing in his words.

She didn't understand what he was asking until she saw his eyes jump from her shoulder to her hip. Lucas must have shown him just how badly she was injured, exposed the scars she was still embarrassed of. She lifted her arms and let him pull his shirt off of her. She closed her eyes when his fingertips gently touched her scars. She angled her head away from him when he began to trace them over her breasts and down across her torso.

His face crumpled as he finished following the white lines down her body. "Kee," he whined. "I'm so sorry. I just...I don't understand. I don't know why they would do this to you."

She went to cover her chest, but was pulled in tightly against his hot, naked body. She wrapped her arms around his shoulders and buried her face in his neck. She inhaled the scent of him, the sweet, fresh smell of pine and citrus. She felt her heart leap to her throat and her eyes stung.

Cain held her to him for a few moments later before pulling back so he could press soft kisses to her lips. "I want to undo everything they did," he whispered against her lips. "You didn't deserve this. I'm so, so sorry." He repeated again as he cupped her face in his hands.

"Cain," she pressed her forehead against his when she saw his eyes mist up again. "I'm sorry that I thought you had planned it. I was so upset, so mortified at what happened to me. And the way Noah was talking made it sound like you had told him everything and I just didn't know what to do."

He pressed his lips against hers again. "I heard what he said and I swear I haven't told anyone your secret, Kee. I wouldn't do that to you. You know you can trust me."

"Then why would they attack her?" Conrad asked sharply, eyes narrowed at the pair. He liked Cain, the beta had always been nice to him, but his loyalty was to Kee. She needed to know the truth and if Cain knew anything, he needed to tell them.

Cain lifted his lip in a snarl at Conrad as he drew away from Kee. "I'm getting tired of you challenging me, Conrad."

"I don't care. Kee's my alpha, not you." He growled back with a hard glare.

He scoffed as he picked up the red shirt Kee had stolen from him and handed it to her so she could cover herself. "She can't be your alpha."

Conrad bared his teeth. "Why? Because she's a girl? Or because she isn't a werewolf?"

"You told him?" He asked incredulously as he whirled on her. "You barely know him! How do you know he wasn't the one who planned your attack?"

"He chose me as his alpha and I trust him, Cain." Kee defended in a calm tone as she stood up and clutched the shirt to her naked chest.

Cain leapt to his feet. "You can't be his alpha, Kee! You're not a wolf!"

"I was born from two werewolves. I have wolf blood in me." She countered irritably.

"Yeah, but you're—," he stopped himself when her face suddenly went cold and distant. Even when they had their little fights, she never looked at him like that. Who was this person?

"I'm what Cain? A girl? You think girls can't be dominant? Can't rule a pack? That's an old way of thinking." She took a step back when he reached for her. "Plus, Conrad is the one who found me. If he wanted me dead, he would have left me to die."

Conrad put his hands on Kee's bare shoulders as he stood behind her. "I helped her get revenge."

Cain was quiet as he processed what the other wolf had said. "Warren's address book. You took it." When Conrad nodded, he glanced at Kee with guarded eyes. "Were you the one who killed Brandon?"

She met his eyes without flinching. "Yes."

"Fuck, Kee," he ran his hand down his face. "There had to be another way."

"Not for me." She retorted simply with a shrug.

"Why?"

"They tried to kill me so I killed them in return."

He looked at her with bitter confusion. "Who *are* you?"

She stiffened under Conrad's hands. "I don't know." She told him honestly. "Someone stronger than who I used to be."

"Kee, what happened to you was horrible and it breaks my heart that it occurred," Cain started in a gentle tone. "But, you aren't a murderer. This isn't you."

"Are you saying I didn't deserve to kill them? That they didn't deserve to die? They tried to kill me, Cain! And they all thought they had! What if I *had* died? Would you still think they didn't deserve it?" She snapped and pulled away from Conrad when he tried to calm her down.

"Of course they would deserve it, but you're *alive*, Kee!" He stressed. "And my wolves are dead instead!"

"Would you prefer it the other way around?" She taunted.

He looked horror stricken at her words. "Of course not! You have no idea how fucked up I was when I thought you were dead, Kee!" He lifted his palms up helplessly. "How many times do I have to tell you that I want you to be my mate? I love you."

"How do you expect me to be your mate when you can't accept what I've done? What I still need to do?" At his startled look, she sighed. "Someone planned this, Cain. I need to find out who did it."

"And then you'll kill them, too?" He murmured.

"Yes," she replied confidently. "Then I'll put this all behind me. Or, at least try to."

"Why do you have to kill them?"

"So they don't have a chance to try it again."

"And?"

"To make me feel better." She admitted when he rubbed his face again in exasperation. "I don't know what else to tell you except that this is personal. I almost died and I'm going to get my revenge."

"Tell me one thing." He demanded, his tone cool. "You thought I was the one who planned this, right?" When she nodded, he clenched his hands into fists again. "Would you really have killed me if I had?"

She sucked in a breath as she hesitated. She had been struggling with that question since she woke up from her attack. "I don't know." She answered, but once the words were out she knew they weren't true. She wouldn't have been able to do it. She could never kill Cain, no matter how much she told herself to.

He tensed and had to stop himself from showing the betrayal he felt. "Give me my clothes, Kee." She opened her mouth to say something, but held up his hand to stop her. He wasn't ready to hear anything else. His heart couldn't take any more strain for the day. "I need to go."

The ache in her chest returned with a painful throb. "Okay." She breathed. She slowly handed him her favorite red shirt. They looked down at the shirt when he reached for it, both of them frowning. She looked away and let go, not watching as he pulled it on.

Conrad pulled off his shirt and handed it to Kee. "Here."

She accepted it with a grateful look and slid it on before stepping out the baggy jeans. "Do you want your boxers, too?" She asked as she handed the pants to him.

He eyed the black boxers on her and shook his head. His shirt was already saturated in her scent and he wouldn't be able to leave if the scent of her pussy was on him as well. He tugged on the jeans and carefully zipped them up to avoid any snagging. When he was dressed, he avoided looking at her as he headed to the door. He grabbed the handle to the door and hesitated. "When you can answer my question, let me know."

She already had her answer, but nodded anyway. They both needed a little more time apart after their revelations. "I will."

He tightened his grip on the knob. "I love you."

"I love you, too."

He gave a small smile, but didn't trust himself to look back at her. He opened the door and left, hoping she would find the answer he wanted to hear. Until then, he had a lot of thinking to do. He wanted to feel she was justified for killing his fellow wolves and he would admit that a part of him agreed with her. However she had killed his pack.

*But this is Kee, the one I want to mate.* Cain thought as he headed out of the club, ignoring the security as they sneered at him. He hated what happened to her. His beast was thirsty for the blood she already spilled in vengeance. But, would he have been able to fight his brothers? His wolf scoffed, and he had to agree. Of course he would have fought them.

He suddenly realized why he was so upset. It was because he had failed her. He should have been the one to kill them in her place *before* they got to sink their claws in her. If she came to him with an answer, he would explain to her the epiphany he had come to. He just hoped she would make the right choice.

# Twenty-Six

Kee sat awake on Lucas' king-sized bed while Conrad snored softly next to her in his human form. She smiled softly at the sight and brushed a few hairs away from his face. He really was too good to her. Since he declared her his alpha, he had been nothing but supportive. He constantly had her back and kept her calm. Her smile faded as she stroked the blonde strands. He deserved a better alpha. He deserved someone strong and reliable, like Cain. She wouldn't force Conrad away from her, but maybe she could convince him to rethink his choice.

She glanced up when the door opened and felt tension fill the room as Lucas made eye contact with her. She peeked at the clock and then back to him. "It's nearly dawn." She commented quietly.

He looked at the antique clock on the wall. "So it is."

"Your throat looks better. Did you find Aubrey?" She asked, trying to ease some of the strain between them.

"No." He hadn't been able to find his bleeder. It was odd considering she spent the majority of her nights in the club, reaping the benefits of her status. She received free drinks and food as well access to any of the rooms upstairs should she need them. None of his staff questioned or denied her unless she broke one of the conditions of their contract.

"Oh, that's weird." She bit her lip when he hummed in response. They lapsed into an awkward silence she couldn't stand. "I was worried you weren't going to come back."

"And I assumed you had left." He retorted as he walked towards his closet, unbuttoning his shirt as he did.

She raised an eyebrow at him. "You thought I left, but still waited until dawn to come back?"

"Perhaps I did not want to know for sure if you had fled with your wolf." He disappeared into the closet for a few moments before reemerging in black pajama pants that hung low on his hips.

She watched him walk towards his couch, trying futilely not to stare at the expanse of his toned chest. "Conrad and I are still here."

"He is not the wolf I was referring to."

Her stomach knotted as he continued to talk in a monotonous, distant voice. "As I said, we're still here."

"So it seems," he commented as he gracefully laid down on his leather couch. He heard her rise from the bed and softly pad over to him. He closed his eyes and made sure his unnecessary breathing stayed even. "Yes, Miss Quinn?"

"Why are you acting this way?" Kee asked as she crossed her arms across her chest. "And why are you sleeping on the couch? Shouldn't I be the one who's mad?"

"You are welcomed to feel any way you wish to so long as you keep it from echoing through the bond."

She uncrossed her arms and threw her hands up. "What did I do, Lucas? Yes, I got mad at you for keeping your doubts about Cain from me! Yes, I was angry that you two were fighting! Was there something else?"

"Everything comes back to Cain, doesn't it?" He asked pointedly.

"What's that supposed to mean?"

"Desiring him to be innocent, wanting to talk to him, needing to stop the fight to save him," he waved his hand in a circle. "You get my point."

"Of course I wanted him to be innocent, Lucas. I didn't want him to be the one behind my attack because I wouldn't have been able to kill him. I needed to talk to him because he deserved to know the truth," she explained. She walked closer and bent so she could poke him in the chest. "And I stopped the fight to save you *both*. I can't stand the thought of losing either of you."

He opened his eyes and grabbed her hand when she jammed her finger in his chest again. "Either of us?"

"Well, yeah," she mumbled when he tugged her closer towards him. "You're both important to me."

"So I am important to you?" Lucas was pleased when she climbed on top of him, straddling his hips and resting her hands on his bare stomach. He sighed softly as her touch cooled the fire of his anger. "You are also important to me. I have grown attached to you this past month."

"We've grown a lot closer." She agreed quietly, drawing circles on his stomach. "And I realize I've been selfish."

"Oh?" He ran his hands down her arms and then rested them on her knees.

Kee caught his curious gaze and nodded. "Lucas, you've done so much for me since my attack. I was so consumed with my revenge that I took you for granted. Conrad, too. I've thought about how much you have helped me and I realized I haven't really thanked you." She glanced away in shame and stared down at his pale, smooth torso again. She swallowed and then peeked back up at him almost shyly. "Thank you so, so much. Really. I don't know how to repay you."

His eyes softened. "I did not help you expecting repayment, Keira."

He stroked her thighs with his thumbs. "I wanted to help you." He admitted unabashedly.

She rested her hands on his shoulders when he sat up, his hands going to her hips. "I still want to repay you," she answered and bit the inside of her cheek nervously. "And I thought of something that only I can give you."

He tilted his head in question. "There are many things only you can give me, Keira." He replied as he ran his hands up to cup her breasts through her thin shirt.

She blushed and swallowed thickly. "I've happily given you that, but I'm always down to do it again," she commented with a smirk. "But really, there's something else that I know you want, but someone told me it will come with some more side effects." She said with a nervous laugh.

His face shifted to a serious expression. "Your blood?"

She dipped her head in a quick nod. "Yeah. I mean, if you don't mind deepening our bond?"

Lucas stared up at her, his eyes searching hers. He cupped the underneath of her jaw and tilted her head to the side, exposing her neck to him. "I would love to sink my fangs into your soft, warm neck," he gently nipped the skin, but made sure he didn't so much as scratch the surface. "I want to taste your exotic blood and swallow your scorching essence."

Her eyes fluttered shut when he gently scraped his teeth over the tender area once again. She felt his cock swell under her and she pressed down against it wantonly. She felt him press a soft kiss to her pulse, but then he abruptly released her jaw. She blinked and looked at him as he pulled back. "Lucas?"

"However, I do not want you to offer it to me because you feel indebted to me." His voice was firm with an icy edge to make sure he made his point. "I told you I would not feed from you again. If you truly want me to, then I will gladly do so, but I will not do it simply because you feel obligated to."

Kee felt her face flush in humiliation. "T-that's not how I meant it at all."

"You are careless with your words, Keira." He scolded as he reclined back against the leather cushions, no longer touching her. "The sun is rising and I must sleep."

It was a subtle dismissal, but she could feel the irritation from him through the bond. It was the first time she had ever felt something from his side of their connection and it hit her like a punch to the gut. She quickly scrambled off his lap and made a bee-line to the bed. She climbed into the bed and rolled over so her back was towards the couch. She burrowed under the duvet and covered her mouth with her hand.

*What just happened? I've never felt him before and when I finally do it was such a hostile thing. He was more than irritated. He was angry.* She thought anxiously.

Lucas stared up at his ceiling as he honed in on the bond they shared. She was such an emotional person. She could never decide what she wanted to feel, her emotions always mixed and jumbled. Currently she was mortified, upset, and sad. What else did he expect? He was still bitter about the entire ordeal with Cain and hadn't bothered to rein in his frustration.

He did not want to share Keira and tonight he understood that she still loved Cain. Really, it had only been short of five weeks since the couple had fought. It had been wishful thinking to assume that any emotional bonds she had with Cain would have been severed when she blamed him for the attack.

Love was a concept he had difficulty understanding. He had people who served him and fawned over him. Perhaps there were even some who loved him, but he had only a small handful of people he had ever cared about. But, love? He couldn't say for sure if he had ever felt the emotion. Every time he had come close to the experience, it had been ripped away from him.

He frowned as his mind took him back to the first woman he cared about as a vampire.

*"Janrie." Lucas cooed as he strolled into the formal living room of him and Florence's manor in England. He smoothed his hands down the leather vest he wore over his dark blue and black striped doublet. The bottom of his brown breeches were rounded out around his knees and disappeared under his tall boots. His hair hung around his shoulders in waves, the black a stark contrast to the white, lace collar that flared around his neck.*

*"Lord Vranas." She greeted with a shy smile and curtsied low. She giggled as he came up behind her, wrapping his arms around her small waist. Despite being dressed in her plain, beige servant's dress and dark brown apron, he always made her feel like royalty.*

*He inhaled the permanent lily scent of her silk skin and smirked. She was almost the same height as him, her pointed ears level with his mouth. Her ash blonde hair was pulled up into a bun and tucked under a white bonnet-like cap. "Tonight?" He whispered.*

*She shuddered against him. "Yes."*

*"Good. I cannot describe it, but the taste of you and your body leave me forever starved." He purred as his hands slid to her hips. His mouth hovered over the exposed skin by her jaw. "You are a goddess, Janrie."*

*"What is going on here?" A cold, feminine voice demanded.*

*Lucas stepped away from the elf servant and looked at his maker. She was dressed in an emerald silk dress that was tight around her torso and flared out at her waist. Long sleeves billowed down from her pale arms, a long stretch of fabric hanging from behind her shoulders like a cape. Her dark red hair was piled up into an artfully sculpted bun, small pins with jewels inserted into it for decoration. Her cheeks had been powdered pink, her lips already a natural light rose color.*

*Light brown eyes glared hard at him as he tried to calm her with his words. "Lady Florence." He greeted sweetly. "I was informing Lady Janrie that I require fresh linen in my room."*

*"Hm," she replied, clearly unconvinced. "Lucas, you are to greet our guests and entertain them as needed until I arrive."*

*"What will you be doing, my lovely master?" He asked cautiously. She never liked him questioning her, but he had always been a curious one.*

*She glanced at Janrie with her emotionless brown eyes. "I have a matter I must attend to."*

*He frowned, but didn't comment on it. Instead, he dutifully bowed to her. "Yes, my Lady."*

*That night after the guests left, he headed back to his room. As soon as he pushed open the heavy wood door, the scent of death and stale blood assaulted his nose. He let out a dreadful sigh, already knowing what awaited him. He stalked into the room and headed to his bed. He saw Janrie sprawled out on his blankets as naked as the day she was born. She had been drained of her blood. Florence had obviously drank her fill before slicing each of the elf's wrists and then her neck, leaving Janrie's head to flop awkwardly to the side.*

*He gently stroked her cold cheek with the back of his fingers before wrapping a blanket around her nude form. On his nightstand was a pile of fresh linen sheets, a note with elegant cursive sitting on top of it.*

'Fresh linen, as requested.

-F'

*He crumpled the note and glanced back at Janrie's pretty, narrow face. It was his fault she ended up this way. He let himself get attached to her and plan a future he knew they couldn't have together. He should have known that the ever jealous Florence would have never allowed another female to gain his attention, let alone a servant from a different race.*

Lucas had been a new vampire at the time, barely half a century. He had thought that he had just been naive. That perhaps he had just been careless with Janrie. After many more cities and finally parting ways with his maker, he ventured back to London centuries later.

He met an intriguing, seductive vampire with ice blue eyes and hair as black as his own. He properly courted her, as was deemed necessary in England during the 1800s, but kept it quiet. He tried to keep his interest in her guarded and he thought it had worked. They were together for a few months and it was spectacular. Sometimes they would attend private shows at the theatre, or perhaps low-key social parties together. They would often feed from the same source simultaneously, draining their victim without a care. They would then indulge in the pleasures of the flesh, fucking like animals next to the empty corpse without a single remorse.

It was beautiful.

*Dressed in a white shirt, deep purple silk vest, and his favorite black tailcoat, Lucas went to call upon his Bridgett. His brow furrowed when her servants did not answer the door within a few heartbeats. He removed his top hat and nervously smoothed back his shoulder length hair before knocking again.*

*After a few more minutes of silence, he tried the door handle and pushed it open when he found it wasn't locked. His stomach dropped when death permeated the Victorian house. The bodies of her servants littered the floor like rubbish, blood and other bodily fluids seeping through the rugs to stain the wood beneath them. With a heavy heart, he hurried up the stairs to Bridgett's room, practically leaping up the staircase. He kicked open her door, the wood flying halfway across the room, and shouted in frustration to see her staked upon her four-post bed.*

*"Bridgett." Lucas murmured solemnly as he pulled the wooden stake from her heart. He set it down on her nightstand and frowned at the pile*

*of crisp, folded sheets. He lifted the white note from the top of it and snarled at the familiar penmanship.*

'Did you require more fresh linen?

-F'

*He threw down the note with a curse and turned from the room. He hadn't seen his maker in seventy-three years; not since they parted ways in France. Apparently she was still keeping tabs on him and clearly he had not hidden his relationship with Bridgett well enough. Once again, he had let himself get close to a woman and it had cost her her life.*

Lucas closed his eyes and rubbed his temples at the memories. Since then, he did not dabble in relationships. He had crafted a mental blockade and kept out any unnecessary emotions. He satisfied his needs and urges for blood and sex, but did not form personal relationships with those he used.

Aubrey was his bleeder, but he only cared for her as much as the contract demanded. He would admit that he favored Giovanni, but that was because he made him. Lucas tried to make it a point to not be like Florence. He wanted to have a good relationship with Giovanni and care for him the way Florence didn't care for him.

However, he cared for his shapeshifter. When he first met her, he simply saw a tool to be used. A rare instrument that only he would have, or know of. It would make him stronger than ever. He had been disappointed to discover she only knew how to shift into animals, but it was still an extremely useful skill. He doubted she realized just how lethal she could be now that she could shift into people.

That train of thoughts brought him back to the question he found himself constantly asking himself since he brought her to Byte. *When did she become more than a tool?*

Slowly she had seeped through his barriers. He did not hesitate to shed his blood to save her life even though he knew it would create a permanent connection with her. Maybe he wanted the bond as a way to feel closer to her, to understand her better. He wasn't sure. What he was certain of was the raw anger he had felt when she admitted she loved Cain.

*If she is a tool, then why am I so livid?* His eyes narrowed at his revelation. Because she's more than that. She has been for a long time. *Then why am I pushing her away?*

He knew the answer. He didn't wish to share her and hated that he couldn't keep her for himself. He let out a silent sigh as he felt his body begin to shut down as the sun crept into the sky. He would have to ponder everything at a later time.

# *Twenty-Seven*

Sitting in Lucas' office, Kee typed away at his computer as she searched for apartments for her and Conrad. It had been a week since the falling out with Cain and Lucas and she was done feeling sorry for herself. Cain hadn't tried texting her, obviously waiting for her to come to him, and Lucas simply wasn't speaking to her.

She could feel him two stories beneath her in the basement, sleeping along with the other vampires of his coven. In less than an hour he would rise and their silent, tense war would continue. She had been sleeping in one of the spare bedrooms on the fourth floor so that Lucas could have his bedroom to himself. Conrad, of course, had followed her.

She sighed and drew her hands away from the keyboard so she could lean back in the leather chair. Her relationships were all sorts of screwed at the moment. *Maybe I should just give up on dating all together.*

She looked down at Lucas' polished black desk and felt her cheeks warm as she remembered the first time they had sex. It had been amazing. He had been careful yet thorough, catering to and satisfying her needs. The other times after that had been intense and rough, but in the best kind of way. He always made sure she came, sometimes twice. They had begun to learn the other's kinks and quirks as well as their limitations and boundaries. They played into the other's desires and found common ground so they were both constantly satisfied.

She felt her pussy clench in desire, her panties going damp.

Kee was completely and utterly confused about how she felt for Lucas. She thought it was just an attraction at first. She had acted on the fleeting desire to have sex with him which then turned into wanting it more and more. However, she couldn't deny the feelings that had come bubbling up to the surface the longer they spent together. And not just from time in the bedroom.

Lucas made her laugh and listened with genuine interest when she spoke about something she was passionate about. Whether it be a book, a movie, or even an opinion, he cared. She found herself captivated when he opened up to her about random moments in his past that were triggered by mundane things. He would casually tell her historical facts about certain foods, or slangs, or even clothing trends when they were brought up. She had laughed when she tried to imagine him in a white powdered wig in France. She loved his smile and his laugh, especially when the tips of his fangs showed. That was when she knew he truly found something amusing.

*What the fuck is happening?* She groaned to herself, pressing her hand to her forehead. *How long have I felt this way? Is it even real? Or only because we're bonded and have been spending time together?*

She looked up when the door opened and smiled at Conrad and Lucy as they came in laughing. Lucy was a petite, arctic werefox. She was almost the same height as Kee, maybe an inch shorter, with hair so blonde it was nearly white. Her eyes were a light, pale green and her skin a flawless cream. She had an enviable beauty, but her personality and humor was what made Kee instantly like the bartender.

Kee had been at the bar quite a few times Lucy worked and had liked her from the start. The fox could nicely turn down unwanted advances and in the next moment completely shut down an egotistical drunk who didn't take her rejection well. Most of the time it left Kee laughing on her barstool. After she found out Cain wasn't behind her attack, she had stopped hiding her appearance in the bar and introduced herself to Lucy. It had only been a week, but Kee could tell they were going to be good friends.

"What's so funny?" Kee asked with a smile as Lucy let out another giggle.

"Lucy was telling me about one of the other shifter security guards. He thought he could take her home and then grabbed her arm when she said no. So, she kicked him in the balls." He answered with a laugh despite his wolf grumbling unhappily.

Conrad had met Lucy shortly after Kee's attack. They had quite literally run into each other in the kitchen when he had come up to make lunch for him and Kee. After exchanging clumsy apologies, he learned that she was one of the lead bartenders at Byte. He limited the truth to his presence and said he was training with Dante. After that, whenever they saw each other around the bar, they would stop and chat for a while. Conrad found the friendship to be a refreshing change from all the vampires around him.

"You should have seen him, Kee!" Lucy said as she plopped down in one of the chairs on the other side of Lucas' desk. "He wasn't so dominant anymore! Down on his knees, grabbing his balls and practically crying like a little bitch. It was one of my finer moments."

Kee laughed. "I wish I could have seen it."

The fox pouted at her. "Where were you last night, anyways? I miss our girl talks at the bar."

"Sorry, Luce, I had to finish packing up my apartment. I have until tomorrow to get all my stuff out so I threw it all in storage until we find an apartment." She replied.

"Wine night soon then? We need to get away from Byte and go somewhere else for a change! Why don't you come over to my apartment? Or, we can break into your apartment when you get the new one!"

"Sounds like a date," Kee winked and turned to Conrad. "Do you have any other preferences for the apartment?"

He shrugged. "I'm not picky, Kee." He then opened his arms and did a little spin, showing off his new security uniform. "What do you think?"

Kee looked at the black jeans that fit well on his legs and the tight black shirt that hugged his toned torso. 'Security' was sprawled across his shoulder blades in white letters, the club's name and emblem stamped in the same color on the left side of his chest. Around his waist was a utility belt that held a flashlight and a high voltage Taser. His honey blonde hair was pulled back into a ponytail at the base of his neck so it was out of the way.

She clapped appreciatively. "What a stud." She grinned when he blushed and looked away. "I know a certain wolf who would definitely appreciate the view."

Lucy giggled, but it sounded forced. "Oh yeah, Cassie will be practically drooling over how your ass looks. Which is *fine*, by the way."

The blush crept down his neck. "You guys are exaggerating."

"We're not," Lucy interjected as she gave him another admiring once over. "The wolf is seriously into you, Conrad. I think she even spilled her tray of drinks one night because she was too busy watching you."

"She's right. I've seen how she looks at you." Kee added with a smirk. "She's from the Inglewood pack, right? Why not give it a go?"

He gave a one shoulder shrug and looked away from her. "I'm not really looking to date. Besides, dating from different packs is risky."

"Why?" Kee questioned. "I don't care if you date someone from a different pack. I want you to be happy, Con."

His amber eyes softened as he turned back at her. "And I'm lucky to have an alpha who thinks that way," he began before giving a soft sigh. "Unfortunately not all alphas have that reasoning. If two wolves mate from two different packs, one has to join the other."

Lucy pursed her lips together. "I've heard about packs like that. It's usually the female who joins the male's because the female's alpha doesn't want an outside threat."

Kee rolled her eyes. "See? This is why I hate alphas and refuse to have one."

Lucy sighed dreamily and cradled her chin in her hands. "And so you became one. It's like a fairytale."

She shook her head with a laugh. "I'm only an alpha because Conrad chose me as his. You can become your own alpha if you need to, Luce."

"No way," she waved her hand in dismissal. "I can hardly care for myself. How am I supposed to care for other people? Fuck that. I'll just remain the stray in the LA skulk. As much as the alpha wants me to officially join, I just can't deal with all those horny foxes."

Kee laughed again and turned back to the computer. She glanced at the desk phone when the speaker crackled to life, asking for her. "This is Keira."

While Lucas was dead to the world, his employees began coming to her for direction. She had tried to tell them she wasn't in charge, but when they pointed out that she was his bonded wolf, she couldn't exactly argue it.

*"Señora, we have a delivery for Mr Vranas."* The security downstairs informed her.

As a precaution, Lucas had various types of wereanimals that guarded Byte at all hours. The club was only open at night, but he wanted to ensure his coven was safe while they slept during the day.

Miguel was their day security and was honestly her favorite. He was born in California, but spent his days off in Mexico with his family. He was always eager to share stories and pictures to anyone who would listen.

"What is it, Miguel?" She asked cautiously.

"*Flores,*" The werebear replied skeptically. "*There's a note, but it's not my place to read it.*"

"Flowers? Anything smell off about them?"

She could hear him inhaling deeply through his nose. "*Not at all, señora, just smells like flores and the human who delivered them.*"

"Weird. Go ahead and send them up."

"*I'll be right there.*"

"Thank you, Miguel." She heard the intercom on the speaker cut out and looked at Lucy's raised eyebrow. "What?"

"You going to read the note?" She pressed.

"No, it's not mine to read." Kee retorted. She tilted her head when the fox stood and shook her head. "What? You think I should?"

"All I'm saying is that I've noticed the distance between you and the boss man. You two used to flirt and look at each other with hunger, but now you two act like the other doesn't exist." When Kee glanced away from her, she sighed. "Look, people generally send flowers for three different reasons: love, apology, and death. If he's seeing another girl, I bet the flowers would be from her." She explained. At her friend's suddenly torn expression, she changed the subject. "It's time for me to set up the bar. I'll see you down there?"

"Probably," she muttered distractedly as her friend left.

*Is Lucy right? Is there another girl?* She shook her head. It wasn't her business.

She quickly stood up as Miguel walked in a few minutes after Lucy left. It was almost comical to see the large werebear holding a small vase with flowers in it. She took the vase from him and set it down on the desk. "Has Aubrey shown up yet?"

"No, señora. Still haven't seen a glimpse of her in days." He answered with a shrug. "I hope she's okay. She's an arrogant thing, but still nice."

She sighed. "I hope so, too. If you happen to see her, will you please send her up here? I know Lucas will want to talk to her once he's awake."

"Of course." He replied with a cheerful wave before leaving.

Conrad walked over to the desk and sat in the chair Lucy had been in. He looked at the dark red vase and the flowers within it. White lilies, white chrysanthemums, and black roses were arranged perfectly within it. He crossed his arms behind his head and grimaced. "That's a bouquet of death."

She nodded. "Nana once told me that lilies represented the soul becoming innocent again after death. And, I think I read somewhere that in Europe chrysanthemums are used for funerals." She gingerly rubbed a petal on one of the black roses. "These have been airbrushed black."

"Black roses are really rare. Most of the time they're dark red with hints of black." Conrad frowned when she grabbed the white envelope from the vase. "You think that's a good idea?"

"No, but he's already mad at me so what harm could it do?" She shrugged. "Pretty sure whatever we had is done anyways."

He gave another heavy sigh. "If you would just talk to him."

"I *tried*," she stressed. "I'm not going to fall to my knees at his feet and beg for forgiveness. I don't roll over for anyone anymore, Con, especially when I didn't mean to insult him in the first place."

He shook his head as he waved his hand at her. "At least read it out loud."

A small part of her had hoped he would have stopped her, but even as she broke the seal he didn't move to stop her. She pulled out the small white card and read it aloud.

*"Lord Lucas,*

*I do hope you're faring well. You've lost one female a month ago, and now you are missing your bleeder. Would you like to meet before I pick off another one? I do feel entitled to a rematch. No tricks this time.*

*Forever your faithful servant,*

*Alexander."*

Conrad tensed, his body going rigid as she finished reading the card. He looked at his alpha as her energy shifted to something deadly. He slowly got to his feet when she just stood there, staring at the card and scanning the lines over again. "Kee, talk to me." He said softly, slightly afraid that everything but her eyes had gone still.

"I'm not reading this right," she whispered harshly. *"You've lost one female over a month ago, and now you are missing your bleeder."* Her hands shook as disbelief washed over her and an ice cold coil of rage began to twist in her stomach. She looked up and saw her wolf flinch as they made eye contact. "What does that mean, Conrad?"

"K-Kee...you need to talk to Lucas. I'm sure he can explain this." Conrad replied quietly and took a few steps back from her as her aura began to expand. It was like a thick, invisible flood rapidly filled the room, drowning his senses in her energy. "Kee." He whined as it dropped him to his knees, the heavy air pushing down on him. He yielded to her aura and titled his head back in submission.

She saw her wolf submitting to her and wanted desperately to pull back from hurting him, but she couldn't control her anger. It was a raw, hungry rage that stemmed from the slap of betrayal. It was so familiar. "Conrad, you need to go." She bit out through clenched teeth.

The office door flung open with a loud bang and Conrad managed to glance at it from the corner of his eye. "Lucas." He murmured hopefully.

The vampire looked at the submissive wolf and then at the furious woman standing behind his desk. Her face was calm, but her aura swelled in the room, her fury pulsating through their bond like a static charge. It shot through the bond and nearly choked him, physically jolted him when he was getting dressed and making him stumble.

His eyes went to the small, white card in her hand. He glanced at the flowers and then looked at her blank face again. "Pull in your wrath, Keira." He chided her like a child. When her gaze remained on the card, he gestured at her wolf. "Look at what you are doing to Conrad. You are supposed to take care of him, are you not?"

Her eye twitched before she slowly looked up at him. "Conrad, leave." She said without breaking eye contact with Lucas.

"I don't want to leave you like this." He replied, his tone strained.

"Everything will be fine. I'll see you downstairs."

Conrad struggled to climb back to his feet. He looked at the irritated vampire as he headed to the door. "Please, make this right." He whispered to Lucas before leaving the room.

Lucas' brow furrowed. Minutes passed and the two never broke eye contact. Finally, he gestured at the card. "Did the wolf beta upset you again? I have to say, those would not be my choice of flowers to send."

"Everything comes back to Cain, doesn't it?" She mocked him from the other night. She let out a low, sarcastic laugh. "This bouquet is meant for you, actually."

He lifted a black eyebrow at her. "And you found it fit to read the attached note?"

She didn't even try to look ashamed. "I did, and I'm glad I did. Otherwise I don't believe I would have ever found out the truth."

"Do not speak in riddles, Keira." He patronized harshly, her anger easily feeding his own through their bond.

She didn't reply, just held the card out to him. He took a few steps forward so he could pluck it from her fingers. He glanced over the note, quickly reading it. He read it again, and then a third time. His stomach plummeted at the implications of Alexander's words and he crumpled the paper in his fist. Clearly, his enemy had his bleeder, but worst of all, he had tried to kill Keira. He looked at her and this time her face showed the fury they both felt.

"It's your fault." She hissed, her hands balled tightly into fists. "*Your fault!*" She screamed and picked up the vase before hurling it at the wall.

He refrained from flinching. "I did not know he was behind it, Keira. If I did, I would have told you and we would have killed him together." He tried to reason with her, keeping his voice calm. If he had fed, his heart would be beating hard against his chest.

"It doesn't matter, Lucas!" She screeched. "This happened because you were too weak to kill your opponent! Look what it did! You lost members of your coven, your bleeder, and he almost killed me! All because you couldn't finish the *fucking* job!"

Lucas glared as she hit him low and hard with her words. "I was trying to avoid a massacre. It is my job as the overseeing lord to do what is best for my vampires."

She snorted at him. "How's that working out for you? Did I not just remind you that he's been killing your brethren? Almost killed me?"

He bared his fangs at her in a silent sneer "You are upset and reasonably so, but you need to tread carefully."

"What are you going to do, Lucas? Kill me? Or maybe you'll have

Alexander try again?" She jabbed angrily.

"Look at what you have become thanks to me!" He suddenly shouted at her. "You are stronger than before, both mentally *and* physically! Your shapeshifting has gone beyond what you have ever been able to do! You have become the perfect weapon and it is because of me!"

She blinked at his word choice. A new sense of betrayal pinched at her heart and her face fell once again into a blank mask. "Is that what I am to you? A weapon?"

His body went tense like a strung bow, his pale skin going nearly white. "Keira—"

"No wonder you helped me so much," she gave a watery, humorless laugh. "You wanted me to become this." She gestured at herself. "Was fucking me part of your plan, too? Or was that added in for my benefit? To keep me from learning the truth?"

His face fell. "You know it was not like that, Keira."

"I don't know anything!" She shouted as her eyes stung. Everything that had happened the past month flashed before her eyes. Everything he did had been done with an ulterior motive. The realization hurt more than the truth about Alexander.

"I trusted you," she cried as her heart clenched painfully. "You were there for me when I needed you. You held me when I was breaking into pieces. You let me develop these...these feelings for you!"

His chest went colder as tears swelled in her eyes, but his undead heart managed to flutter with her confession. "Your feelings are not one sided. Do not toss this away; let us talk about it."

"Talk about it? You mean like how I tried to talk to you after you had a tantrum?" She shrank away to the other side of the desk when he tried to approach her. She wiped furiously at her face, wiping away the tears before they could fall. "How can I trust anything you say?"

"I was upset by what happened and needed time to think about it." He stopped walking towards her and watched as she scrambled to keep space between them. "Do not forget that I did not plan your attack, Keira." He pointed out. "Do not pin that on me."

"You didn't plan it, no, but you're the reason it happened. You used what happened to mold me into exactly what you wanted me to be, didn't you?" She accused.

Lucas remained quiet as he carefully chose his next words and tried to hide his emotions from their bond. "I knew you could be more than what you were. I did what I thought would help you achieve your goal."

She scoffed. "And you would just reap the benefits, is that it?"

He clenched his jaw. "Yes."

Kee's eyes fluttered shut and she quickly shook her head to stop the rising emotions. She held on to her anger and tightened her resolve. She wouldn't break. Not now. Not ever again. She slowly walked around the desk, making sure to keep a wide distance between them. "I can't do this."

"What is that supposed to mean?" Lucas questioned and watched as she headed to the door. "You are just going to leave?" He tossed the crumpled note on his desk and gestured at it. "We know who you have to kill to finally put this behind you. We can do it together."

"No, I will do it alone." She paused at the door frame and shot him a frigid glare over her shoulder. "I'll succeed where *you* failed." With that, she left the room and disappeared down the hallway.

The vampire stared at the open door as his mind raced. The more he thought about it, the angrier he became. With an animalistic snarl, he knocked everything off his desk, grabbed the edge of it, and easily flung it at the wall where it broke and fell to the floor alongside the shattered vase.

If he got to Alexander first, he would make sure he paid dearly for the havoc he created.

# Twenty-Eight

*Stay calm, stay calm. Breathe, just breathe.* Kee repeated to herself like a prayer as she rushed down the stairs to the main club area. The bar was already starting to get packed, Lucy and another bartender busy making drinks. She slipped past a group of girls celebrating a bachelorette party and headed straight to the front doors.

Conrad turned when he felt his alpha approaching. He made the next person in line step to the side so Kee could slip out past him and the crowd. He apologized to Dante, who was working the door with him, and followed after her. "Kee, wait!"

She turned towards him after she was a few feet away from the club and shook her head. "I can't be here tonight." She told him.

"What happened?" He asked as she pulled out her phone and clicked on the Uber app. "Where are you going?"

She put in the only address she could think of and confirmed her pick up spot before shoving the phone back in her pocket. She ran shaking her hands through her hair and looked up at him. "I'm a weapon to him, Con. I've become exactly what he wanted me to be."

His face scrunched up in confusion. "Lucas? That can't be it. There has to be more to this."

She shook her head. "It's his fault I was attacked, Conrad. Remember when you first met Lucas in my living room? When we were talking about Alexander? He didn't kill him when they fought and people are suffering for it. His brethren, Aubrey, me, and God knows who else."

"Kee, he didn't plan your attack." He tried to point it out to her. "This is all Alexander."

"It's his fault!" She shrieked, causing some people in line to look over at them. She tried to rein her hysteria back in as Conrad led them a few a more feet away from the club. "If he had killed Alexander none of this would have happened."

"That may be true, but he didn't mean to hurt you." He said softly. "He cares about you, I know he does. I can tell by the way he looks at you."

She shook her head as a blue sedan pulled up alongside the curb in front of her. "No, he cares about his tool." She told him as she opened the back door to the car.

"You need to think this through, Kee. Think about the last five weeks very carefully." He pleaded.

"I'll try, but I make no promises." She looked at him and softened her eyes at his torn expression. "I'm not leaving you. I'll be back. We have apartment hunting to do, remember?"

"I'll hold you to that." He saw her nod and then slip into the car, closing the door afterwards. He watched the car drive off and sighed heavily as he turned back to Byte.

Dante finished snapping a wristband on a human male as Conrad came back over to him. "Everything alright? She seems upset."

He shrugged. "She is, but I'm hoping she'll get over it."

"I couldn't help but overhear your conversation." The vampire checked the ID for the next person in line while Conrad patted them down. Dante secured a wristband around the patron's wrist and ushered him inside before looking at the wolf again. "Let me start by saying that Lord Lucas has never paid so much attention to a person before."

Conrad met his gaze. "Gio briefly mentioned something similar."

He shrugged. "I have been a follower of Lucas for nearly a century, not as long as Giovanni, but long enough to know that everything he does is for a reason." He told him as he checked another ID. "He's hard to read and other vampires are always looking to overthrow him. Did you know he was once considered to be the representative for the state?"

*Holy shit, for all of California? That's one step below the council.*

"I didn't know that. But, what does this have to do with Kee?" The wolf questioned cautiously.

"Maybe nothing, but people look for weaknesses in their enemies to exploit them," Dante replied. "Lord Lucas does not get close to people for that reason." His eyes narrowed with seriousness. "I doubt he forgot that with your alpha."

Conrad furrowed his brow. "What are you trying to say?"

He shrugged. "I'm saying none of us knew about Kee until he brought her here already half-dead from the attack. If we, his coven, didn't know about her, how did his enemy?"

He went silent as he thought about it. "Someone told Alexander about her." He concluded. When Dante dipped his head in a nod, he growled. "But, who?"

"That is the question, isn't it?" Dante asked as he held out his hand to check another ID.

Hours passed and the line outside Byte was practically nonexistent now that most of the customers were inside. Conrad instantly reached for his phone when it vibrated in his back pocket. He looked at the screen, expecting to see Kee's name and cursed when it wasn't.

"Hey, Dante, I'm going to take a fifteen real quick." He informed his partner for the night.

"Have a good break." The vampire lazily responded, his eyes on the Sci-fi book in his hand.

He nodded and then walked down the sidewalk to where Kee had been picked up. When he was far enough away from the bar, he brought up his messages and opened the new one.

*If you miss a check-in call one more time I will show Amelia just how displeased I am.*

Conrad felt his blood boil. It scorched through his veins like lava and made its way to his beast, making it snarl with rage. The bastard knew exactly how to get to him. His fingers began to tighten around his phone, but he stilled them before they broke it. He violently shoved his wolf down and called the sender.

He answered on the first ring. *"How nice of you to call."*

Conrad grit his teeth at the sarcastic tone. "I'm sorry, but I'm at work."

*"And yet here you are calling me."* The other man pointed out coolly.

Conrad took a slow breath to try and calm his anger. "Yes, I saw your message and took a break in order to call you. I don't want Mia to get hurt over a misunderstanding."

*"The only misunderstanding is apparently your check-in time,"* came the growl of a reply. *"You should have taken your break when you needed to call me. That would have been the smart thing to do, wouldn't it? Or, are you going to tell me someone else was hurt as well?"*

"I can't control how busy it gets, *sir*." He snipped, instantly regretting it when the line went quiet for a few moments. "And, again, I'm sorry for last time. But as I explained, I couldn't leave the girl to suffer. She was having a panic attack. I couldn't leave a pack member like that."

*"Don't forget about who your pack really is."* He warned. *"And quite*

*frankly, I don't really care for your excuses, Conrad,"* he stated in a bored tone. *"I doubt Amelia does either."*

His hand tightened on the phone again as his beast whined. He closed his eyes tightly and swallowed his pride. "Please, let me talk to her." He wasn't above begging when it came to his Mia.

*"Perhaps you should have thought a little more about her before you missed your call."*

"I'm calling now. Please."

*"Maybe I'll feel generous if your information is useful."*

He pinched his lips together as he tried to carefully tell the alpha a half-truth. "Another wolf was killed a week ago," he began. "I'm still trying to figure out who is behind it, but I'm getting closer." Throughout his reports, he tried to hide Kee's involvement in any of it. He refused to get her killed for his own selfish needs. It was the least he could do.

A snarl echoed into the phone. *"Who was the wolf this time? Another one of rank?"*

"Future rank," he explained. "Noah was to be Cain's beta once he took over the pack."

He let out another growl. *"What does that bring the death toll to? Four?"*

"It brings it to three," Conrad corrected carefully. "And one attack that almost killed a fourth."

*"Ah, Cain's mate, right? He almost lost his bitch and then lost his best man, what a shame."* The other male observed quietly.

If Conrad didn't know any better, he would have thought the older wolf had sounded almost sympathetic. "He's a strong wolf." He mumbled back.

*"Hm, it's good he's next in line then, isn't it? Tell me, how exactly are you close to figuring out who is killing my wolves? What have you found out?"*

He swallowed nervously as he thought of a way to cut Kee out of the equation. "I know you think Warren has plans to go against you, but I think someone else was behind the attacks. A vampire."

The other end of the phone was silent for a moment, but when he spoke again his voice was low. *"And why do you think that?"*

"Lucas, the lord of the city and county, received a threat today from his enemy. It was about losing a wolf a month ago," he stated vaguely. "I think he was referring to Cain's woman. She works for Lucas, at his club." He hastily added.

*"And it was from another vampire?"*

"Yes, I saw the note and the signature. Alexander and Lucas had a power struggle last month and it seems Alexander is still bitter about losing."

*"I know about the fight. That is what started all this. But why would a vampire bother with killing wolves if they are on the same side? Why wouldn't Alexander just go after another vampire under Lucas' care?"*

"I'm not sure, Liam." Conrad admitted, but he continued in as if he hadn't spoken.

*"Did the LA wolf pack have a change of allegiance? Is that why he went after my wolves? Why else attack them? Something doesn't add up here."*

As much as Conrad hated the other man, he would admit Liam wasn't a fool. The pack had ambushed Kee and she had killed them for it. *But what connected the wolves to Alexander? How did he control them?*

He suddenly tensed when the obvious solution hit him so hard he lost his breath. It all clicked into place the more he thought of it. After all, why had he been sent to LA in the first place? *Warren.* Alexander didn't have power over the wolves, but their alpha did.

*What if Warren was the one who ordered the attack for Alexander?*

*Dante suggested that someone had told the vampire about Kee. It had to be Warren.*

He had to tell Kee.

"Sir, that's all I have for now." Conrad briskly told him.

*"Keep looking into this, Novak. If vampires are involved with the deaths, this will be messy."*

"Yes, Liam." He replied dutifully, but he was dying to get off the phone and call Kee.

*"You have earned yourself a few minutes with your Mia. If you still want it?"* He asked almost flippantly.

His heart clenched in his chest. His need to get off the phone was instantly pushed aside and replaced with desperation to stay on longer. "Yes! Yes, please!" He cried. He didn't care if he sounded like an eager dog awaiting a treat from his owner after performing a series of tricks. He would happily do a hundred more just to hear her voice. "Please."

—

*What am I doing here?*

She had been staring at the one story house for minutes, awkwardly standing on the sidewalk. With a deep breath, she forced her legs to move. She followed the pathway up to the porch and hesitated before knocking softly. It was quiet on the other side of the door and remained so as the seconds ticked by. Feeling silly, she turned to walk away when she suddenly heard footsteps. She bit her lip when the door swung open and looked down, unable to meet his gaze. "Sorry to come by—"

"Kee?!" A stunned girl's voice came instead of a rumbling baritone.

She snapped her head up to see Katie standing in the doorway, her mouth hanging open in shock. "Katie?" She asked in confusion. *Why is Katie at Cain's house?*

"Oh my lord, you're alive!" The wolf cried happily as she closed the distance between them and hugged her tightly. "I can't believe it! Wait until Cain sees you!" She pulled away and shouted, "Cain!"

Nerves slicked Kee's palms as she stared dumbfounded at the girl. Did Cain move on? She swallowed thickly and took a step back. She didn't blame him. She couldn't. Not after everything they had been through. Not after everything she had done to his pack. Not after she was so conflicted on her feelings for Lucas.

"You know, I think this is bad timing. I'll come back later." She muttered, making Katie give her a weird, disbelieving look.

"Are you kidding me? Do you know how happy he'll be? We all thought you were dead!" Katie exclaimed.

*He already knows I'm alive.* She shook her head and took another step back. "You can tell him on your own. I'll just, um, talk to him later."

Katie didn't hear the woman's soft spoken response, her eyes were glued to where Cain would be coming down the hall. She beamed when she finally saw him and stepped away from the door to let her alpha take her place. "Cain, look! It's Kee! She's here!"

Cain stepped into the entryway and saw a wide-eyed Kee staring back at him. "Kee." He breathed her name like a sigh of relief. It had taken everything in his willpower to not text or call her the past week. He was barely able to sleep, her attack haunting him and his mind spinning as he anticipated her answer.

She looked between the two wolves and lifted up her hands in front of her. "I'm sorry to interrupt you two. I just—I don't know. I wanted to see you. But, you're busy and that's fine. I should have called. But, um, instead I just came over. I didn't think. I'm sorry."

The beta heard her rambling and couldn't help the nostalgic smile that turned up his lips. "It's not what you think, Kee." He told her tenderly. He quickly reached out when he saw her starting to step back away from him. He gently grabbed her wrist and pulled her to him, pressing their bodies flush against each other. Keeping one hand on her lower back, he cupped the back of her neck with the other and gave her a feather-light kiss. "Tell me your answer." He breathed quietly against her lips.

She made a small noise in her throat. It was a sound of relief and longing. "*No*. It was always no." She barely got the soft words out before his lips were on hers again. She wrapped her arms tightly around him, holding him almost desperately to her. He lifted her from the ground like she weighed nothing and carried her into the house, Katie shutting the door behind them.

Katie stared after them longingly as her alpha carried his woman down the hall towards his room. Hope budded and blossomed in her chest so fast it was almost painful. If Kee was alive, then there was a chance that Wyatt was, too. Any day he could come strolling back to her, showing up on her doorstep just as Kee had!

Happy tears spilled down her cheeks as she pulled her phone out of her back pocket. She found Natalie's name in her text messages and felt a giddy laugh bubble out of her mouth. *I can't wait to tell the pack!*

CPSIA information can be obtained
at www.ICGtesting.com
Printed in the USA
FSHW010504221021
85669FS